The MARVEL House

KATHY NICKERSON

MARVEL HOUSE
Copyright © 2018 Kathy Nickerson

ISBN: 978-1727594454

This book is a work of fiction, and all the characters and details are imaginary. Any resemblance to people the reader knows or loves is purely accidental. And, quite probable.

For more information on Kathy Nickerson, please visit www.KathyNick.com.

Cover artist: Becky West

Printed in the United States of America

To Wendell—my husband, lover, partner, and friend.
Thank you for choosing me every day since 1973.

ACKNOWLEDGMENTS

Every book is a group effort, more of a symphony than a solo. For The Marvel House I owe thanks to more people than I can list, but here are a few:

Ada Jewel for helping to name my characters. You launched the story on that car ride.

The HCC Writers Guild for being my tribe and keeping me inspired.

My concept editor, Amy, for your honest, clear, encouraging direction.

My everything-else editor, Molly Rose. Thank God for your love of all things grammar.

My partner in publishing, Anna of ScribblesandScribes.com. You never let me misplace a comma, and you refuse to let me give up as an author. Your touch changes everything for the better.

Becky of artsywest.com for the gorgeous cover art.

All the dear readers who continually ask if I'm writing another book. "Why, yes, I am. Always."

Our wonderful grandchildren. You understood when I had to miss ballgames and concerts and Saturdays to take care of bookish things.

Felicity and Serenity who remind me always to keep chasing the dream. One of us is sure to catch it someday.

Ryan and Charity, Joseph, and all the cousins in the household on Lake Street. Thank you for being a true house of Marvels this year. Well-done. I wish I could have sent you a Madge.

And my husband, to whom this book is dedicated. Thank you for being my patron in the arts and my partner in everything.

Chapter One

Wednesday, September 14th
Sixty Days to Go

Madge DuPree rang the doorbell of the Marvel house, pulled back her shoulders, and gripped the handle of her small suitcase. She hoped these people weren't huggers.

Her next thought was that the woman who opened the door wore her skirt too short and her makeup too heavy, but Madge simply said, "Here I am."

"Good. That agency must be fast. First thing my lawyer has gotten right in this divorce. I just got back from dropping off the kids, and I have a meeting downtown at lunch. We barely have time to get you settled." The woman pulled Madge inside and grabbed her suitcase. "Here," she released Madge's arm long enough to retrieve a notebook from the entryway table and thrust it forward. "I made lists. Phone numbers. Daily schedules. Things like that. I was up half the night putting it together." She kept talking as she turned and walked into the dining room.

Madge followed, but she paused in the dining room and brushed her hand across the rosebud wallpaper beside the staircase.

The woman glanced back over her shoulder. "I know," she said. "That wallpaper is ancient. Old houses are supposedly full of character. But this one has so many quirks. We've been working on it since the day we moved in. I wanted to peel that paper off and do something neutral." She stopped and looked around the room. "I guess someone else will do it now."

Madge pulled her hand back. She thought the wallpaper suited the room. It fit with the wooden staircase and the curved banister. What color was neutral these days, anyway? In her day it had been beige. Surely they wouldn't paint the dining room beige. Heavens. Beige would ruin the place.

"And here is the kitchen," she heard the woman say from beyond the doorway. Madge stopped dawdling. She took a breath and forged ahead, even though her knees complained. They had been complaining more every day since she turned seventy-five. Along with her back, her hands, and her sciatica.

Madge followed the sound of the woman's voice into a kitchen with glass-fronted cabinets and stainless steel appliances. She stopped and held onto a dark counter-top that extended into the middle of the room.

"Are you okay?" the woman asked.

Madge nodded. She was far from okay, of course. This room should have been smaller. And warmer. She had expected white wooden cabinets with a green countertop. Formica, if she remembered correctly. The stove should have been across the room, and a teakettle should have been singing on it.

"I know it looks a little overwhelming," the woman said. "I think we got carried away with the remodel in here. It might be a little modern for such an old house. But you'll figure out all the gadgets. Don't worry."

Gadgets were the least of Madge's worries.

"I'm Alex, by the way. Alex Marvel. I don't know if they told you." Alex opened a side door into the garage and swept her manicured hand in an arc. "There's the car. Fully fueled. The keys are on a peg here by the door. I printed off a Google map to the kids' schools and daycare. The car has navigation, of course."

Madge clutched the notebook and wondered what Alex meant by all that. She didn't have time to ask, though, because they were whipping around and heading to the other side of the house.

"This guest suite has rarely been used," Alex said. "We added a bathroom and small bedroom in the renovation. But my mother-in-law prefers a hotel on her rare visits to the Midwest. So, it might be lacking some amenities. You'll just have to make a list of anything you need, and I'll pick up supplies. My number is in the notebook." With that, she swung open the door to a small sitting room and stepped inside.

Madge almost smiled. The room was her favorite shade of blue. They had kept the bay window, and it filled the space with light. On the opposite wall, a wingback chair and round ottoman sat near the fireplace. The small table with a china lamp would be the perfect place to do her *Word Search* puzzles.

Alex walked to a built-in bookcase and pulled open doors to reveal a television. "We had this installed at Christmas in case of guests. No one has ever used it."

Madge thought the television might be only slightly smaller than a movie screen, although she hadn't been to the movies since Clark Gable. She also wondered what her friends from the Glory Circle would think if they could see her now. She imaged walking into church for Tuesday morning Prayer & Share and overhearing their conversation.

Grace Colby would probably make a remark about the chair being too soft. Grace always had an opinion. Madge didn't remember for sure when Grace became such a curmudgeon. After her husband got sick, probably. But, Madge didn't want to analyze Grace Colby right now. She moved on in her imagination to how the other Glory Circle Sisters would respond if they could see this place today.

Evelyn would shush Grace and comment on the lovely color. Erma would echo whatever Evelyn said. And Bess, well poor Bess would just be confused, as usual.

Alex interrupted Madge's thoughts by pointing toward another doorway. "The bedroom and bath are through here. They are small but adequate, I think."

Madge wandered around her new digs one more time. She looked at the bed so big she could sleep on it sideways and the bathroom just two steps away. "Oh," she said, "I believe I can make-do."

"Good. I'll let you unpack. Then, we can meet in the kitchen in say, thirty minutes? I want to go over a few things before I leave."

"I'll be there in ten."

Really, if she had known housekeepers got a set-up like this, Madge might have gone into this line of work years ago. She put her Bible on the small table and then tucked her few clothes into the drawers she found inside the closet. She hung her jacket on the rack and placed her extra pair of shoes on a shelf. Then she stood back and looked at the ridiculously empty space. "Should have brought the bigger suitcase," she said.

Madge hadn't wanted to carry much into this situation, though. Just get in and get the job done. That was her plan. She needed two-thousand, four-hundred dollars and eighty-nine cents to get her Oldsmobile out of hock at the repair shop. Then she had a few court costs to pay. And something the judge called reparations. Those dollars would go to the owner of the ice cream truck that had smashed the radiator on her Olds.

She still didn't know why the nincompoop hadn't pulled off the street before he stopped. She had only looked down for a second. Then, BAM! Steam, smoke, and ice cream bars everywhere. What a ruckus.

This temp job for sixty days would be just the thing, though. She could earn the cash and pay everyone off. Then, she could get out of here and back to the solitude of her normal life. She didn't need much wardrobe to do all that.

Chapter Two

Wednesday, September 14th
Sixty Days to Go

Madge found Alex standing in the kitchen a few minutes later. She sipped from a tall mug and pointed toward a machine in the corner. "Coffee?"

"No, I've had my quota," Madge said.

"Such self-control. I'm on my third cup, and I'll need more before the day ends. Okay, let's go over the schedule for today." She pulled out another stack of papers. "The kids get out of school at three and three-fifteen. The older girls have dance, tutoring, and volleyball so you don't have to get them today. Their father will swing by on his way here tonight and pick them up. The daycare doesn't close until five, but they charge by the minute after that, so don't ever be late. It is exorbitant."

"Do they have names?"

"The daycare people?"

"The children."

"Oh. Right. I forgot you haven't met the kids yet." She looked around the room as if her family might materialize at any moment. "I thought we had a picture somewhere." She grabbed her phone and started sliding her finger around. "Here. This was taken earlier in the summer, so they've grown some."

Madge looked at the tiny picture. She could barely see four

little girls on a playground. No one smiled for the camera.

"Aspen, Quinn, Peyton, and Grace," Alex said. "They aren't any trouble individually." She looked at the photo a little longer. "There are just so many of them. It adds up, you know?"

Madge didn't know. She never had children. When the Glory Circle Sisters volunteered to teach Sunday School or make crafts at Vacation Bible School, Madge always signed up for kitchen duty. She wasn't particularly good with children. Or people in general.

Alex pulled the phone back. "Here, let me get a picture of you. It's Madge, right?" She pointed her telephone and pressed a button before Madge had time to respond. "I need to send it to the daycare giving you permission to pick up the baby." She tapped away on the telephone screen as she spoke. When she finished, she slid the phone into her back pocket.

"I know this is a crazy set up," Alex said. She snapped a lid on her coffee cup. Then she reached for a leather bag and began stuffing papers inside. "It would have been much simpler if the girls could have just gone to their father's apartment this week while I'm out of town. I think the judge must be losing it. You know what he did, right? Did the agency tell you?"

"Well…"

Alex saved Madge from having to answer. "We spent weeks with our lawyers trying to divide things fairly." She paced the length of the kitchen as she spoke. "We settled on the scuba gear and the Christmas china and who should be responsible for health insurance and orthodontist fees. Just working out the calendar for the Cardinals' season tickets took us three sessions."

She stopped pacing and looked at Madge. "And we had custody all worked out, too. Joint custody. Equal share. One week at their dad's apartment and the next week with me downtown. We would sell this monstrosity, split the profit, and be totally out of debt for the first time in our lives. But do you know what the judge did? Do you? Did they tell you why I suddenly need a housekeeper and nanny?"

Madge waited. She wasn't sure Alex was looking for a response. Besides, she'd rather not have the discussion about how she knew these things.

"He gave the kids this house." Alex threw her hands in the air and waved them around. "That's right. Four little girls who can't even remember to brush their teeth are now in charge of a house with a double mortgage. And we, the grown-ups who have real lives and jobs and commitments, we shall be moving back and forth with our suitcases every other week."

Madge did know about the unusual arrangement. She thought it was kind of wild, too, but she didn't plan to agree with Alex Marvel out loud. The tangled mess had given her the perfect opportunity to earn some cash, so she felt rather grateful to the creative judge.

Alex slammed a final notebook into her bag. "So, I will live out of my suitcase for the next sixty days until my lawyer files an appeal. He better fix this thing or else…"

Alex seemed to run out of breath with the last statement. She sagged against the refrigerator.

Madge ran her finger along the counter and flicked a crumb. The wise thing at this moment would be to stay silent. To keep her nose out of the business going on in this house. Head down. Do the work. Earn the cash. Get out. But Madge had never been good at keeping opinions to herself. Maybe it came from living alone and having no one to boss.

"Well," Madge said, "maybe that judge doesn't believe in divorce."

Alex crossed her arms. "Who cares? It doesn't work like the fairies in Peter Pan, you know. Not believing doesn't make it go away."

"No. But, my friend, Catherine, had a granddaughter who almost got divorced once. They worked it out."

Alex pulled her bag onto her shoulder. "Look, I appreciate your interest. I really do. Right now, though, all I need is a housekeeper. Not a marriage counselor."

Madge picked up a tea towel from the counter. "I was simply making conversation. None of my business what you do." Of course, it had become her business the minute she stepped across the threshold. She needed this experiment to last the full sixty days or she would come up short on cash. Then she couldn't fix the Oldsmobile. She could just see Grace Colby smiling and suggesting Madge ride the OATS bus to get groceries. Madge snapped the tea towel. She didn't plan to ride any old lady bus, nor did she plan to give up one iota of the independence she had worked so hard to gain. She needed the Marvels to stick to the plan. Which, she supposed, meant she needed them to get this divorce. She tried not to think about that.

"I'll just tidy up the kitchen," Madge said. "You better be on your way." She walked toward the sink where breakfast dishes sat in a crooked mess. What did she care, anyway? Sixty days was fine by her. Once she collected her pay, her zany employer could do whatever she wanted.

"I'll be back in a week," Alex said. "You have all my numbers. And the girls' father will be here in the evenings if you need anything else."

Madge waved the tea towel, "Have a great trip. We'll make out just fine." She turned the faucet and ran water full blast to drown out any more conversation.

A few minutes later, Madge stood in the center of the clean kitchen wondering what to do with her day. She also wondered for a couple of moments whether she ought to pack up her suitcase and call a cab.

"Lord," she said, "these people are a mess. You could have gotten me a job cleaning for some old maiden lady. One without a cat. But, no, You set me down in the middle of a soap opera. I don't even watch that trash on television, and now I'm livin' it. I hope You know what You're doing."

She stood in the kitchen another moment, considering her predicament. Finally, she said, "Okay. I'll give it a try." She looked around the room. "If I'm staying, I better get to know the lay of the land."

She started in the laundry room and then moved to what she supposed they would call the living room. Or maybe the family room. She didn't think either description fit a house with such a fractured family. This wasn't any kind of living, with parents coming back and forth every week.

Madge walked into the dining room and stood at the bottom of the staircase for several minutes. She ran her hand over the smooth, wooden banister. A person's upstairs seemed kind of private. Eventually, she climbed to the first landing, but she jumped each time a stair creaked. "Quit being a ninny," she told herself. "You have every right to explore the house. It's research." She marched up the final steps, ignoring every creak and groan.

Upstairs, she opened the first door and saw two beds covered in pink spreads. All the trappings of little girlhood sparkled in the room, and Madge felt a smidge of regret about making money from the divorce. She shut the door and silenced the thought.

Across the hall, she found what she considered a typical teenager's room. Lots of purple. More books than toys, and a desk stacked with electronic gear.

The next room sat pristine under the eaves. The closet and bureau were empty, the bed neatly made. Madge felt like she had stepped into a cool forest and she immediately labeled this The Green Room.

At the opposite end of the hall, Madge found the master bedroom. She shook her head at the giant bed. She could probably share with five people and never touch toes. She expected marriages had lasted longer back in the days when beds were smaller.

The doors to the walk-in closet stood open, and hangers dangled at odd angles. Dirty clothes sprawled out of a hamper onto the floor. In the adjoining bathroom, toiletries sprawled across the counter. Make-up and hair products spilled from every drawer. The trashcan overflowed.

Madge backed out of the bedroom and shut the door firmly behind her. She decided a woman's bedroom should remain private. No need for the housekeeper to venture there.

For lunch, Madge found half a loaf of whole wheat bread and the last three slices of deli ham. A tomato would have been nice. Maybe some pickles. But the refrigerator was as empty as one would expect from a person who had been planning to move out next week. Madge found a notepad and started making a grocery list. She hoped the man of the house had some cash. She didn't plan to spring for all the grub herself.

Chapter Three

Wednesday, September 14th
Sixty Days to Go

An hour later, Madge awoke in her soft chair. "Must have dozed off," she said to herself. "All this excitement, I suppose." She checked her watch and then checked it a second time. "Drat. The thing must be broke." She worked her way out of the chair, which proved much more difficult than falling into it, and went back to the kitchen. The glowing clock on the microwave indicated that Madge's watch was working just fine.

"Well, shoot. I better get started if I'm going to make a practice drive to that day care center." She grabbed her purse and looked at the three sets of keys hanging beside the back door. She finally decided on the one with a pink key ring. Sure enough, one click opened the door of the car waiting in the garage.

Madge scooted behind the steering wheel and looked at the map taped to the dashboard. It had yellow-highlighted lines squiggling in three different directions from the "You are Here" star. Each line led to what must have been a school. Madge read the names and decided on the one marked Toddle Time as the daycare center. She studied the street names and looked at all the turns. Finally, she hit the button on the remote control and the garage door slid up with a groan. As if it knew this was a bad idea.

Madge backed out with a couple of quick jerks and paused at the end of the driveway. Left or right? She looked at the map. She looked at the sky to find the sun. Although she had no idea why. She'd never understand what that had to do with left and right.

A right turn would take her back into familiar territory, and she might be able to wind around and find her way to the schools from there. Maybe. A left turn would take her deeper into the part of town known as Cherry Hills. Some folks called it the snobby part of town. Madge sat in the driveway a few more seconds. Finally, she backed out and turned left into Cherry Hills.

She drove several minutes looking for the first turn on the map, Pebble Trail Drive. She never found a sign for it, though. Eventually, she took a turn she hoped would lead her back out to the main road. If she could find Broadway, she could orient herself. Or maybe find a gas station where she could ask directions.

Twenty minutes later, Madge had found nothing but a tangle of streets sprouting from one another with no path out. The drivers in Cherry Hills were so rude, too. All that honking. And nobody wanted to share the road. They swerved into her lane half the time. Finally, Madge turned right, rounded a corner, and found herself in the open on a four-lane road. She steered the car into the parking lot of an office building so she could catch her breath.

"Lord," she said, "this is a pickle, and You are gonna have to get me out of it. I admit I might have jumped a little quick into this situation, but yesterday it seemed like You were pointing me straight toward this job. Can't you do a little pointing toward the daycare now?"

She leaned back and took a breath while she watched a young woman climb out of a car and walk toward the office building. She wondered what kind of work went on inside. She leaned forward and squinted, trying to read all the names listed on the sign.

Suddenly, she stopped and slapped the steering wheel in victory. "Hot dog. You have landed me right in the parking lot of that little lawyer who hired me. It's a miracle." Madge grabbed her handbag and worked her way out of the car. Then she hustled across the parking lot as fast as her stiff joints would allow.

Madge barged off the elevator and greeted the young receptionist. "Am I glad to see you," she said.

"Excuse me?"

"Madge DuPree," she said as she picked up the bronze nameplate from the desk. "And you are Paige Rosedale. Is that Miss Rosedale or Mrs.?"

"Miss, but how can I…"

"I thought so. You look so young. First job? Right out of college? Or are you taking night classes?"

Miss Rosedale reached for the nameplate. "I am taking some classes, but this is certainly not my first job."

"Uh huh. First job that doesn't come with a large order of fries on the side, I bet."

"I'm sorry," she pulled the nameplate out of Madge's hand and centered it on her desk again. "How can I help you?"

"Your boss, Mr. Charles Jackson Oakley the Fourth, hired me yesterday."

"I think I would have remembered you," Miss Rosedale said. "Are you sure this is the right office?"

"Absolutely. I met Mr. Oakley downtown yesterday. He hired me right on the spot." Madge didn't offer any more details, and she hoped Miss Rosedale wouldn't ask.

"And, Mr. Oakley hired you to do what?"

"I'm a housekeeper-slash-nanny for his client Mrs. Marvel."

"Oh," Miss Rosedale stared at Madge for a moment. "Well, unfortunately, Mr. Oakley is in a meeting right now. May I do something for you?"

"I hope so." Madge pulled out the map and slapped it on Miss

Rosedale's desk. "Can you tell me how to get right there?" She pointed to the daycare dot.

"I'm not very good at maps," Miss Rosedale said.

"You and me both, Sister," Madge shook her head. "But I've got to get there to pick up the baby before five. They charge by the minute. Maybe your boss can help." Without waiting for permission, Madge turned toward the office and reached for the door.

Miss Rosedale tried to intercept, but Madge barreled through and stepped into the room just as Mr. Oakley threw his arms up and gave a shout. He dropped the video-game controller when he saw Madge.

"Sorry to interrupt," she said, "but I think it is in your best interest to help me keep my job."

Mr. Oakley, who also looked like he could be working behind a fast food counter, reached for his jacket as he spoke. "And what job exactly would that be?"

"You don't remember me? You kids need to pay better attention. No wonder your waiting room is empty. You have to lean in with people and give them your focus. You hired me yesterday as a housekeeper for Mrs. Marvel. You know, the case where the kids got the house."

"Ah, the housekeeper. Yes." Mr. Oakley pulled on his jacket. "I remember the agency sent you to the courthouse before I'd even had time to get my car. Kind of amazing."

"I was in the neighborhood," Madge said.

"Good. And how can I help you now?"

"Well, I can't find the daycare. I've been driving around in circles, and I started praying for help. All of a sudden, I ended up right here in your parking lot and I saw your pretty, young secretary walking right in the door like a guardian angel pointing the way."

"She's an administrative assistant."

"And pretty."

"Well," he straightened his tie, "I'm afraid I don't understand how I can be of service just now. As you can see, I'm quite busy."

Madge raised her eyebrow and looked at the game controller. "I see."

Mr. Oakley cleared his throat and pulled a file folder closer to the edge of the desk. "I was just clearing my head for a minute. It's a proven device."

"I'm sure. Now, I need to find the daycare center. Before five o'clock."

"And why do you think I'm the person to help you?"

"Well, because Divine Providence obviously guided me here for one thing."

"I don't know." He pointed out the window. "We're in a pretty central location and only a few blocks from the Marvel house."

"And, number two, you wouldn't want me to lose my job and mess up this whole experiment. That might look bad for your career. I mean, Judge Hightower did make the order, and I've heard he is pretty important in the state."

Mr. Oakley wrinkled his eyebrows. "Judge Hightower recommended you, didn't he?"

"Well, you asked for my references, so I gave you his card." Madge let the sentence hang, hoping that excused her from telling a straight out lie.

Mr. Oakley shook his head and looked at the map. Then, he picked up a pencil from his desk and made a couple of marks. "We are here," he said. "All you need to do is go out to Broadway and make a right. Then three blocks to Pine and turn left. That will take you to Grand. They have a new roundabout at Grand and Elmhurst. That's a little tricky. You want to exit onto Jamison, which takes you to Poplar. Got it?"

He looked up to see Madge frowning.

"Was that a left or a right out of the parking lot?"

Mr. Oakley sighed and looked at his watch, then back at Madge. "Have you ever navigated a round-about?"

"Not that I'm aware of," Madge said, "but I've taken a number of interesting detours. Sometimes on purpose."

He rubbed a hand across his eyes and then straightened up from the desk. "Come on," he said as he tucked the map into his pocket. He led Madge through the office and back into the reception area. He tossed a set of keys at Miss Rosedale and said, "Just lock up and follow in my car, okay?"

She grabbed her purse, jacket, and coffee cup in one smooth move. "Sure."

Madge noticed the eager look in the girl's eyes as she followed her boss toward the door. She didn't think the silly lawyer noticed a thing.

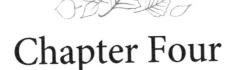

Chapter Four

Wednesday, September 14th
Sixty Days to Go

Mr. Oakley got into the car and told Madge to buckle up. He handed her the map once he had snapped his own seatbelt. "I'm going to drive," he said, "and you pay attention. Watch the map and the street signs so you can stay acclimated to where we are. That way you can drive it yourself tomorrow without any trouble."

Madge did her best to comply, but the shops looked so interesting in this part of town. They passed a car lot with *Barton Motors* flashing in blue neon. Madge loved her Oldsmobile, but a shiny Mustang did catch her eye.

On the next corner, she saw a store with fancy party dresses in the window. So sparkly and short. Who could wear such things? Why a girl ought to be embarrassed to show that much leg. And look at the price of gas. It's up three cents. Mr. Oakley interrupted her thoughts.

"And that's Grand. The roundabout is coming up in a couple of blocks. It's tricky but really smooth once you get the hang of it. Everything clear so far?"

"Oh, yes," she said. "Just fine."

A few minutes later they entered the roundabout, and Madge gripped the door handle. "Whoa," she said. "What on earth? A turnstile in the middle of the street? How do you know where to get out of this thing?"

"You just go with the flow of traffic," he said. "Don't stop; just flow. Pull in when it's clear, circle around, and peel off at your exit." He said this as he turned the car to the right and whizzed out of the circle onto a quiet street.

Madge closed her eyes to stop the spinning in her head. When she opened them again, they had parked in front of a large, red, brick building with a colorful sign out front announcing the home of Toddle Time.

When Madge didn't move, Mr. Oakley said, "Aren't you supposed to go in and get the kid?"

"I thought maybe it was a drive-through."

"I don't think they do that."

"Oh."

She sat a bit longer and looked at the building. Finally, Mr. Oakley spoke again. "Do you want me to go with you?"

Madge slammed her purse against the dash as she gathered herself together. "Of course not. I'm perfectly able." She knew she didn't look so able as she climbed out of the car with her stiff knees and tromped up the sidewalk toward the glass doors. A sign beside the door instructed her to buzz for admittance. What a world.

The woman who greeted Madge in the hallway looked like she'd spent one too many hours in the bouncy house. The noise level coming from the room behind her could drive anyone mad.

"May I help you?" the woman looked over her shoulder as she spoke, and Madge wasn't sure she had made contact.

"I'm here for a pick-up," Madge said. She didn't know the routine in these situations. "Marvel. I'm the new housekeeper."

"Oh, right. I think Mrs. Marvel sent a release form earlier. Just a second while I check the computer." The woman scurried across the room and punched keys on a keyboard that swung out from the wall. Madge saw her own face appear on the nearby screen, red hair flying in all directions. She looked rather wild-eyed and frightening. Mrs. Marvel should have warned her so she could have posed. She wouldn't give a child to the woman in that photo.

"Okay. Everything looks to be in order. I'll just get Baby for you."

Madge watched the daycare worker hurry away and thought she was much too eager to get rid of one of her charges. Within seconds, the worker emerged from the noisy room with a blonde toddler on her hip. The child looked at Madge with huge, blue eyes and promptly began to wail.

"Oh, it's okay Baby," the teacher said. "This is your Nanny. She's a sweet lady and is going to take you home for your din-din."

Madge resisted the urge to call the teacher a dimwit. Why would she tell the kid something like that? The baby had never met Madge in her life.

"Go ahead and cry, Kid," Madge said. "I'm an ugly stranger, and you shouldn't want to go with me any more than the Man-in-the-Moon. But we're stuck with it. So, let's go." She scrawled her name on the electronic tablet where the teacher indicated. A few minutes later, she stood on the sidewalk with the screaming child.

Mr. Oakley came around to the side of the car and opened the door. "What's wrong with the baby?" he said.

"Probably thinks she's being kidnapped."

"Well, let's get her home so she'll feel better." He reached out for the toddler and plopped her into the car seat. Then he and Madge both stood looking at the contraption.

"How do you close it?" Madge said.

"I have no idea."

He fiddled with the snaps and straps for a few minutes while the toddler continued to wail. Finally, Miss Rosedale jumped out of the car behind them and came around to the other door. "Need some help?" she asked.

"I have no clue how this works," he said.

"They are kind of confusing at first. Here, watch. This crosses over here and goes in this, and it all snaps together like that." Miss Rosedale had the baby latched into her car seat in moments. "What's her name?" Miss Rosedale asked.

Madge consulted the notebook from her purse. "Grace. I think"

Miss Rosedale pulled a blanket and book from a pocket underneath the seat and said a few soothing words. Within seconds, Grace had stopped crying and snuggled against the headrest.

"How did you do that?" Mr. Oakley asked.

"Magic."

Madge felt a new admiration for this administrative assistant. "You must have children of your own," she said.

"No, not at all. Just nieces and nephews."

"Oh. No children, though?"

"No. I told you I'm not married."

Madge raised her eyebrows and managed to poke an elbow in Mr. Oakley's ribs as she straightened up. "Imagine that. Such an able administrative assistant. And not even married."

He rubbed his side and frowned at Madge. "So, you're good now? You can manage to get back to the house?"

Madge looked over the hood of the car, trying to figure out exactly where she was in relationship to anything familiar. Finally, she turned to Mr. Oakley and said, "Not a clue."

He groaned.

"I'm sorry. I'm not used to all this city driving. Too many streets with silly names and intersections with triple lights, and that round-thingy-majiggy. I hate to admit, but maybe they should have taken my keys instead of just suspending my license."

Mr. Oakley had been walking away during the speech, but he stopped and turned around slowly with one hand on his heart and one on his head. "They suspended your license? Who suspended your license?"

"That other judge. The rude one."

"Here in this district?"

"Of course, here in this district. I don't have any trouble driving at home where things make sense. We don't put one-way streets in silly places."

Miss Rosedale stepped closer. "Why did the rude judge suspend your license?"

"Because of the ice cream truck, I suppose."

Both Mr. Oakley and Miss Rosedale waited for the rest of the explanation. Madge finally went on. "If the driver would have pulled all the way off the street or kept his music playing or something, I probably would have seen him."

Mr. Oakley leaned forward. "But?"

"But he didn't. So, when I dropped my lipstick, I leaned down to get it. It wasn't one of those Avon samples, you know. It was a good drugstore lipstick and cost me plenty."

"What happened then?"

"Well, how could I know the driver would be taking a lunch break right there on my side of the street? Shouldn't he have pulled into a gas station or something?"

"You hit an ice cream truck," Mr. Oakley said. "That's why you lost your license."

"No. Well, yes, I did smash into the truck. Slightly. But that was just a fine. The license was because I didn't stop for the cop."

"You ran from the police?" Miss Rosedale put a hand over her mouth.

"Not on purpose," Madge said. "So many flashing lights and strange noises downtown. How could I know he was aiming that siren at me? I figured it out after a few blocks."

Mr. Oakley moaned and paced in a circle while Miss Rosedale reached out and put her hand on Madge's arm.

"Is today the first time you've driven with your suspended license?"

Madge crossed her arms, stuck out her chin, and spoke with a slight huff. "Of course it is. I only drove because it seemed like an emergency. Couldn't leave the kid here all night."

"You might have told us you didn't have a valid license," Mr. Oakley said. "That might have been a pertinent fact in your job interview."

"Nobody asked me. Housekeeping doesn't usually include chauffer services. And I didn't hear anybody say anything about running a carpool. Taking care of the kids after school and doing some light housekeeping. That's what you said on the elevator. Just someone to take care of the kids and do some light housekeeping."

"In the elevator? We didn't talk in the elevator." Jack tilted his head at Madge as if trying to remember all the way back to last Friday. "We met in the lobby when the agency sent you over."

He leaned forward and looked directly into Madge's face like a real lawyer in a courtroom. "The agency did send you over, didn't they?"

"Well, not exactly."

"What did happen? Exactly."

"I sort of had an appointment at the courthouse about the ice cream truck, and I kind of ended up in the wrong room. So confusing that building."

"Go on."

"So, I sat in for just a few minutes on this really interesting case between a husband and wife who were dividing up their earthly goods." She looked at Miss Rosedale and said in a lower voice, "So sad this divorce stuff. Everybody suffers." Miss Rosedale nodded.

"Anyway, the whole place got in an uproar when they finished because the famous judge pulled a Solomon and gave the kids the house."

"Pulled a Solomon. What is that? I don't get the reference," he said.

"It's from the Bible," Miss Rosedale told him. "I'll explain later."

"Well, it was great stuff," Madge said. "Afterwards, the cranky little judge in my courtroom didn't do nearly as well. He slapped all kinds of things on me. Expensive things. Things that will keep me from driving if I don't earn a boatload of money right away. So when you and Mrs. Marvel rode down in the elevator with me and then sat at the next table for lunch…."

"The cinnamon rolls. You recommended the cinnamon rolls."

"I did. Someone had just told me they were the best ever, and he was right, wasn't he?"

"He was."

"So, I overheard you and Mrs. Marvel talking, and I knew you needed a short-time housekeeper. I needed a short-time job. It seemed like a good fit."

Mr. Oakley stood unblinking for a few seconds. "So," he finally said, "you accosted me in the hallway and impersonated a credentialed housekeeper from a reputable agency. Great. This is great. Plus, you came from traffic court. My first case. My first real client. And I've managed to get tangled up with traffic court. Aiding and abetting. This is probably aiding and abetting."

"Oh, I don't think so," Miss Rosedale said. "She didn't actually drive while you were in the car. In fact, you prevented her from driving at all. If you just take her home now, and I follow you, the whole thing will be completely legal."

"That's right." He started to smile. "I didn't even see her drive to my office. I don't actually know for sure how she got there." He turned to Madge. "Don't say another word about how you got to my office." He turned back and paced in a tight circle. "I'll just drive her home, and that will be the end of it." He fake-slapped his head and started strolling toward his car as if he had just secured world peace. "Man, that was a close one," he said, as he climbed into the driver's seat and left the two women standing on the sidewalk.

Madge looked at Miss Rosedale who smiled and shrugged before turning toward the other car. Once Madge had buckled herself into the front seat beside Mr. Oakley he said, "You know I have to replace you with a real housekeeper."

Madge shrugged. "Maybe you do, maybe you don't. Mrs. Marvel already left for her business trip. She's gone all week." Madge pulled her purse onto her lap and reached inside. "She gave me the notebook. That's pretty much a signed contract."

She watched Mr. Oakley considering the situation. She could tell he might waver, so she decided to push him the rest of the way off the cliff with something that wasn't a complete lie. "And I do have that recommendation from Judge Hightower."

"So, you have housekeeping experience?"

Madge thought about her two-bedroom house on the corner lot, sitting empty now while she stayed with the Marvels. She kept it neat, at least by her own standards. "Of course I have experience," she said. She hoped he wouldn't ask about kids.

"Well, I suppose you win for now. I don't have time to replace you today, but you are on probation. We will see how things go. Now, watch closely as I drive you home, Ms. DuPree."

"It's Madge. People just call me Madge."

"Okay, Madge. Pay attention to the street signs."

"What do they call you?"

"Excuse me?"

"I don't think anybody actually calls you Mr. Charles Jackson Oakley the Fourth, Esquire, or whatever. Even if you did earn the title at a fancy school. So, is it Charlie or Chuck?"

"Neither." He pulled into the street and frowned as he made the first turn. Then, he looked at Madge who was still waiting for a proper response. "It's Jack."

Chapter Five

Wednesday, September 14th
Sixty Days to Go

An hour later, Madge heard a car pull into the garage. She braced herself. Now would be the test of this whole scheme. She had to convince Jack to let her keep this job for the next sixty days. Once he filed the motion to get the house back from the kids, everything could change. In the meantime, Madge needed to put on a Mary Poppins hat.

Doors slammed, voices rose, and the rest of the Marvel family came tromping through the laundry room door. All three girls stopped when they saw Madge.

The father of the clan came through last, carrying a duffle bag along with his briefcase. He bumped into the shortest girl because he was attempting to check his phone at the same time and didn't realize the parade had stopped.

"Whoa, what have we here?" he said.

Before Madge could answer, he went on. "Girls, this is Madge. Or should we call you Mrs. Whatever? I don't know the actual etiquette. We've never had a housekeeper/nanny type person."

He was all smiles about the situation, though, so Madge decided to be generous. "Madge will do," she said. She didn't know the etiquette either. She had never been a housekeeper/nanny type person, nor even a live-in-the-same-house-with-someone-else person.

"Great. Hi, Madge, I'm Luke, and these are my girls; Aspen, Quinn, and Peyton. I see you've met our little bonus already." He nodded toward Grace in the high chair.

"I have. I fed her some crackers when we got home, but I think she's still hungry. What does she eat for supper?"

All four faces stared blankly at Madge. Finally, Luke said. "I have no idea." He looked around the kitchen. "I'm always stepping on Cheerios, so I guess she eats those."

The littlest sister said, "She likes Cheerios."

Madge didn't think the baby was surviving on Cheerios, but she decided to keep the thought to herself for now.

"So, how about the big people?" Luke said. "What are we having for dinner?" He looked at Madge with eager expectation.

She raised her eyebrows and replied. "Cheerios?"

The tallest girl dropped her school bag and pulled open the pantry door. "Mom let the groceries run low because we were supposed to be at your place this week. I don't think we have much."

"Besides Cheerios, we have one can of green beans, a bag of rice, and various boxes of snack crackers, to be exact," Madge said. "I did an inventory."

"Sooooo," Luke said, "Did you think about doing some shopping, too?"

"Nobody told me I'd have to do the shopping. And they certainly didn't leave me any money to do it with."

"Fair enough. Okay." He looked around the kitchen and then at the sad faces of his girls. "Pizza! Who wants to order pizza?"

"I do, I do," the younger girls yelled in unison and started shouting out their favorite toppings.

The girls scattered within minutes of the phone call to the local pizza place. Madge wiped the baby's face and then let her down to play with toys in the family room. Luke had plopped into the big, leather chair and had started flipping channels, oblivious to the little people around him.

Madge decided to wait in the kitchen for supper. She grabbed a *Word Search* puzzle book from her purse and pulled up a stool at the bar. At first, she couldn't concentrate. The pressure of feeding an entire family made her queasy. They wouldn't be able to eat pizza every night. Maybe she should call Emily. Before Catherine died, Emily did all her housekeeping. She would have tons of recipes. Probably even some to feed a family. Madge shook her head and muttered. If she called for a recipe, Emily would soon know all about the accident and the Oldsmobile and this plan to earn money. She could imagine what Emily would say, too. The same kind of things she used to say when Madge wanted to drive Catherine to Prayer & Share on Tuesdays.

"You women need to call for a car. You're too old to be driving on icy streets. If you asked me, the Glory Circle Sisters ought to just cancel on a day like this."

Madge had almost worked herself into a dither with those memories when a child suddenly appeared at her shoulder.

"Are you doing homework?"

"What?"

"Homework. Is that your homework?"

"No. It's a puzzle."

The little girl climbed onto a stool next to Madge and leaned over the book. Her long hair completely obscured the page. Madge tried to remember if this was Quinine or Pittsburgh. Or Philadelphia. She realized she couldn't actually remember any of their strange names.

"It doesn't have any pieces."

"It's a word puzzle. The words are the pieces."

"Oh. How does it work?"

"Well, you have to find the words listed on the page." She pushed aside the hair. "They're all scrambled up. Like maybe they are upside down or backwards, or even catty-cornered, like this one." She drew a long circle around the word "cosmetologist."

"Wow. That is a long word. You must be a really good speller."

"Well," Madge couldn't remember ever being a particularly good speller in school, and the compliment silenced her for a moment.

"I'm a bad speller. I always have to do retakes."

"What's a retake?"

"You know, we have a spelling test on Tuesday, and if you get all the words right, you don't have to take it again on Friday. I always have to retake."

"Oh, well, that's nothing. Practice makes perfect, they say."

The little girl turned solemn eyes on Madge and shook her long hair like a curtain. "Not for me. I've never gotten a perfect."

The doorbell rang, and Madge thanked Heaven for saving her from the trauma of a little girl's spelling sorrows. As she waited for someone to answer the door, she wondered again how she had gotten herself into this mess. And, if she could survive.

The oldest girl finally came leaping down the stairs to retrieve the pizza, and soon all three girls were grabbing paper plates and gooey slices. They scattered again as quickly as they had invaded, leaving three slices of pizza behind.

Luke appeared in the kitchen and grabbed two of the slices without ever taking his eyes off the screen in the next room. "Have we got any Pepsi?" he asked. "Or did the kids drink it all?"

"I have no idea," Madge answered, and she did not stir from her spot.

Luke stumbled into a stool as he maneuvered around the table and reached into the fridge, all the time keeping his eyes toward the next room. He lost sight of the television just long enough to disappear into the fridge and resurface with a can of soda in triumph. "Yes! Last one."

Within minutes, Madge was alone with the last slice of pizza. Baby Grace toddled back into the room and came all the way up to Madge's knee. Evidently, she had decided to warm up to the hand that fed her. Madge tore a tiny piece of cheesy crust and offered it to the little mouth. "Do you eat pizza?"

Grace devoured her offering in a quick bite.

"I guess you do."

Madge and Grace split the last piece of pizza, which suited Madge just fine. She could not imagine what would happen to her digestion if she ate a whole slice of greasy pepperoni at seven o'clock at night.

She carried Grace into the living room a little while later and waited for a commercial break before interrupting Luke. "What time do the girls go to bed?"

He grinned. "Ah, again, I have no idea. Aspen could probably tell you. Their mom normally takes care of that kind of thing." Grace yawned as her dad spoke. "That one looks pretty sleepy right now."

"I thought so, too. Do you want to do the tuck in?"

"Uh, not tonight, I guess." He pointed at the briefcase lying untouched on the table beside him. "I brought some work home, and I should be getting to it."

"I expect so." Madge left the room without saying all the other things that came to mind. She found the two little girls playing in their room. "What time is lights out?" she asked.

Madge actually saw the thought process work through their little minds. *This lady doesn't know what time we go to bed. We could get away with anything.*

"Nine-thirty?" The smaller one spoke with a question in her voice.

The bigger sister slapped her arm and said, "Ten. She means ten. We go to bed at ten."

Madge looked at the clock on the pink dresser. "I'm betting more like eight-thirty. You have five minutes to finish that game. Then go brush your teeth or whatever you do before bed."

She heard the groaning as she went down the hall and Sister

One saying to Sister Two, "You shouldn't have said 'ten', she wasn't going to believe 'ten'."

The oldest sister didn't hear Madge knock on her bedroom door. Finally, Madge opened the door and stepped all the way in. The girl jumped off the bed and jerked wires from her ears.

"I knocked," Madge said, "but you couldn't hear me."

"Right. I was listening to music," the girl crossed her arms and looked away from Madge.

"I'm putting the baby to bed. Do you know if your mom does anything special? A book or toy or anything?"

The girl softened suddenly. She walked over and held out her arms to the baby. "I can do it," she said. "I do it lots of times when my mom is late at work or something."

Madge stood aside and watched as the girl, whose name she absolutely could not remember, carried Grace into the next room. She had missed this nursery on her scouting expedition. The small door looked like another closet, which it might have been at one time. Madge watched the ritual of special blanket, white lamb, and "Goodnight Moon." She could handle that in a pinch. Although she couldn't remember ever reading to a child.

"Now we sing," the girl said.

Madge gripped her hands together behind her back. Singing. The thought sent her straight back to the velvet curtains and polished floor of the eight-grade recital. She almost caught a whiff of the Evening in Paris perfume from the blouse Mrs. Clemmons wore. The teacher's voice still echoed in her mind as it had in the auditorium that night. "Since you have a little problem with pitch, Dear, we shall let you lead the pledge tonight instead of singing with the class."

Madge popped back from the memory in an instant and nodded. She managed to hum along for the first line of "Jesus Loves Me" and then pretended to cover a cough. Fortunately, Grace settled down with a thumb in her mouth and did not make a peep. Afterwards, Madge and the-sister-with-no-name tiptoed out of the room and closed the door on complete silence.

"That's it," the girl said. "She's a good baby. She makes my mom tired sometimes, but that's just because she wasn't planned."

Madge cleared her throat and squinted at something on the far wall. "Well, she's all tucked up now. That's good. Now, what about the little girls? What do they need?"

"Nothing. They're allowed to watch a movie for a few minutes before bed. Then they turn it off and go to sleep."

"A movie?"

"Yes. For ten whole minutes." Both little girls stood in the hallway giving Madge wide-eyed stares. Their faces were still damp from tooth brushing, and they wore matching princess nightgowns.

"Okay. I'll just see you to your room," Madge said. She followed as the girls scrambled into their twin beds and plopped face-forward toward the television perched on their dresser. The bigger sister held a remote control. She looked at Madge.

"I've got it," she said. "You can go to your room or whatever."

Madge accepted the dismissal and backed out into the hallway, but she kept the door cracked just long enough to see Julie Andrews and the Von Trapp children appear on the famous staircase. The movie choice surprised her. She had expected some kind of cartoon.

Before going to her room or whatever, Madge paused again at the doorway of the first bedroom. The girl had left her door open slightly this time, and Madge saw her propped against pillows, earpieces in place and a book in her hands. She also noticed a raggedy teddy bear peeking from beneath the covers. She considered knocking again, or about just going in. She thought this girl who seemed the most self-sufficient of the lot was the one who probably needed tucking in the most. Something in the set of the shoulders kept Madge from intruding, though. She understood that posture. She owned it.

Chapter Six

Thursday, September 15th
Fifty-nine Days to Go

Madge didn't set an alarm for Thursday morning. She had always managed to wake up by six, no matter how late she went to bed. She thought that would give her plenty of time to pour the last of the Cheerios into bowls and manage whatever details would be required to get the girls out the door for school.

Wrong.

The shortest sister brought the first crisis when she appeared in the kitchen at six-fifteen with a wadded up shirt. "It's red day."

"Sounds fun," Madge didn't look up from the bowls where she was trying to make the cereal come out even.

"My red shirt is dirty."

"Wear a different one." Madge searched in the pantry to see if a box of Wheaties might be hiding. She could stack some Wheaties on the bottom to make the bowls look fuller. No luck.

"I don't have another one. This is my red school shirt. My only one. I have to wear it today or I won't get to do specials."

"What kind of specials?" Madge pulled some graham crackers from the back of a tall cabinet and considered the possibilities.

"Art. Music. And Recess." The last word came with the threat of actual tears.

Madge stopped and crossed her arms. "If you don't wear that particular red shirt, they won't let you go to recess? What kind of school do you go to?"

"It's progressive," the oldest sister said as she entered the kitchen. "This is school spirit day. They do it every year. We did it when I was a kid. She gets to go to recess. She just has to go last, and she might not get to take part in some of the relays because they are based on colors and stuff."

"Give me the shirt." Madge wanted to box somebody's ears for this foolish idea that made extra work for busy parents. Instead, she scrubbed the dickens out of a stain on the front of The Only Red Shirt.

She handed the wet shirt to the big sister. "Toss this in the dryer, Willow. It will be ready by the time breakfast is over."

The girl stared as if Madge had ordered her to eat raw squid.

"What?" Madge said.

"My name isn't Willow. It's Aspen."

"Oh, sorry. Wrong tree." Madge scribbled on a small notepad while Aspen stomped off to the laundry room.

The middle sister came downstairs while Madge was dividing milk into equal, tiny portions. Madge paused and snuck a peek at the notepad. "Good morning, Quinn."

"Can I have a Pop Tart?"

"We don't have any," the younger sister said. Madge looked at the notepad and reminded herself the speaker was named Peyton. Though why anyone would name a child after that scandalous soap opera she could not imagine.

"Daddy has all the Pop Tarts at his house along with the Cherry Hi-C 'cause we were supposed to be there this week."

"Why didn't he bring that stuff here?"

Aspen came back into the kitchen and picked up a bowl of cereal. "Stop begging for stuff and just eat."

Quinn slumped into her chair. "We were supposed to have Pop Tarts today. And nobody checked my spelling."

"Give me the list," Aspen said. "I'll check you while we eat."

Quinn shook her head and Madge noticed the back of her hair had turned into a giant rat's nest of tangles. "I don't know it. We should have done it last night."

Another threat of tears. Madge couldn't think of anything to help with spelling words at this late date, so she changed the subject. "I'll go to the market today. Pop Tarts tomorrow. We'll check spelling tonight. How's that?"

"That is great." Luke came down the staircase and hopped the last two steps. "I love the idea of somebody going to the store." He peeled some cash off a small wad and handed it to Madge. "I'm not sure if Alex left you any grocery money, but this should get us by until she comes back on the weekend. There is a Super Shopper just a couple of miles down on Dodge. Take the Trenton exit because Pacific is closed for repairs." He grabbed a cup of coffee as he gave directions, and Madge listened without taking notes.

He paused with a packet of sugar in mid-air. "You need to write any of that down?"

"Actually, I'm in need of a constitutional today."

"A what?"

"A walk. I need a good walk. Isn't there a grocery store near-by?"

Luke squinted and looked at the ceiling as if the answer might be hiding above the cupboards. "No, not really. Not unless you count the Gas & Go a few blocks down on the corner. I think they sell milk and stuff."

"Okay. I got it," Madge said.

"You sure? Because I could write it all down. Or punch it into the navigation for you."

"I've got it," Madge said. She swiped a damp cloth across the baby's face and lifted her from the high chair. She handed the semi-clean bundle to Aspen and spoke to Luke. "And you better get this circus loaded or everybody is going to be late according to the notebook."

The dryer dinged as she spoke and Peyton made a dash for the all-important red shirt. Aspen grabbed a diaper bag for Grace and pulled her own backpack on the other shoulder. Madge looked at Quinn's ratty hair and said, "Ponytail. Fetch me one of those do-hickies you use for a ponytail." A few minutes later, the entire clan had loaded into the car with almost-clean clothes and almost-respectable hair. Madge gave a brief wave, closed the kitchen door, and dropped into a chair. She had no idea breakfast could be so stressful.

Madge took almost an hour making out the grocery list. Luke had left her enough money to cover a few meals, but she knew she couldn't carry home more than a couple of sacks. She didn't expect the convenience store to have much in the way of supplies. Even so, she went into the garage and looked around for some kind of contraption to bring home the goods. Maybe a child's wagon.

She found two pink scooters and a purple skateboard. "Well," she said, "the mother of invention then."

Twenty-minutes later, Madge DuPree started down the street pulling a cart made of scooters and skateboard held together by jump ropes. The thing wobbled a little on the sidewalk, but she trusted it would steady itself once she loaded some weight. She almost wished the other Glory Circle Sisters could see her now. They would be so proud of her creative genius.

Although Madge had made up the part about needing a constitutional, she felt her head clearing as she walked. It wouldn't do to let Evelyn know about that. Evelyn was always telling them they needed to stay active to prevent stiffness and keep their brains young. She and Tom had actually joined some kind of health club and started taking classes.

Classes, for pity sake. Madge could not imagine pulling on one of those tight, skimpy outfits and prancing around the room with a bunch of college girls trying to stay fit.

"Lord, You just zap me straight into Glory before it comes to that," she said. "Because I'd ruther have arthritis and join Bess in the daffy club."

These ruminations had led Madge nearly two blocks, and she caught herself almost smiling as she strolled along. She stopped herself, though. That mental picture of Evelyn in a leotard had done it. The smile certainly had nothing to do with fresh air and exercise. The minute Madge earned her money, she would be cruising to the store in her Olds and leaving these walking shoes behind.

On the next block, Madge saw a house with gorgeous purple hydrangeas, and a smile popped all the way out before she could stop it. Fortunately, she saw the convenience store just ahead on the next corner, which saved her from breaking into song and making a complete fool of herself.

Madge hated shopping. Always had and always would. Way back in the day, the other ladies had sometimes suggested a trip downtown together to make a day of it. Madge had gone along, just to have something to do. She often sat in the shoe section and pretended to consider new pumps while they flitted about the various departments trying on hats and gloves and dresses. Such fal-de-ral. Of course, she wouldn't have admitted to any of them that her pension check didn't stretch far enough each month to cover a new pair of shoes, let alone a matching bag. Not when they all had husbands doling out the cash.

She swatted those thoughts out of her mind like a pesky fly on a hot day and surveyed the store in front of her. For just a moment, Madge thought about pulling her scooter cart inside, but she didn't want to appear too much like a bag lady. Instead, she parked it discreetly beside a tree at the corner and prayed no one would steal it. She looped the rope and tied it in a double knot just to make the get-away difficult if they did.

No carts inside, of course. So Madge started loading things on the edge of the counter and telling the check out girl, "I need a couple more things," every time. She finally stopped with two gallons of milk, three boxes of pop tarts, some hotdogs, cheese, bread, canned stew, and a huge box of Cheerios. At the last minute, she added a bag of cookies and some M&M's. If Luke Marvel wanted more Pepsi Cola, he could figure out how to drag it home himself.

Once she had paid for her loot, Madge looked at the bags and then at the door. Finally, she looked at the checkout girl. "You got anybody who can help me carry it out?"

"Uh, no not really," the girl said. A line had already started to form behind Madge.

She looked over her shoulder at the man who stood next in line. He kept studying the phone in his hand as if it held the secrets to the universe. Behind him, a woman with a toddler on her hip rocked back and forth and stared at the magazine rack.

Madge grumbled and grabbed one sack with each hand. "I'll come back for the rest," she said. After two trips, she had the cart loaded and the groceries evenly distributed for balance. She gave a slight tug, and the contraption rolled forward smoothly as if it had been designed for just such a task.

Even with that success, no unexpected smiling bothered Madge on the way home. The purple hydrangeas looked less glorious as she trudged past. She hadn't realized the trip to the store was downhill, but it must have been a slight grade because she was most certainly pulling uphill now.

The skateboard broke free one block from home. Madge watched it roll across the street and bang into a garbage can. The gallon of milk still perched on the board wobbled, righted itself, and then tumbled off the other side and bounced three times before landing in the middle of the street.

The loss of the skateboard from the center of the cart left the whole thing unstable. The sack with M&M's rolled across the sidewalk, breaking open and scattering candy in all directions.

Madge left the milk to fend for itself and started retrieving other items from the bag. She heard tires screech as a driver swerved to avoid the milk. She heard the splat when the driver obviously failed. She waited a few seconds before looking up from the sidewalk.

A woman in shiny, red high heels slid her long legs out of the car and walked around to assess the damage. She turned to Madge. "I don't think it left a dent," she said. "But the milk appears to be a total loss."

Madge looked at the pool growing beneath the front tire of the little sports car. "Pity," she said.

The woman looked over Madge's mess on the sidewalk. "Let me pull out of the street, and I'll give you a hand." Before Madge could protest, the driver had jumped back in, roared the engine, and pulled the car neatly to the curb. Madge heard the red heels clicking on the sidewalk as she bent to corral her groceries.

"Are you going far?" the driver asked. "Because I could give you a lift with the rest of these. I don't think your cart is going to make it."

"No, thank you." Madge waved toward the Marvel house. "I'm going right there."

"To Alex's house?"

"Yes." Madge pulled back slightly and looked at the stranger again, warily this time.

"Are you a relative I haven't met?"

"I'm the housekeeper." Madge said it with as much dignity as she could muster, considering the groceries at her feet and the milk running in the gutter.

"That doesn't make any sense." The woman reached into a slim bag slung across her body and pulled out a card. She handed it to Madge. "Alex never mentioned a housekeeper. And I have no idea why she would need one."

Madge pulled back her shoulders. "And what business is that of yours?"

"I'm Mara Lynn Harper, Alex's closest friend and her real estate agent. I'm here to sell the house."

Chapter Seven

Thursday, September 15th
Fifty-nine Days to Go

Once they got all the groceries inside the house and the skateboard back to the garage, Madge felt obligated to offer a cup of coffee. And a cookie.

"So, Marilyn, there might be coffee left in the pot."

The realtor pointed to her name on the business card Madge had dropped on the bar. "It's Mara Lynn, actually. I'm named for both of my grandmothers in an effort to stop a feud. So embarrassing. But that's another story. And, yes, I'd love a cup of coffee before I put the sign up in the yard."

"Uh-huh."

Madge poured coffee. She set creamer and sugar on the bar near where Mara Lynn had made herself at home.

"Thanks, this will really help." Mara Lynn stirred her coffee and propped her chin up with her hand. "This is so hard. I love this house, too. It has the perfect combination of antique charm and modern upgrades. The woodwork is amazing. And the fireplace. I can hardly stand to see it go. It will, though. Quickly and at a good price."

"Uh-huh." Madge didn't want to say anything more. No need to muddy things up with her feelings about this particular house.

Mara Lynn took a long sip and twirled the cookie on her saucer. "I helped them move in," she said. "I actually picked out these countertops when they finally redid the kitchen."

Madge certainly didn't want to talk about what they had done to the kitchen. So, she changed the subject. "You're an old friend, then?"

"I've known Alex since we were five, but she became a little sensitive about the term 'old friend' once we hit thirty."

"Best friends?"

"No," she squinted and fiddled with the cookie some more. "Alex didn't like that term, either, because it made us sound like sixth-graders. Alex likes language to be precise. It's the teacher in her."

"Teacher? I thought she worked for some kind of big company."

"Oh, she does." Mara Lynn gave up and took a bite out of the cookie. After she had chewed and swallowed, she said, "She's a pharmaceutical rep and doing quite well. She had to leave teaching after Peyton was born. That's when Luke lost his third or fourth job, and they just weren't going to make it. Somebody had to be the grown-up."

She stopped and covered her mouth. "I'm sorry. That was a rude way to speak about your employer. I'm so sorry. I shouldn't have said anything. It's the emotions. I swear I should not have taken this contract even though the commission will be great. I should have sent Alex to someone else. Ugh. I have to get my professional head back in the game."

"Well, after all," Madge said, "you aren't best friends."

Mara Lynn's shoulders drooped and she leaned against the barstool. "No," she said, "we're First Friends. First and forever."

They sat in the beautiful kitchen for a long time after that. A clock somewhere in another part of the house ticked off the minutes. Madge finished her coffee, but Mara Lynn merely sipped hers. It was not the kind of silence a person felt the need to break. Madge couldn't think exactly how to describe it. She thought about how she might tell this story later to the Glory Circle Sisters, and she couldn't find the right words for this silence.

Not uncomfortable. But not exactly pleasant. Sort of as if they were waiting for something, yet knowing perfectly well that nothing was still to come. Madge tried to remember when she had sat in this kind of silence before.

And then, she knew. The quiet ticking. The coffee and cookies. The almost-sacred waiting for something that would never come. It had been the day of Catherine's funeral. She and the other Glory Circle Sisters had gathered with family and friends afterward. No one had spoken that day, either. They had just sat together like this and mourned.

Madge looked up and saw Mara Lynn staring into her coffee cup like a woman in mourning. As much as Madge knew the feeling, she couldn't give into it. The possibility of losing the house brought up all kinds of things Madge couldn't deal with right now. She needed to focus on the one thing that mattered most. If Mara Lynn sold this house, Madge would lose her job.

"So," Mara Lynn said suddenly. "I'd better get to it. I wanted to drop off the sign while I was in the neighborhood today. I'll come back later with some papers for Alex to sign. We actually have some pretty good prospects lined up already."

While she spoke, Mara Lynn stood and carried her cup to the sink. Madge followed. She thought about suggesting Mara Lynn just drive herself right on down the street and come back in about sixty days. Instead, she said, "Need help?"

"Well," Mara Lynn looked at Madge with some questions on her face.

"Don't worry. I'm old, but I'm strong," Madge said. "I can still fetch and tote. Come on."

The two of them set out to tote the heavy, wooden yard sign from Mara Lynn's trunk onto the Marvel's front lawn. Madge wished Mara Lynn worked for a company that used those little, metal signs like a garage sale. Instead, she had brought the old-fashioned kind with a wooden shingle that swung from a post.

The women managed to lug it all the way to the sidewalk before they dumped it. Mara Lynn brushed dirt from her skirt and slapped her hands together to remove any remaining dust. "That will do for now," she said. "I'll come dressed for manual labor another day and pound the thing into the ground. We might actually need a post-hole digger. I don't know. Now I have to see a client a few blocks away. It was nice to meet you, Madge. I had no idea Alex planned to bring someone in for the transition, but I think it's a good idea."

"Pure genius on somebody's part," Madge said.

After the little sports car had sped off down the street, Madge spent a few minutes pretending to examine the grass at the edge of the sidewalk in case anyone was watching. When it seemed like things were clear, she grabbed one end of the "For Sale by Regency Realtors" sign and started dragging it toward the garage.

"Lord," she huffed out on her first try. "I'm no Samson; but if You want to send down some supernatural strength, I'd take it right now. I don't know how You feel about Alex selling this house, but I'll tell you what I think. It is a stupid idea. You can't raise kids in an apartment downtown."

Madge stopped pulling and stopped to catch her breath. The next words came stronger. "If she has to sell it, I guess that's her business. Although I don't know what Luke will think. And why do I care what Luke will think? Why do I care where those kids live after I'm gone? I don't care two whits."

She bent to grasp the sign again. "Could You just hold it off for sixty days? I don't want to end up like Bess, stuck in a retirement home, dependent on anyone and everyone to get me where I need to go. I need my wheels, not to mention my freedom." She stood up, stretched her back, and looked at the sky. "I'm counting on You."

It took three hitches for Madge to pull the sign all the way into the far corner of the garage. She looked around for a tarp or rug of some kind but came up empty. Instead, she settled for draping a beach towel over the sign. For good measure, she dropped a deflated volleyball and a box of hockey gear on top. She moved the skateboard and scooters around so they partially blocked the view.

Madge didn't think she felt guilty exactly, but she found herself rather jumpy the rest of the day. Sounds around the house seemed louder, and she checked the garage twice to see if the heap looked as obvious as she thought.

Yet, when the girls tumbled out of Luke's vehicle later, nobody said a word about the strange sight. Instead, they wondered what was for dinner and whether or not she had bought treats at the store. Luke just wondered if she had replenished the stock of Pepsi.

"Sorry," she said. "I decided this could be a bring-your-own-bottle house. I figured if I tried to stock the right drink for every adult, I'd drive myself mad. I'll shop for the meals, but you two will have to bring in your own specialties."

Luke gave her a half-salute. "Fair enough. I'll just run down to the corner right now and do that. Pepsi and chips. Maybe some chocolate donuts. I might even share." He tickled Peyton as he walked toward the door and ruffled Quinn's hair. "And maybe a box of cigars, what do you think? Should I get some cigars?"

"Nooooooooo," the girls said together, but they were laughing.

"He's in a jolly good mood," Madge said.

Aspen looked up from the floor where she had been playing with Grace. "Yeah. Weird. I've got homework. And, Quinn, you better work on spelling."

The girls pulled backpacks toward the bar and started spreading out books. Peyton wandered off toward the family room with Grace puttering behind. Madge decided to work on her *Word*

Search. She was chewing on the end of her pencil a few minutes later when she felt Quinn leaning in.

"Lunch."

"Lunch? It's time for supper, kiddo."

"Not the food. The word. It's right there," Quinn said. She traced the letters from right to left in a reversed line.

"Well, so it is. Good for you. How did you find that one?"

"We had that word last week. I missed it."

She turned back to her own paper and hunched over it.

Madge watched a few minutes. She had never worked a puzzle with a partner before. The very thought went against her stand for independence. Even so, she tapped Quinn with the pencil. She pointed to the next word, which probably wasn't from a grade school spelling list, and said, "How about this one?"

Quinn looked at the word a few minutes and then traced her finger across the page. She didn't take long before she pointed to the upper left corner. Madge handed Quinn the pencil, and she made a slow, steady circle around the word. They continued working the puzzle together until Luke returned from the store. When Madge got up to make macaroni and hot dogs, Quinn kept working.

Chapter Eight

Friday, September 16th
Fifty-eight Days to Go

"The girls will catch a ride home with the carpool today," Luke said at breakfast the next morning.

"We have one of those?" Madge wondered why she bothered with maps and whirly-go-rounds if the neighborhood already had transportation worked out.

"Sort of. We don't actually use it very often because if you ride, you have to take a turn driving. Neither one of us is that reliable."

Madge thought that sounded like an obvious statement.

"Anyway, the girls are covered after school. I'm taking off a little early today since it's Friday. I'll bring Gracie home and grab my stuff before Alex gets here. I don't want to drag bags to work with me. We didn't have time to work out the transition details, but since you are here, I guess it doesn't matter that much. I'm sure Alex will be late."

"I'll be here," Madge said. She handed Quinn the spelling list they had been working on over breakfast and watched while she folded it and pushed it into her book bag. "Watch out for the silent 'e'," Madge said. "It's sneaky."

Quinn nodded and followed her dad toward the garage, leaving her breakfast untouched. Aspen stacked bowls by the sink before she grabbed her own book bag. "Thanks for breakfast," she said to Madge as she walked toward the door.

"Just doing my job," Madge said, "but you're welcome." She was not accustomed to being thanked by a teenybopper, and she didn't exactly know how to respond. After the family left, Madge wondered if Aspen always acted so politely or if she wasn't accustomed to having breakfast.

One thing for sure, Madge had never done spelling words so early in the morning. She taxed her brain most days by watching *The Price is Right*, but she usually got the price wrong.

Madge would have told anybody who asked that she was flexible, not stuck in her ways like Grace Colby who couldn't be bothered to trade visiting days at the nursing home if it interfered with her hair appointment or her cleaning lady. Madge didn't have a cleaning lady.

Evidently, being flexible with the Glory Circle Sisters was a little like that exercise routine they do from chairs. Being flexible in this house felt more like being an acrobat in the circus. Madge hoped she could keep up.

Madge also felt a slight edge of dread about living with all these emotional females. She knew she had a reputation among her friends for being somewhat mouthy. She couldn't help it if she had the right opinion in most discussions. Even so, she would walk backwards out of a room and go around the block twice if it meant she didn't have to talk about her feelings.

Thinking about her friends reminded Madge that she needed to write some letters. The other ladies were expecting her to come back home on Monday. She thought she had a few stamps in her purse, and she was going to use paper and envelopes from the stash she found in a kitchen drawer. She could pay for them if anyone complained.

She started with Emily. They weren't exactly friends, and

Emily wasn't even a member of the Glory Circle, but somewhere in the last couple of years Emily had taken on the role of checking in on Madge. It was totally unnecessary, of course. Madge thought Emily needed something to do after Catherine died. She had kept house for Catherine so long, she probably felt lost. So, Madge tolerated Emily's phone calls and her stopping by on the way to the store and her frequent questions about Madge's health and her plans.

Madge sat for a long time with her pen hovering above the page.

"Dear Emily," she began. "Have decided to stay in Cherry Hills for a longer time than expected. As you know, I only came to spend a week with my nephew, Ben, and his wife, Nancy, but something came up. Got into a bit of a scrape with my car and need to earn a few dollars for repairs. Came across a great job as a housekeeper with a nice family. Short-term thing. Just the ticket."

She stopped and scratched out the word ticket. No need to bring up anything related to court. Finally, she slowed her pen and wrote more carefully.

"So, I won't be coming home for about two months. I'll get my mail forwarded to this address. It's my current place of employment. I'm sure you have some things to say about that. If Catherine was still alive, I know she would have all kinds of advice for how I should behave myself. And I would ignore it. I'm sure you have a few words to say on her behalf. So, feel free to save yourself the postage, and let's pretend you said it all, and I agreed. Then we can both go on and do whatever we please. Regards to your husband. Hope he is well. As husbands go, he isn't a bad sort."

The next letter went to Ben. She thought hard about how to put things so he and Nancy wouldn't come rushing over to yank her out of the house and back to their apartment. She settled on breezy.

"Ben, all is well. Employers are a mess but doing fine by me. You and Nancy enjoy yourselves and don't worry. Try out that new Italian place I heard the bailiff talking about. I'll keep in touch about the car. Let's make sure that repair shop where they towed it has a good man. I don't want any shyster trying to take advantage of an old lady. Regards, Your favorite (and only) Aunt Madge.

P.S. Probably best if you don't write to me at this address. Might worry these folks to see a letter from the judge. I'll keep in touch."

She wrote a few lines to Evelyn next. The Glory Circle didn't have an official president, but Evelyn always led at Prayer & Share. Everyone looked to Evelyn if a decision couldn't be made between peach cobbler and blueberry crumb cake for Pastor's Appreciation Day. She would always break the tie, and nobody complained.

So, Madge wrote her by default and explained the situation.

"Tell the girls not to worry. I won't stir up too much trouble while I'm here. And, if I do, you all can come over and straighten it out later. I'll see you sometime around Thanksgiving."

Once her letters were sealed and addressed, Madge walked a couple of blocks and dropped them into the mailbox she had noticed earlier. When she got back to the house, she sat in Luke's big, leather chair just to rest her eyes from the strain of writing.

The strain wore off at about four o'clock when a door slammed. Madge tried to remember why she was reclining in a room with a stone fireplace when suddenly a small face came into view.

"I forgot silent 'e'."

Madge struggled to pull the lever on the recliner and sat up, working hard to orient herself to place, time, and people. The little girl came closer. "I got a seven."

"Seven's a good number," Madge said.

"Out of twenty-five."

"Well, that's not so good." She remembered now. She bore some responsibility for this child. "Should we study some more?"

"Too late." Quinn waved a piece of paper like a white flag. "This is next week's list. We gotta start on it already."

"Okay," Madge said, "let's start." She felt rather proud of herself for remembering Quinn's name. Maybe she could handle spelling. Another door slammed, though, before Madge could read the first word. She heard Grace crying and Luke shouting.

"Madge! Madge! Can you take her? I've got to pack my stuff and get across town before five."

Luke handed the screaming baby to Madge and then tore up the staircase. Madge attempted a soothing jiggle. "Okay, Grace, it's okay. We'll find something to eat. Stop crying now."

Grace did not stop. And, she did not eat. Grace kept crying the whole time Luke threw clothes into a suitcase and rummaged around downstairs for various sports equipment and magazines.

"What's wrong with her?" Madge asked when Luke stopped at the refrigerator.

"I have no idea. She was like this when I picked her up. The daycare said she wouldn't eat her lunch today. They tried to call Alex and tell her something was off, but it went straight to voicemail. I'm the emergency number, but they didn't call me. I don't know why." He spoke the last words while holding a football in one hand and a golf club in the other.

"I have no idea, either," Madge said.

"Hey, I'm a responsible guy. These are for networking. Guys

make deals on the golf course all the time. I might get my big break on the eighteenth hole." He grinned at Madge, stuffed the football under his arm, and reached in the pantry for the Cheerios. "Here, Gracie, how about your favorite?"

Grace stopped crying long enough to stuff a bite of cereal into her mouth.

"See? I can take care of things," Luke said. He took two steps toward the staircase before Grace started crying again. He looked back at Madge for a few seconds, then shook his head and kept walking.

Chapter Nine

Friday, September 16th
Fifty-eight Days to Go

After Luke went upstairs, Madge tried walking circles in the kitchen, bouncing Grace on her shoulder. "I'm not going to sing you a lullaby," she said. "We'd both feel worse if I tried that. I can't really tell you a story unless you want to hear about the time Bess thought the neighbors were stealing her electricity. Or maybe how I broke the windshield on my Olds one winter scraping ice. Catherine rescued me and splurged on a fancy town car to get us around the rest of the month."

Grace kept crying, and Madge thought about joining her. She didn't know a child could make you feel so helpless. She also wished she hadn't mentioned the windshield. The memory made her miss Catherine, and it reinforced the helpless feeling. Nobody would be hiring a town car this time.

Before Madge could wade any deeper into her muddle, Aspen came downstairs. "I can't even hear my music over the crying," she said. "What's wrong?"

"No idea," Madge said. "Neither your brilliant father nor the trained staff at Toodle Time knows, either. So we are stuck."

"Toddle Time," Aspen said. She reached out and brushed damp hair away from Grace's face. "She's really hot. Do you think she has a fever?"

Madge put her hand on the baby's forehead. "Maybe. Or maybe she just worked herself up." She waited a few seconds before asking the question she'd been wondering for a while. "What do you think your mother would do?"

"I don't know. Cry with her probably. She gets exasperated rather easily in these situations."

Madge raised her eyebrows both at the use of such vocabulary and at the way this child seemed to understand the adults around her. "Well, I might try rocking her," Madge said. "I've heard babies like rocking."

"I'll get her blanket."

Luke came through the kitchen with a duffle bag and a large suitcase just as Aspen bopped up the stairs. He stopped when he saw Madge holding Grace. He stood in the middle of the room, a bag in each hand, while Grace cried and Madge patted her back.

"I think someone should rock her," Madge said.

"Good idea."

"Someone she knows."

"Yeah, probably so." Luke didn't move.

"Someone like her father," Madge finally said

"I don't know how to rock a baby," Luke said. "I never did that part."

"Well, neither did I, Buster." Madge turned Grace around to face her father. "But, I think it comes with the territory when you procreate. So figure it out."

Luke dropped his luggage and took Grace. With a free hand, he caught the blanket and stuffed bunny Aspen tossed toward him.

"Okay, Gracie," he said. "Let's see who's on the sports channel tonight. Maybe we can find a good game to watch while we rock."

Madge tried not to roll her eyes. She stood in the kitchen with Aspen and listened to the rumble of the television and the wailing of the baby. After a few minutes, the crying stopped. Madge could only hear the ballgame and the whisper of the rocking chair brushing against the wall.

She and Aspen peeked around the corner together. Grace had fallen asleep snuggled against Luke's chest. He didn't seem in a hurry to make his golf game anymore.

Madge pulled Aspen away from the door. "I didn't know he could do that," Aspen said.

"Neither did he." Madge led the way to the kitchen and opened the refrigerator to start supper. She handed Aspen the last of the hotdogs. "Dump those in a pan and add some water."

"My mom will be home tonight, and she can go to the store tomorrow."

"That's good."

"Unless she's too tired."

"She'll probably be pretty tired from all that running around at airports and such. It's a fright."

"She does it all the time," Aspen said, "so she's used to it. But she might be tired anyway. She has to stay up late when she travels because she has lots of meetings and dinners and stuff."

"Uh, huh." Madge didn't like the direction of this conversation. She knew all about women who traveled for business. Late night meetings in bars. Lonely businessmen across the hall in fancy hotels. She might be past her own prime, but she knew about such things. "Maybe you better check on your little sisters," she said. "I haven't heard anything from upstairs in a while, and quiet can mean trouble."

"Okay. But I think they are playing. They like to go to their room after school."

Madge frowned. "They just stay in their room to play? What about going outside?"

Aspen looked out the window. "I don't know. We usually go to our rooms."

Madge put her hands on her hips. "You have a backyard that's better than a park. Why aren't you out there playing every day?

I even see swings."

Aspen didn't look out a second time. "Yeah. Our dad built the swings. But they fought about it afterwards because he should have spent the money on tires for the Lexus. Sometimes he's impulsive."

Madge felt rather impulsive at that moment. She had an impulse to spank a couple of grown-ups who had such conversations in front of their children. "Well, that's a bunch of nonsense," she said. "Swings are a lifetime investment. Your dad knew exactly what he was doing. And you girls ought to be out there trying to fly to China on an afternoon like this."

"Flying to China?" Aspen gave Madge an almost-smile.

"Sure. That's what you do on a swing as good as those. You pump hard and kick your feet, and pretty soon you sail so high you can see China. Don't tell me you've never tried?"

Aspen shook her head, but she smiled for real now. "That's silly."

"Maybe. But it's more fun than hiding in your bedroom with gizmos and gadgets stuck in your ears," Madge said. "Making you deaf before you're twenty, by the way."

Aspen opened her mouth as if she might respond, but the rumble of the garage door interrupted. Instead of arguing with Madge, Aspen dropped the hot dog package and shouted up the staircase, "Mom's home!"

The sound of little feet rushing from upstairs joined the sound of car doors slamming, and within moments, the kitchen bustled with a family reunion. Aspen held back from the hugs and hellos. She took her mother's briefcase and nodded when Alex asked if she had a good week.

Madge noticed that Alex kept her phone in one hand and looked at it several times even as she listened to the little girls chatter about school and friends. "That's good," Alex said after every question or remark. She kept the same tone of voice even when Quinn admitted her poor spelling grade.

"It's not good. Seven's not good, Mommy."

Alex looked up from her phone. "What? I'm sorry, Quinny; I had to finish up this message from work. What's wrong with seven?"

Aspen stepped in before spelling could become the center of attention. "Gracie is sick."

"What?" Alex dropped her phone on the counter. "What kind of sick? Where is she?"

"It's just a little fever," Madge said. "I'm sure she will be fine. Her Daddy rocked her to sleep."

Alex stopped moving and stared at Madge. "He did what?"

"He rocked her," Aspen said. She pointed toward the family room. "She's sleeping."

Alex kicked off her heels and crept around the corner where Luke had actually stopped rocking. Madge and the girls followed a few steps behind. They reached the doorway just in time to see Alex pull the blanket away from Grace's sweating face.

"What are you doing? She's burning up. You don't swaddle a child with a fever like that. You'll make it worse. Does she have a rash? Good grief. Give her to me. She needs a tepid bath and some Tylenol. Did anyone give her Tylenol?" While she spoke, Alex pulled Grace off Luke's lap and started toward the staircase. The baby woke and whimpered. Then, seeing her mother, she snuggled down and stuck her thumb in her mouth.

Luke stood and yelled at Alex as she climbed the stairs. "We didn't give her Tylenol because a fever is the body's natural way to fight off illness. She was doing just fine. We were doing just fine." His voice trailed off as Alex slammed the bathroom door. The sound of water running in the bathtub almost drowned out his next words, but Madge heard him say, "Besides, I didn't have any idea where we kept the stuff."

The transition went even less smoothly as the evening wore on. The tepid bath did wonders for Grace who was soon giggling and splashing.

"The nap probably helped," Madge said as Luke walked through the kitchen.

He grabbed a duffle and swung it over his shoulder. "Right. Thanks for trying. Tell Alex I left some cash on the dresser in case she didn't have time to get any. I don't think we have anything to feed the girls for supper otherwise."

He came back for his second bag just as Alex appeared on the landing. She waved the cash over the banister. "Did you sleep in my room all week? And did you just leave your stuff lying around for me to pick up? I'm not your maid anymore, Lucas! Next time you are here, you sleep in the green room. I thought we made that clear." She tossed the cash and a pair of running shoes over the banister and stomped back up the stairs.

Luke walked over, picked up the money, and flipped through it for a few seconds before he handed it to Madge. "Stick it in a jar somewhere," he said. "You might need it for something when Her Majesty isn't around."

Chapter Ten

Saturday, September 17th
Fifty-seven Days to Go

Madge rose at her usual time and waited an hour for someone to appear in the kitchen for breakfast. Eventually, she remembered this was Saturday. Obviously, the Marvel house operated on weekend time. She ate a piece of toast, drank her coffee, and then went back to her room. She sank into the tufted chair and felt her sore back relax against the soft fabric. She rested her feet on the matching ottoman and wondered if this is how it felt to be royalty. She also wondered if the queen ever felt this exhausted. "You know, Lord," she said, "this job is tougher than it sounded."

Around nine, Madge heard someone stir upstairs. She thought it came from Grace's room, but, she didn't move immediately. She assumed the mother of the house would respond.

Thirty minutes later, Madge heard the television in the family room. Again, she waited a few minutes for more sounds of family life. Finally, she gave up and hauled herself out of the chair.

Quinn, Peyton, and baby Grace scrunched together on the

sofa with a fuzzy blanket. They didn't pull their eyes away from the television when Madge walked into the room. Aspen sat curled at the other end of the sofa with the remote in hand. Her tousled hair and pink slippers made her look more like the little girl she should be. She looked up at Madge. "Cartoon Day."

"I see. Anybody want breakfast? We've got toast."

The little girls didn't stir, and Aspen shook her head. "Maybe later."

"Okay." She waited a minute, wondering if she should insist on some form of sustenance. Could children skip breakfast? What about Grace? Would it stunt her growth if she went without a meal? Finally, Madge reminded herself this was not her problem. She was just the housekeeper. In fact, Saturday and Sunday should probably be her days off. Nobody had even talked about such things, but they shouldn't really need her when one of the parents was home.

With that, she turned and marched back to her room. She would turn on her own television and find something besides cartoons to watch. Maybe an old movie or the *Andy Griffith Show*. Maybe some documentary on the royal family. She saw one about the Queen once.

Sometime later, Madge woke up when she felt a bump against her knee. Her first thought was that she had missed the end of the movie and would never know if Mr. Smith beat the crooked politicians in Washington. Of course, Jimmy Stewart usually won the day and the girl, so she probably knew how it ended. Her next thought was to wonder why this small person was standing in her house.

Madge rubbed her hand over her eyes and became conscious enough to remember she wasn't in her own home. This little person leaning against her knee was baby Grace. Madge reached out and offered her hand. "You want some milk?"

Grace accepted the hand and pulled toward the kitchen. Soon, all four girls had wandered into the room and gathered around the bar for a late breakfast.

"What is this?" Peyton asked.

"What do you mean?" Madge slathered butter on another piece of bread and sprinkled it with cinnamon and sugar.

"This." Peyton held up the last corner of her toast. "What are we eating?"

"Cinnamon toast. Haven't you ever eaten cinnamon toast?" Madge shoved the pan under the broiler and straightened up with her hands on her hips.

Peyton shook her head and Quinn said, "It's even better than Pop Tarts."

"My, my. What a compliment." Madge poured more milk into Quinn's cup and winked at Aspen as she turned toward the stove.

"We've had it," Aspen said. "They just don't remember."

"I'm sure you have."

"Had what?" Alex appeared in the kitchen wearing a loose tee shirt and something Madge did not consider pants.

"Cinnamon toast," Madge said. "Want some?"

"No thanks. Just coffee. Lots of coffee."

Peyton stuffed a bite of toast into her mouth and said, "Can we go to the zoo today?"

"The zoo?" Alex shook her head while she poured coffee into a tall mug. "Sure. Right after we fly to the moon and stop off at the North Pole."

"Hurray! Let's do it."

"She's being sarcastic," Aspen told her sister.

"I was being realistic," Alex said. "We can't go to the zoo because it costs money, and we need to save our money for school shoes right now."

"If we went to the zoo," Peyton said, "would Madge come with us?"

Madge stopped buttering bread. She glanced up to see how Alex would handle this one.

"Madge?" Alex looked confused as if Peyton had asked to bring along the family dog. If they had one. "Well, no, probably not," she said. "Madge works for us. We wouldn't expect her to go out of her way to come along on a social outing."

Madge felt the sting. It surprised her because she hadn't planned to care about these people. Being classified as the help, though, not even worthy of a trip to the zoo, took the breath right out of her.

"Besides," Alex kept talking, "nobody is going to the zoo. I have an appointment to get my hair done in about thirty minutes, and then I need to fill out a million travel reports. I have to return phone calls, check emails, and schedule all my things for next week. Plus, you girls need to clean your rooms."

All three girls started whining at once, and Alex held her hand up like a policeman directing traffic. "I am ignoring all complaints," she said. "File them with someone who cares."

"You don't care about the zoo?" Peyton said. "They have new elephants."

Madge wished this zoo talk would stop. It wasn't helping her feel any better.

"I care a great deal about elephants," Alex said. "But they live a long time. Those same elephants will still be at the zoo in a few weeks when I get through this busy season at work and my bonus comes through. I promise."

Madge handed Peyton another piece of toast. In the same moment, she decided to change the subject.

"Somebody needs to go to the store," she said.

Alex frowned. "Groceries. I forgot we would need to restock groceries." She looked around the kitchen for a few seconds and then back toward Madge. "I don't suppose you would be up to that task?"

Madge crossed her arms. She wasn't good enough to tag along on a social event, but she was perfectly fine for sending to the store. She searched her mind for some way out of driving the car.

Finally, she remembered something she had heard on television once. "Seems like it might be outside my job description," she said.

"Right." Alex tapped her coffee cup. "I can see where restocking the entire kitchen might be a bit much. Well, I'll just have to stop on my way back after I get my hair done. Once I'm restocked, I'll create a master list. You can use it to make sure we don't run so low again."

Alex took a long drink of coffee. She had barely swallowed when she spoke to Madge again. "You are staying here with the girls, right? You weren't counting on the day off or anything were you? Because if I have to drag all of them along this will take four times as long."

So, that answered the question of whether or not she had weekends off. Madge thought about complaining. The zoo comment still bothered her, and she thought about stating her rights, although she wasn't sure what they were. Instead, she thought about how much faster she would earn her get-out-of-hock money if she worked seven days a week. She could probably shorten this job by a week or even more.

"Oh, I wasn't counting on anything," Madge said. "I'll be here."

If she had known how long a Saturday at home with four children could become, Madge would definitely have counted on something else. Like a root canal. Her one real task was to oversee the cleaning of rooms while she did her own small load of laundry. It should have taken an hour, tops. However, the girls managed to drag their chore out until the middle of the afternoon with whining, complaining, and procrastinating.

Once, Quinn appeared in the laundry room holding a sparkly, pink shoe in her hand. "This isn't mine," she said.

"And, I'm pretty sure it isn't mine." Madge continued folding towels.

"But it was on my side of the room. And Peyton won't pick it up."

Madge stopped and studied the situation. "So, you walked all the way downstairs, through the kitchen, and into the laundry room carrying a shoe you didn't want to pick up and put in the closet which was two feet away? Just so you could tattle on your sister?"

"Because she wouldn't pick it up. And it's hers."

Madge stood amazed at the third-grade logic. "Fine. Go drop it on the floor again. Exactly where you found it. Tell Miss Peyton that Madge said to pick it up if she ever wants to see a slice of cinnamon toast in this house again. Or else."

Quinn pumped her fist in the air and ran for the staircase shouting, "Peyton, Madge said…"

Those magical words continued throughout the day.

"Madge said you have to give me a turn with the remote."

"Madge said everybody has to share that package of gum."

"Madge said I can, too, play football when I grow up."

And, finally, "Madge said Mama should be home any minute, and we can ask her about painting our toenails."

At supper, which consisted of rotisserie chicken and packaged salad around the bar, Madge decided to ask her own question. "What time should I be ready to leave for church in the morning?"

Alex put her salad fork down and took a sip of water from her bottle before she answered. "Well, let's see. Tomorrow…"

"We don't go," Aspen said.

Alex shot Aspen a look. "What she means is that we probably won't go tomorrow. Things get so hectic right after school starts that we find it difficult to keep up. Sunday ends up being our only day to catch up and get ready for the week. Of course, you can go to service anywhere you like tomorrow. You really should take a day off. Or at least a half-day. Would Sunday mornings work best for that? So you could go to your own church?"

"My church is across town. If I tried to fight the traffic, I'd have to go straight to the altar and repent." Madge thought about the situation for a moment. She hadn't actually told a lie. If she took Alex's car to church with her suspended license, she would need to repent.

"I could probably call my nephew," she said. "They go to some big church downtown. I could go with them."

Alex stared at her phone, as usual, and only half-listened to Madge. "Oh, that's good. That would be fine. We'll probably just hang around here getting ready for the week. You feel free to go visit your nephew for the morning."

"I might do it," Madge said. "Where *is* the telephone, by the way?"

"Your telephone? I haven't seen it." Alex looked up just long enough to glance around the room before she returned to her screen.

"Not my telephone. *The* telephone. I thought it would be on the wall in the kitchen, but it isn't there, so I can't figure out where else it would be."

"Oh, you mean a landline? We haven't had a landline in years. Don't you get reception here on your cell?" This time Alex actually looked at Madge.

"If you mean one of those little purse phones, no. I don't have one. Never saw the need."

"Well, that is a problem. How will I reach you if I need something?"

Madge thought how proud all her friends would be if they could see the half dozen responses she did not give to that question. Instead, she said, "Well, yes. Or, if I need you. For instance, if the baby gets sick again or something."

"Well, yes, that, too. Of course." Alex tapped her finger against her own phone for a moment. "I'll just have to pick up one of those pre-paid phones next time I'm running errands," she said. "My lawyer can tack it onto the settlement costs."

"Brilliant idea," Madge said.

Chapter Eleven

Monday, September 19th
Fifty-five Days to Go

Madge didn't go to church on Sunday. She felt like a heathen for the first hour of the morning, but after that, she relaxed enough to admit that having a "catch up day" was a pretty good idea. She just wouldn't make a habit of such a thing. She used Alex's phone to call Ben's wife Nancy and let her know she would be staying with the Marvels for the day. "Yes, everything was fine," and "No, they didn't need to come to take her for a drive."

When Monday morning hit with a fury, Madge was glad she had taken the proverbial day-of-rest. Having Mom in the house didn't make the morning school rush any less hectic. In fact, it seemed to raise the stress factor a few notches.

"Did you pick up that notebook I need for science?" Aspen spoke between bites of cereal and didn't look up from the textbook propped against her backpack in the center of the table.

"Shoot," Alex said from the laundry room. "I knew I forgot something. We are completely out of dryer sheets."

"What about my notebook?" Aspen shouted the question this time.

Alex shouted back, "I didn't see a notebook on the list."

"I told you as you were getting in the car."

"If it's not on the list, it's not in my head by the time I get to the store. You know that." She came into the kitchen with a couple of tee shirts looped over her arms. "Madge, could you add the notebook to your grocery list for this week?"

Madge reached for a notepad beside the sink just as Aspen came to drop her empty bowl on the counter. She stared at Madge's list. "Why do you have our names on your grocery list?"

"What?" Madge moved her hand so the neatly printed names at the top of the page were less visible.

"You have our names at the top of your grocery list."

"Are you buying us treats?" Quinn asked.

Aspen pulled Madge's hand away and flipped back the pages of the notepad. "Our names are on every page." She looked at Madge and frowned. "You can't remember our names, can you? You have to write them down so you don't call me 'Willow' or 'Maple Tree' or something."

"Aspen, that's a terrible thing to say," Alex reached out and pulled Aspen toward her. "You apologize."

"No, she's right." Madge smoothed out the page. "I'm not ashamed of it. I wrote down all your names the first day because I couldn't keep anyone straight. Heaven's sake, I never met anyone with interesting names. All I ever knew were Harrys, Gertrudes, and Elmers. I met a Perdity once, but she went by "Aunt Goose" most of the time."

Quinn giggled and Alex smiled. "Not really."

"Really. I don't know who came up with it, but some little child had once called her 'Aunt Goose', and it stuck. Anyway, fancy names are something new for me, and I couldn't keep them straight. So, I wrote you down. Even after I knew your names, I kept copying you to the top of the page every day. I suppose it became a habit."

"Well, I think that is a nice habit." Alex pulled Aspen in and wrapped her arms around the stiff shoulders in an unusual display of affection. "It's pretty special to be at the top of someone's list every morning, don't you think?"

Aspen shrugged, but she didn't pull away. Quinn jumped up and ran to the counter. "I want to see my name on the list. Where am I?"

Madge pointed to the spot. "I didn't mean to make a federal case of it," she said.

"Well, I think it is both sensible and sweet," Alex said. "I like knowing the girls are on your list."

"Let's go with sensible. I'm not usually known for sweet." Madge picked up her pencil and tried to bring the conversation back to business. "What about this notebook? Do I need to know anything special like color or number of pages or anything?"

The bonding moment dissolved, and the rest of the school rush flew by in its typical blur. Madge eventually found herself alone with a few dirty dishes and the sound of the washing machine for company. She had finished her chores and settled in to catch *The Price is Right* when she heard the kitchen door open and close.

"Just me," Alex yelled. "I forgot the file with all my expense reports."

Madge met her at the foot of the stairs as she ran back down. "What about school pick-up today," Madge asked. "Are you doing it?"

"Oh, sheesh. We forgot to work out the schedule didn't we?" She glanced at her phone to check the time. "If you can cover this afternoon, we could work out the rest of the week when I get home tonight. I'll probably be late. I don't think anybody has after school stuff today, so it will all be their regular times. Could you do that?"

Madge tried to run various scenarios through her mind in the few seconds it took Alex to walk across the kitchen. She felt like her brain was caught in the roundabout on Grand Avenue, though. Finally, in desperation, she said, "say, would you have time to drop me somewhere?"

Alex stopped and looked up. "Drop you? Sure. But don't you want to take the extra car? I'm using my company car all week."

"No, I want to meet up with someone. So I won't need my own wheels."

"Okay," Alex said. "I have a few minutes." Although she didn't sound as if she really did.

When they reached the intersection near Jack Oakley's office, Madge pointed to a bakery in the strip mall across the street. "Right there is good," she said.

"You're meeting a friend at the bakery?"

"I want to check prices on their day-old sales."

Alex pulled in and stopped without putting the car in park. "Okay, here you go. Are you sure you will be okay? Your friend doesn't seem to be here yet."

"Listen; when you get to be my age, you know how to navigate your way around a situation. If anything goes wrong with the plan, I'll work it out."

"Okay, but the first thing I'm going to do today is get you that phone. I don't like leaving you without a telephone."

"Do you know how many decades I've lived without a telephone in my purse? I think I can manage a few more hours. Now get yourself to work and let me get about my business before those bagels get another day older."

Once Alex and her company car were out of sight, Madge hoofed it to the corner and crossed the street.

"I know I came pretty close to telling a big one or two this morning, Lord. I do want to check the price of bread, but I'm not going to have time now. So You just take that into account, okay? Give me a little break, under the circumstances."

She still felt a little short of breath when the elevator doors eventually opened and coughed her out into Paige Rosedale's reception room.

Miss Rosedale looked up from the book on her desk and smiled. "Hello, Ms. DuPree. How can we help you today?"

Madge wasn't accustomed to such a greeting, and she almost forgot her errand. "Hello," she said. She stood for a moment wondering if someone was going to offer crumpets and tea or something. Finally, she said, "I wonder if I might see Jack, I mean Mr. Oakley for a few minutes."

"Let me check and see if he is available." Miss Rosedale turned slightly so that Madge couldn't hear her voice and spoke into the telephone. She turned back in a few seconds with the same, polite smile. "I'm sorry. Mr. Oakley is on a call right now, but if you would like to schedule something with him later this week..."

"I'll wait." Madge plopped down on one of the stiff chairs, folded her hands together over her purse, and stared straight ahead.

Miss Rosedale turned back to her computer and began to type. Every few minutes she looked over the top of her computer toward Madge. After fifteen minutes, she spoke again. "Could I get you something? Some water? Coffee?"

"Nope."

"It might take a while," Miss Rosedale said. "Are you sure you don't want to make an appointment?"

"I'll wait."

Chapter Twelve

Monday, September 19th
Fifty-five Days to Go

Madge waited thirty minutes before Miss Rosedale finally jumped up from her desk. "Just let me go check on that call," she said. "Maybe I can give you some idea how much longer it will be." She slipped through the door to the main office with a quick knock.

Madge could hear voices on the other side, but she couldn't make out the words. A few seconds later, Miss Rosedale emerged. "Good news," she said. "He is almost done."

Jack opened the door in that same moment and spoke to Madge. "Let's see what we can do for you today, Ms. DuPree. I can spare a few minutes. Miss Rosedale, if that next call comes through, please hold it as long as you can."

Madge caught the confused look on Miss Rosedale's face before she recovered and said, "Right. I won't interrupt you unless it's urgent."

"Don't worry," Madge told her, "My business won't take five. I need a carpool this week."

Both Jack and Miss Rosedale frowned. "A carpool," Jack finally said. "To take you where?"

"To the elementary school, the junior high school, and that

Toodle Time place every afternoon. The mom covers morning drop-offs."

"Toddle Time," Miss Rosedale said, but Jack just kept frowning.

"I don't understand how we can help you."

"Well, she expects me to pick the kids up every day this week. Nobody ever mentioned that in the job description. Nobody ever asked if I had a license. And you seemed all hot and bothered about that when I mentioned it, so I thought you'd better help me pick those kids up this week."

Jack looked at Madge as if she wasn't actually speaking English. Then he turned to Miss Rosedale as if she might translate. She did. "Ms. DuPree needs to pick the Marvel children up at school this week, but her license has been suspended by the court for that little mishap with the ice cream truck."

Jack squeezed his eyes shut. "Oh, yes. The ice cream truck. Everyone managed to leave out that little detail, as I recall." He lifted his hand the way a person would swat at a fly and said, "Well, I guess you will just have to come clean with your employer, Ms. DuPree, and let her know that you are unable to fulfill that part of the job."

Madge copied his hand motion with her own flip of the wrist. "Well, I guess you will just have to notify Judge Hightower that your client can't obey his rules for the next sixty days because she doesn't have a housekeeper anymore."

Jack opened his mouth again, but before he could speak, Miss Rosedale intervened. "How about this: What if I take an hour every afternoon this week to go along as a chauffeur? We could make the school and daycare run together. That way Ms. DuPree is technically picking up the children, but she isn't driving without a license. I can help her get acclimated to the route, and it gives her a little time to come up with a solution together with Mrs. Marvel."

"Sounds like a plan," Madge said.

"Well," Jack rubbed his hand across his chin as if he actually needed time to consider all the pros and cons of the suggestion. Or as if he had some other pressing business for his administrative assistant.

"I could drop off any papers that need to be filed in court at the same time," Miss Rosedale said. "That way it wouldn't be a waste of company time."

"Good point. If you combine it with errands you already need to run for the office, it won't even be taking much extra time." He paused just long enough to seem dramatic. "Things could probably hold together here for a little while."

Madge and Miss Rosedale both looked around the empty, silent office. "Yes, probably," Miss Rosedale said with a straight face.

Jack turned with that and disappeared behind his office door. Within seconds, Madge could hear the sounds of a terrible battle being waged.

"Gaming helps him think," Miss Rosedale said. "It's a proven strategy."

"I'm sure. Now, on to more important matters. You have to stop calling me Ms. DuPree. My name is Madge."

"And mine is Paige. At your service, Madge," she said with a sweet smile.

And so, the Paige Rosedale School Pick-up and General Aid Service was born. Madge tacked on the General Aid part because she also had to rely on Paige to figure out how to get to the schools, where to park, and how to navigate the sticky questions from Aspen who was the first passenger to climb aboard the unusual train.

"Hi, I'm Paige, a friend of Madge."

"Why are you driving my mom's car?"

"Well, as I said, I'm a friend of Madge's, and I'm just helping her out with some errands today."

"And why isn't Madge driving?"

"Madge isn't entirely familiar with this part of the city yet, so I came along to help her out until she feels more comfortable. I'll probably help all week."

Aspen clicked her seatbelt, but she kept staring at Paige in the rearview mirror. "Does my mom know about this?"

"Well, not exactly." Paige spoke a little more slowly this time as she maneuvered the Lexus out of the pickup line and into traffic.

Madge huffed and swiveled around in the seat. "Look, Kid. I had a little trouble with the law a while back, and they are holding my license for ransom. Until I earn a few more bucks, I can't get it back. I haven't exactly discussed that with your folks yet. So, until I do, Paige is going to be our chauffeur. And that isn't going to be something we necessarily talk about at supper. Or breakfast. Not until I have time to work out a few details and talk to your parents."

Aspen stared at Madge as if she had just admitted to a bank robbery.

Madge waited only a few seconds before she said, "So, are we good?"

"Yeah," Aspen said. She didn't say anything else until after Madge had turned around and Paige had driven several blocks. Finally, Aspen spoke again. "You didn't, like, murder anybody or anything, did you?"

Madge laughed and Paige hit the brakes a little harder than necessary at the stop sign. "Oh, my goodness," she said. "Madge had a minor traffic violation. Mr. Oakley would never send someone with a dangerous background to your home. That is ludicrous."

"Just checking," Aspen said.

Madge laughed again. "You've got spunk. And imagination. That's good to see. I was afraid all those hours with your eyes crossed in front of a screen and your ears blocked by gizmos with wires might have killed your imagination. Glad to hear it's still in there somewhere. You ought to use it once in a while to have some fun."

"I have fun."

"Doing what?"

"Stuff."

"I haven't seen you do anything fun since I've been in the house. I'll admit I don't know for sure what girls your age do for fun these days. But there has to be something besides the zombie stare."

"How was school today?" Paige changed the subject with a question that even Madge knew was destined to die before it reached all the way across the back seat.

"Fine."

That ended the conversation until their next stop where Quinn and Peyton tumbled into the car. Once introductions had been made, Peyton chattered about some recess drama, and Paige knew exactly when and how to respond to keep the story going. Madge sat amazed at the skill and wondered if she should pull out her tablet and jot down notes. She didn't suppose she could capture the actual how-to's of this thing. Paige just seemed to have a natural skill for talking to little kids. Madge would never get a ribbon for that at the fair.

When they pulled up at Toddle Time, Madge took a deep breath. "Okay, here goes nothing," she said. "Or a whole lot of loud something."

This time, Baby Grace reached out instantly for Madge and snuggled down on her shoulder when the attendant handed her over. Madge didn't suppose it would be appropriate to shout. Even though she felt as if she had, indeed, won some kind of competition.

Paige spoke into her telephone a few minutes later, and her phone dialed the office. Madge shook her head and muttered, but she actually felt quite in awe of the system. When they pulled up to the Marvel house, Madge saw Mr. Oakley sitting in his car across the street, ready to pick Paige up and take her back to work.

"Thanks," Madge said to Paige. "I suppose I owe you one."

"It's fine," Paige said. "I think you showed great initiative in figuring out a solution to the problem. My dad would say you'd make a good Marine. 'Improvise, adapt, and overcome.' That's their motto."

Madge liked that. She felt something like a soldier in battle in this house. She watched the girls parade through the side door while Paige unbuckled Grace.

"They seem sweet."

Madge turned and took the baby. "I don't know any real-life kids to compare them to, but they haven't put a frog in my bed yet. They watch a lot of *Sound of Music*, though. Worries me just a little. They might be storing up some tricks."

Paige laughed and patted Madge's arm. "I don't think you have anything to worry about. I'll see you tomorrow. I'll just come here and pick you up, okay?"

"Okay," Madge said. "Lord willing and the creek don't rise. Oh, shoot!"

"What's wrong?" Paige turned around at the edge of the sidewalk.

"I was supposed to pick up groceries. And a notebook."

Paige looked at her phone to check the time and then across the street at Mr. Oakley's car. "Do you think it can wait until tomorrow? I could come early, and we could run to the store."

"It will have to wait. I'll put on my flak jacket and take the barrage." She gave Paige a quick salute, hefted Grace higher on her hip and turned toward the house.

Groceries ended up being the last thing on anyone's mind by the time Alex got home, though. Even Aspen forgot about her science notebook when her mom walked in with two giant bags of exotic-smelling food.

"Mom got Chinese," she shouted up the steps to her sisters. Soon the girls swarmed the kitchen counter, reaching over one another, grabbing at the small containers and shouting for more sauce or another egg roll.

Madge stood back and watched as even baby Grace took part in the feast with real enthusiasm. Eventually, Alex turned from the noise and held a carton toward Madge. "Want to try some?"

"I'll have a sandwich," she said. "I'm not that cultured." Madge had actually tried Chinese one Sunday when Evelyn and Tom took all the Glory Circle Sisters out for lunch. Tom never flaunted his money, but he also didn't blink at the prices that day. Even so, Madge had scanned the menu trying to find something less pricey.

The others had all ordered before Madge finally settled on the Chef's Special, thinking that might be economical. Instead, it was spicy. Madge sat up half the night eating Tums and watching the shopping channel. She couldn't look at rice now without thinking about Wonder Mops.

By the time the last egg roll had disappeared from the kitchen at the Marvel house, bedtime had already come and gone, too. Alex started shooing the girls upstairs while she gathered cartons for the trash. "What about spelling?" Quinn asked.

"What about it?"

"When are we going to study my words for tomorrow?"

"You should have done that after school," Alex said as she cleared the counter.

Quinn climbed on the rung of a bar stool to get her mother's attention. "I did study them," she said. "But somebody has to quiz me."

"Well, you should have asked Aspen. Or Madge. You knew

I'd be home late. We can't do it now."

Quinn sat on the stool and crossed her arms. "Nobody can help me."

"You have to take responsibility for your own stuff in life, Quinn. That's what smart girls do. And you are a smart girl. Tomorrow morning, Aspen will quiz you while we drive to school. Now, off to bed." She kissed the top of Quinn's head, grabbed a full bag of trash, and walked away toward the garage.

Quinn looked at Madge with the threat of real tears. Madge felt as useful as the dry dishrag in her hand, but she gave it a shot. "We'll spell a few over breakfast," she said. "I expect you'll get 'em."

"I won't. I never do." With that, Quinn slid off the stool and trudged upstairs. In a few seconds, Madge heard the strains of "so long, farewell" coming from the Von Trapp children. She thought about waiting for Alex to return to the kitchen and giving the clueless woman a piece of her mind. But, what did a childless housekeeper know about raising kids? Instead, Madge escaped to her own room and closed the door on this particular battle.

Chapter Thirteen

Tuesday, September 20th
Fifty-four Days to Go

"I've had a brilliant idea!" Paige tossed both arms in the air the second Madge opened the front door the next afternoon. She stepped inside and slipped out of her heels almost in the same movement.

Madge watched as Paige pulled a small bundle from her handbag and unrolled a pair of slippers. When Paige saw Madge staring, she said, "I carry my ballet flats everywhere. You never know when you might actually need to walk."

"You could probably wear walking shoes from the start," Madge said.

"Um, no, I couldn't. Oh, I should be able to wear them. We should have come far enough by now that a strong woman could wear sensible loafers and be taken seriously. But, no. If you want to get anywhere in the corporate world, you wear heels. And, a pencil skirt. So you can't actually move your legs to climb the corporate ladder. You have to crawl up it hand over hand, which is a pretty good description of what we do anyway." She stopped talking and narrowed her eyes at Madge. "But I'm not bitter."

"I can see that." Madge had held a job or two in her day, and she knew how things worked. Well, she knew how they worked

KATHY NICKERSON

once upon a time. Nobody had worn spikey high heels at the chicken processing plant, but nobody in a skirt ever moved up to management, either.

"So," Madge finally said, "what is your brilliant idea? I've got a grocery list to accomplish."

Paige jumped up and waved her arms again. "That's it. The grocery list. I'm going to teach you how to shop online. Barker's has an online shopping service, and they deliver. How crazy is that?"

Madge tried to absorb all the words in that sentence. Mostly, the word "crazy" stood out.

"Okay, I can see I've thrown you. Where's the computer? Don't tell me they all have laptops. Surely there's a desktop computer somewhere." As she spoke, Paige wandered around the kitchen.

Madge finally walked over and pulled back folding doors in one corner of the kitchen. Alex had spent hours at the built-in desk one night, paying bills, sorting receipts, and playing endless games of solitaire.

"Perfect," Paige said. "Let's get you online. Did Mrs. Marvel sign you up with a Barker's card for shopping yet?"

In fact, Alex had given Madge a grocery store card just before she left the house that morning, along with a long list and the new telephone with a number Madge had already forgotten.

Madge pulled up a kitchen chair beside Paige and watched as pictures and advertisements flew by on the computer screen. Eventually, a form popped up and asked for all kinds of personal information. Madge grudgingly gave out things like her birth date and the Marvel's address. When it came time to select a password and security question, though, she grumbled.

"The password needs to be something no one would guess. Nothing obvious like your middle name and your age."

"Oh, nobody would guess that," Madge said. "I've lied about it so long I'm not sure I remember it."

"They say it's smart to use a full sentence like, 'I'm going shopping now.'"

"How about if we just use 'password'? Thieves aren't going to get much good out of my grocery list."

Paige agreed, but obviously against her better judgment. She held firm on the three security questions such as the maiden name of your first-grade teacher or some such nonsense. Madge huffed at each of them. Finally, the third question asked, "The person you most admire, living or dead."

Madge didn't answer right away. She wanted to growl about that one, too, but she found the growl wouldn't get beyond the strange feeling in her throat. She reached into her pocket to see if she had a cough drop. No luck. Finally, she cleared her throat and managed to say, "Catherine."

"Do you want to put a last name?"

"No. Just Catherine."

"Okay. We're in. Now your profile is set up. I've told the computer to save it, so when you log on, it will be there automatically."

Madge stared at the machine with all its whirling pictures. "Maybe you should write some of this down."

"Okay," Paige grabbed a nearby notepad. "What should I write down for you?"

"Step one. How do I turn the machine on?"

Two hours later, Madge held an impressive how-to manual. She and Paige had strolled the grocery store aisles on the computer and dropped all kinds of goodies into the imaginary basket. Just as Paige lifted her finger to click 'checkout', Madge spoke. "Don't forget the notebook. We have to get a science notebook."

"Right. Spiral bound notebooks. That should be easy enough."

"And a calendar."

Paige stopped punching keys and looked sideways at Madge. "A calendar? It's a little early. I don't think they are out yet."

"Not a New Year's calendar. A this year's calendar. I need one for checking off the days so I can keep track of when my paycheck is due. And when my car should be finished. And when my sixty days is up."

Paige leaned against the chair and folded her arms. "I see."

"What? I just need a calendar. A small one. To keep on the counter here in the kitchen or something. Maybe one of those that sticks on the refrigerator. That shouldn't be too hard to find."

Paige sat looking at Madge a few more seconds. Long enough for Madge to feel like she had asked for something slightly indecent. "I'll pay for it out of my own money if that's what's bothering you."

"No, I think it's perfectly fine for the Marvel grocery fund to supply the house with a calendar. I suppose you have a right to keep track of the days according to your contract."

"Okay. Let's get a calendar."

Paige leaned forward and hunched over the keyboard. Pictures flew past on the screen so fast Madge couldn't keep up, but suddenly Paige said. "Got it! On sale for $1.99. What a steal. Now, all your items are being packaged and sealed and will be on their way to the Marvel house courtesy of a driver in a well-marked van. What do you think about that?"

Madge sat back. She felt almost as tired as if she had walked the aisles. She looked at the capable and lovely Paige Rosedale and suddenly wanted to show some gratitude.

"I think," Madge said, "we should write a how-to book for your boss."

Paige frowned. "What do you mean?"

"He's a dunce."

"He's brilliant," Paige said. "And dedicated. What makes you say such a thing?"

"He hasn't noticed you're a girl, has he?"

"He's busy," Paige said. She stared at the keyboard and ran

her fingers along the tops of the keys. "Besides, fraternization would be inappropriate."

"Says who? In my day, young men like Jack would have been on the hunt for a girl like you. What's wrong with him anyway? Doesn't he like girls?"

Paige burst out laughing. "Jack definitely likes girls. He has just been too busy to think about them for a few years because of school and opening his office. I'm sure he'll get around to it."

Madge raised her eyebrows and her nose. "Well, if I were you, I wouldn't be waiting for him to get around to it. I'd be moving right on and getting myself a life."

"I'm not waiting around," Paige smoothed her skirt and shook her head. "That's silly. I don't know what made you think that."

Madge raised her eyebrows again. "Whatever you say." The ringing of the front doorbell prevented her from offering further advice. "Mercy, that was a fast delivery."

"Too fast," Paige said. "It must be someone else."

Madge peeked through the tiny space in the leaded glass before she swung the door wide and said, "Emily? What on earth are you doing here?"

"Hello, Madge. Albert needed a few things from the hardware store, and it's on the way between here and there." She waved toward the car where her husband sat waiting. He tipped his hat toward Madge, and she lifted her hand in a slight wave.

"Do you want to come in?"

Emily looked over Madge's shoulder to where Paige stood in the entryway. "I don't want to bother if you have company."

"No bother. We have an hour before we start picking up the kids."

Emily frowned. "So you both work here?"

Paige stepped around Madge and stuck out her hand. "Hello, I'm Paige Rosedale, administrative assistant at the Oakley Law Firm. I'm just helping out one of our clients with some details today."

"It's just Emily," Madge said. "She knows the scoop. Paige works for Mrs. Marvel's lawyer. She's my carpool driver."

"Well, that's a relief," Emily said. She shook Paige's hand. "I'm a friend of a friend. After I got Madge's letter, we worried about her driving children around in traffic."

"We?" Madge spoke with the slightest edge in her voice.

"Well, Albert and I, of course."

"And who else? Grace Colby? Evelyn?"

"You have to admit, Madge, your sudden employment is a little strange. Even for you."

"I'll give you that," Madge said. "But, as you can see, I'm perfectly fine. I have a lawyer's assistant looking after me. My accommodations are rather highfalutin, but I'm getting used to them. I've figured out how to run the high-class washing machine, and Paige is teaching me about the computer."

"Well, glory be," Emily said.

"You want some coffee?" Madge waved again toward the car. "You could even ask your husband to come in if you want. I could show you around the place. Lots of fancy renovations that might interest the two of you."

Emily looked over Madge's shoulder again. "No, I don't think so. We really are on the way to the hardware store. I don't think it would be a good idea to come in right now. I just wanted to see that you were okay."

"And now you've seen."

"Yes, I guess you are just about as okay as ever."

Madge laughed. "That's about right. I never get completely there, but I'm close."

They walked to the car together, and Madge leaned in and spoke a few words to Albert.

After they drove away, she stood a long time on the sidewalk, watching the empty street. Paige eventually joined her.

"You're fortunate," Paige said, "to have friends who care so much."

Madge huffed. "They care to know my business, that's all. Emily will report back to all the others now, and they can talk about me to their hearts' content."

She turned toward the house and walked a few steps in front of Paige. She didn't want to sound mean. They would talk about her, just as they talked about each other. Nobody meant anything by it. The visit had thrown her off balance, though. Seeing Emily here in the driveway, remembering all the times she had warned Catherine and Madge to be careful about various things. The whole episode made it harder for Madge to pretend she had this situation under control.

Chapter Fourteen

Tuesday, September 20th
Fifty-four Days to Go

School pick-up went smoothly, although Aspen still refused to add anything to the conversation. Once they got home, Madge handed over the science notebook.

"Hey, thanks," Aspen said. "It's perfect."

"You better thank Paige tomorrow. She picked it out."

Aspen stuck the notebook in her backpack and pulled out her ear gizmos. She disappeared up the staircase without saying anything more. Peyton wandered through the kitchen looking for a snack, and her eyes grew wide when Madge produced a packet of gummy dinosaurs from the pantry.

"Where did we get these?"

"Aisle 12, Seasonal Specials, Back-to-School and Lunch Box Supplies," Madge read from her list.

"Huh?" Peyton stuffed another bite of prehistoric sugar into her mouth.

"The grocery store," Madge said.

Quinn came up behind her sister, but she shook her head when Madge offered a bag of treats. "You sick or something?" Madge said.

"Just not hungry."

"That sounds like a sickness to me."

Quinn shook her head and walked toward the family room where she slumped on the sofa and flopped her head onto one of the wide arms. She didn't even reach for the remote before Peyton could grab it.

Madge thought about poking around a little more. Maybe the child was actually sick. After all, Grace had that fever recently. But, what did she know? She wouldn't have a clue what to do about it anyway. She would just get busy in the kitchen and wait until their mother got home.

That event happened three hours later. Madge had about given up and fed the children without Alex, but they had discussed having a family supper tonight. Alex said it was important they sit down together, so Madge did her best to hold off even the obviously starving baby.

When Alex rushed in the door, though, she had her cell phone pressed against her face, and she held up a warning hand so no one would try to talk to her as she handled the obviously important life or death situation.

"Okay, fine. That will work. Just leave the papers on my desk, and I'll sign off on them in the morning. I told you this would happen if you gave Dianne that territory. She isn't ready for the pressure. You better put one of the seasoned team members in there pretty soon, or you are going to regret it."

Alex slipped off her jacket and tossed it on a chair with one hand while holding the phone with her other shoulder. Then she peeled off her heels and stretched her back. All the while, she appeared to listen to the other side of the conversation. "Well, yes, of course I mean someone seasoned like me. I bid for the job along with about six other people, and I know I could have done it. I could have grown our market share in that demographic. I could have..."

The rest of the conversation faded out as Alex walked upstairs. She left her briefcase, jacket, and shoes in the kitchen.

They were the only parts of her near the table thirty minutes later when Madge announced supper. The girls hustled downstairs with plenty of racket, but Alex failed to appear.

Madge and the girls sat at the table and stared at one another, then at the food, then at the walls for another few minutes. Eventually, Aspen said, "I think she is still on the phone."

"Okay," Madge said as she picked up the mashed potatoes. "Let's eat. I'm starved."

Everyone's appetite had miraculously survived the uncomfortable scenario. By the time their mother did appear at the table, all four girls had mostly devoured the baked chicken, potatoes, and green beans. Madge offered Alex the final spoonful of each.

"Well, thanks," Alex said. "Fortunately, I had a yogurt in a meeting this afternoon, so I'm not that hungry."

"It was your idea to have dinner together," Aspen said.

"Right." Alex put her hands together in a prayer formation and took a breath. "I wanted to make sure you all understand that on Saturday, Mara Lynn will be coming over to help me pack my things."

Peyton spoke in a small voice. "Will we go with you?"

Madge felt a sudden urge to jump and run. All the way back to the solitude of her own home where hearts didn't break on a daily basis. Instead, she tried to hijack the conversation.

"How about the rest of this chicken, Quinn? You still hungry?" Her diversion failed, though. Alex kept speaking words she had obviously practiced like a sales pitch.

"Not this time. I'm going to stay in Mara Lynn's guesthouse above her garage until we sort out all the house business. With Madge here, you don't have to scoot around to a different place all the time. You get to stay right here in your own room, and your daddy and I will come back and forth to be with you. So, next week, he will be here again, and I'll be at the guesthouse. But, you can call or email me any time if you need something."

"And you would come back?" Aspen lifted her chin as if offering a dare. "If we needed something, you would come back?"

Madge tried counting the green beans left in the bowl. Anything to block out this conversation. She counted twelve beans before Alex spoke again.

"Well, actually, I meant if you needed me to contact Madge about something or attend a concert at school or anything. I probably wouldn't actually need to come back with your dad here."

"That's what I thought."

A few seconds of silence followed, and Madge thought they might have survived this round with only a few flesh wounds. Then, Quinn spoke.

"Would you come if I needed help with spelling?"

Madge felt an actual pain in her chest. She looked at Alex to see if the woman felt any remorse whatsoever. Alex had leaned down to check her phone. By the time she looked up, Quinn had retreated behind a tall glass of milk.

"Spelling? Did you say spelling, Quinn? How did it go this week?" Alex asked the question but kept her eyes on the phone in her lap.

"I got six."

"Great. Keep up the good work."

Quinn slipped out of her chair and walked toward the family room without making a sound. Aspen frowned at her mother. "Six is terrible. It means she got almost twenty of them wrong, Mom. Quinn can't spell."

Alex looked up and seemed to notice her family for the first time. "What? What did you say about spelling?"

"She said Quinn hit a rough patch today," Madge said as she grabbed plates and shoved Aspen with her elbow. "We'll take a look at it in the morning and have her right as rain. You go ahead with your business."

"Right. Okay. I just have to make a couple of quick calls. You girls go ahead and get ready for bed once the table is clear."

Madge and Aspen cleared the table without speaking. Grace played with the mashed potatoes on her tray until Madge whisked her away for a face washing. Then she handed Grace off to Aspen for pajamas.

Madge started the dishwasher, wiped down the counters, and swept the floor while Alex sat at the table with the phone attached to her ear. Finally, Madge gave up and climbed the stairs to make sure Aspen had tucked Grace in and that the little girls had what they needed.

Grace had fallen asleep within seconds, apparently. Aspen gave Madge a nod and closed her own door without any further conversation. The little girls argued for just a minute over who pushed the button to turn on the movie last night. Peyton won, and Madge thought that was a sign of how distracted Quinn must be over this spelling trouble.

When Madge finally came back downstairs, Alex had disappeared. Madge leaned against the staircase and listened for sounds overhead. She thought she could hear the shower in Alex's room, which meant she must have come upstairs during the remote control battle.

"Lord, somebody ought to talk to that woman about kissing her children good-night," Madge said. "Even a dried-up old prune like me knows a mother should kiss her children at bedtime."

She had one foot on the first step when she rethought the idea. A shower for Alex could take thirty minutes, and Madge knew she didn't have that kind of stamina tonight.

She gave up and turned toward her own room. She slapped all the light switches a little harder than necessary as she shut the house down for the night.

Chapter Fifteen

Friday, September 23rd
Fifty-one Days to Go

Madge opened the new calendar the next morning while the family scarfed down breakfast. She understood why it was on sale. Besides having only three months left, it was all flowers, birds, and curly words. She had just wanted a calendar, for goodness sake. Not a daily Hallmark card. She had to assemble this one like a little tent. Once she managed to push all the tabs into all the slots, it sat up by itself and promised an "Uplifting Quote of the Day!" She perched it on the windowsill above the sink.

"What's that?" Aspen said.

"It's a calendar. Haven't you ever seen a calendar?"

"Not like that."

"Yeah. Neither have I."

Aspen reached for the calendar and read the words aloud. *"But those who wait on the Lord shall renew their strength; They shall mount up with wings like eagles, They shall run and not be weary, They shall walk and not faint."*

Madge took the empty cereal bowl from Aspen's other hand and waited for whatever comment must be coming next.

"That's very poetic."

"It's from the Bible," Madge said.

"I thought so." Aspen looked at the words again, maybe reading them to herself. She spoke again without looking up from the calendar. "Are they true?"

"What do you mean?"

"I mean is it real? If you do that, wait on the Lord, whatever that means, can you fly like an eagle?" She looked up, and Madge wished with all her might that Pastor Cleveland was standing in the kitchen. She would even have taken Grace Colby for back up right now.

Madge hadn't been born on a church pew like some of the other Glory Circle Sisters. She never made a big deal of it, but faith had been a surprise to her in middle age. She didn't think her friends understood the difference. Sometimes she thought this connection with God meant more to her because she didn't expect it.

At this moment, though, she wished she had been one of those ladies with a baptismal certificate and a shoebox full of Sunday School awards.

"Well," she said to Aspen, "I don't know about the flying part. But the Bible is true. Every word."

"If every word is true, you can fly." Aspen spoke the sentence like a dare, and Madge knew she couldn't win. She looked out the window and wondered what Catherine would have said to such a thing. Then, suddenly, she knew.

"Well, yes, I guess you can," Madge said.

"You can fly?" Now Quinn and Peyton joined the conversation. All three girls stood at the sink waiting for Madge to explain the mysteries of trusting God and flying like an eagle. God help her.

"All I know," Madge said, "is sometimes life has socked me in the belly so hard I didn't think I could take another breath. Times like when my best friend in the world died of a heart attack."

"Your friend Catherine?" Aspen said.

Madge frowned at the girl. "How do you know that?"

"You talk about her. You don't realize it, but her name comes up a lot."

"Well. Yes, Catherine. She was like my sister, only better." She looked at Quinn and Peyton. "Because we never fought over anything. So, when she died, the world felt ugly and sad."

"Did you cry?" Peyton asked.

"That's not the point of this story." Madge crossed her arms and looked out the window again. "But, on the days when I wished I could call Catherine or drive over to her house," she had to stop for a moment and let her voice catch up. "On those days, I would sit down and close my eyes and run the lines of a church song through my mind. After a while, I'd kind of get up above the sadness. I think you could call that flying."

Aspen looked out the window and spoke slowly. "Kind of like flying to China on a bad day?"

"Exactly like."

No one moved for a few moments until Madge became aware of the clock ticking in the hallway. "Okay, no more philosophizing. Get your stuff together or you'll be late for school."

After the girls left, Madge turned back to the kitchen and tried to decide where to start. Alex had turned the house upside down. She had declared a vow of simple living once she got a new place, and she said she would probably take only the barest necessities to the apartment at Mara Lynn's.

"Once I get a permanent place," she told Madge, "I'll furnish it with pieces I truly love and need."

Yet, boxes and bags kept stacking up in the hallway, creating an obstacle course for Madge when she tried to return clean laundry to the girls' rooms. On Friday evening, Madge almost tripped over a huge box as Alex shoved it into the hallway. Madge staggered against the wall and dropped the basket of socks she had spent all evening sorting.

"I'm so sorry, Madge." Alex leaped up from the closet floor and grabbed a handful of socks. "I didn't hear you coming."

"I'm crafty that way," Madge said.

Alex dropped back to the floor and leaned against the wall. She looked at the tiny princess socks in her hand and then at the box. "Photo albums," she said as if she had been caught eating a chocolate bar under the covers after curfew. "And old journals."

Madge thought about sitting on the floor, too, since a conversation seemed to be brewing. But two things stopped her. The first was arthritis. She knew for sure she could never get back off the floor without two strong men to help her. The second thing was privacy. She had a feeling this conversation was about to invade somebody's carefully constructed fence around their private life. Madge knew if the gate swung open, she might actually have to walk inside. She preferred keeping to her side of such a fence.

"I know it doesn't fit the simple lifestyle," Alex said. She looked at the hallway filled with boxes. "None of this does."

Madge leaned over to pick up more socks with the hope that she might yet escape the conversation, but Alex kept talking. "At first, I convinced myself I was taking them out of spite. So Luke wouldn't have the pictures. Or, out of self-protection so no one else could read the journals. They go back years. All the way to college. But if that is the real reason, why didn't I just throw the journals in the trash?"

Madge felt the gate creaking open, and she worked faster. If she could just get the last of those socks picked up, she could get out of this conversation and back to her own, private life.

"I don't want to burn them." Alex almost whispered the words just as Madge grabbed the last pair of striped socks.

"Nope, you shouldn't burn the past," Madge said. "You get as old as me and you have to look stuff up just to know what happened. Now, I better get these socks put away before the girls go to bed." With that, she hustled down the hallway and effectively slammed the gate behind any further conversation.

She felt a tiny bit bad. She could hear some random phrases running through her mind. Words that indicated she should have offered the woman a hand up off the floor, figuratively speaking. The words were probably from a Hallmark commercial, maybe from Pastor Cleveland. Possibly from Grace Colby. The last thought silenced all the words, thank goodness. Madge had never taken advice from Grace Colby, and she certainly wasn't going to start now when the woman wasn't even in the room.

On Saturday morning, Madge made her own breakfast just at daylight. She knew from all the thumping overhead that Alex had been up half the night, so she didn't expect the lady of the house to appear before noon. And the little girls would want a couple of hours of cartoons before breakfast.

So, Madge settled into her chair with a new puzzle book, a freshly sharpened pencil, and a Cary Grant movie on the television. She placed her coffee and toast on the side table and prepared to indulge. She was working hard on the puzzle and enjoying Mr. Grant's predicament when something bumped her elbow. Madge looked over her glasses with a frown and saw Quinn squinting at the puzzle.

"Jellyfish," she said.

"Where?"

"Top to bottom, right there." Quinn pointed to the left side of the page.

Madge studied the book for a moment and drew a slow oval around the word. "Uh, huh. I see it."

"And there's 'seahorse'," Quinn said pointing to the bottom of the page.

Madge circled the word as Quinn crowded in closer. With a sigh, she scooted over and handed Quinn the pencil. As she did, Madge noticed the door of her room swing just a little wider. Peyton stood sleepy-eyed, still in pajamas, wearing one slipper.

"Do you have cartoons?" she asked.

Quinn looked up from the page, her pencil poised as if waiting for the answer.

"Well, I suppose I do," Madge said, "but I was kind of watching this movie."

Peyton came in and leaned in against Madge's other knee. "What's it about?"

"Well, there's this girl, you see." Madge stopped. She wasn't really all that sure. She hadn't been paying a lot of attention in the beginning, and then Quinn had come in. She picked up the remote control and started pushing buttons. "Let's see if this television has any cartoons."

Chapter Sixteen

Saturday, September 23rd
Fifty-one Days to Go

Just as the first cartoon ended, Aspen appeared in Madge's doorway. She carried Grace, along with a blanket and a bear. Madge hadn't even noticed when Peyton moved from leaning against her knee to sitting on her lap. She motioned for Aspen to come in and reached up to add Grace to the pile. Aspen and Quinn snuggled down at Madge's feet with a shared afghan.

Madge didn't know exactly how much time passed while they sat that way. She had certainly seen enough ponies and rainbows to last until her next birthday when she finally heard Alex in the kitchen. "There's your mom," she said. "We better get breakfast."

Nobody moved, so Madge gave up and hit the button to turn off the TV. "No," the little girls both said, "we haven't seen the part where she wins the dance contest yet."

"You mean you've seen this one?" Madge started trying to scoot the girls off her lap to see if either of her legs had any circulation left.

"About fifty times," Aspen said as she stood. "Children have a high tolerance for repetition."

"Do they?" Madge wondered where the girl had picked up

that tidbit. It was probably true, but she didn't think the phrase was original. They did find something quite original when they walked into the kitchen a few minutes later, however. Alex in an apron.

"Hi," she said as she held up a spatula in one hand and a pitcher of batter in the other. "I thought we'd do pancakes."

The little girls shouted their approval and fought each other for the best stool at the counter. Even baby Grace tried to pull herself into her high chair. Aspen, however, stood with arms crossed in the middle of the floor. "Why?" she finally said.

"Because we like pancakes. And it's Saturday. And nobody has to go to work today." Alex turned back to the stove and poured batter in a curly pattern on the hot griddle. "I'm even making them into designs. Remember how we used to do that?"

"No." Aspen still didn't move. "I don't remember the last time you made pancakes, actually."

Alex kept her eyes on the batter. "Well, that must be because you slept through breakfast. Because I've made pancakes a lot. And I'm making them today. So, pull up a stool."

Aspen didn't move. "It's because you're leaving today."

Quinn and Peyton turned from their place at the bar and stared at their mother. Madge searched her foggy brain for anything to change the subject. Evidently, rainbow ponies had hypnotized her, because nothing else came to mind.

Alex flipped the pancakes and kept her back to the room. "I'm not leaving," she said. "I'm taking my things to Mara Lynn's today. But that is not leaving."

"Are we going with you?" Quinn said.

"No." Alex scooped a pancake onto a plate and handed it toward Madge. Madge recovered enough to accept the plate and add a pat of butter before carrying it to the bar. She waited to hear how Alex would get out of this one.

"There won't be room in the car today for all my boxes and all my girls. Mara Lynn and I will take things over today, and I'll get all settled next week, and then you girls can come see it when it's all set up. We'll have a girls' night and you can sleep over."

"Where will we sleep?" Peyton asked.

"In the guesthouse. That's where I'll be," Alex said.

"Do we have bedrooms there?" asked Quinn.

"No, the guesthouse doesn't have bedrooms. It's just one big room. We'll put pillows and blankets on the floor and look out the huge windows to watch the city lights as we fall asleep. It will be fun." With that, she swooped up two more pancakes and shoved them at Madge with an appeal in her eyes.

"So, who wants syrup?" Madge said. "Lots or a little? Just tell me when."

The change of subject worked for everyone except Aspen. She did move from her spot in the middle of the floor, but only to help Grace into her high chair. After that, she stood in the doorway and shook her head when Madge offered a plate of pancakes.

Nobody mentioned the guesthouse again while they ate. Aspen eventually disappeared upstairs. Once the little girls had gobbled up every last, sticky bite Alex washed their hands and told them they could finish watching cartoons in the family room.

Mara Lynn appeared at the side door just as Madge lifted Grace from her chair. Mara Lynn came in and dropped a kiss on the baby's soft hair. "Hi, precious girl." Then she looked at Alex, "Everybody having a good Saturday?"

"We had pancakes," Alex said as she collapsed on a stool.

Mara Lynn looked around the messy kitchen and laughed. "Nice try, Lex. But I don't think you're ever going to earn that Betty Crocker Homemaker of the Year Award."

Madge tried hard to be silent, melting into the background like a good housekeeper. She gave a slight harrumph, though, despite her best intentions.

Mara Lynn turned to her with another laugh. "It's true," she said. "Alex won the award our senior year in high school. We all took a test without even knowing why. We thought it was for a scholarship or something, I think. Strange questions like 'should you wash liver before you cook it?' Alex evidently got the highest score."

"I guessed," Alex said with a sigh.

"And she won this adorable little charm bracelet at the senior awards ceremony. Other people were getting scholarships to Brown, and Alex got Betty Crocker Homemaker of the Year. It was a riot. We never let her live it down."

"Never," Alex agreed. "And now, when I try to do a simple thing like make pancakes on Saturday morning, you wave it in my face."

"Indeed." Mara Lynn picked a tiny piece of pancake off the edge of the griddle and popped it in her mouth. "Yum. Wish I'd gotten here earlier. Do you still have that bracelet somewhere? Retro is so in, you know."

Madge didn't wait to hear more about the bracelet or the award. Instead, she stepped in and offered to clean the kitchen. She still didn't know her role when the mother of the family was in the house. She supposed she could have just escaped the turmoil by retreating to her room and turning up the volume on the television. But, that space had been invaded once already this morning.

In her vast years of experience, one thing Madge had learned was that pretty much nobody would bother you once you stuck your hands into a dishpan. The sound of water running in the kitchen seemed to guarantee a person some peace and quiet. She was right about that. Once she offered to clear, every member of the family, including baby Grace, disappeared.

She could hear rumblings overhead, so she knew the women were discussing the move. No one appeared on the staircase with boxes for what seemed like hours. Madge had wiped the last counter and just reached for the broom and dustpan when Mara Lynn came stomping down with a suitcase in both hands.

"I talked her out of taking all her earthly possessions on this first trip," she said.

Madge nodded and started sweeping. She did not want to have this discussion.

Mara Lynn shouted up the steps. "Are you coming?"

A muffled voice responded from upstairs, but Madge couldn't make out the words. She moved over near the pantry as if that corner needed a deeper cleaning than the rest of the kitchen.

"I can't hear you. Are you coming down? I'm breaking my back with these suitcases."

Alex came bumping down the steps with the handle of a wheeled bag in one hand and a garment bag in the other. "I still need to go back for some shoes," she said.

"You can surely get by for two weeks with the ten pair we packed."

"Ha, ha." Alex threw the garment bag on the counter and slumped over it. "I hate, loathe, and despise moving."

"I think that quote is supposed to end with money," Mara Lynn said.

"If everything that is supposed to end with money did, we would all be in better shape."

"Indeed." Mara Lynn hoisted the suitcases. "Which reminds me. I think someone stole the 'For Sale' sign I left in your yard. I planned to come back and pound it into the ground, but it's gone. Why would somebody steal a 'For Sale' sign? Who does that kind of thing?"

Madge kept sweeping and glancing around the kitchen for an escape hatch.

"Teenagers probably," Alex said. "On a dare. Don't you re-member the wild things we did?"

"We never stole property," Mara Lynn said. "Somebody ought to pay for that sign. It better not come out of my commis-sion." She walked toward the garage with the suitcases.

Madge couldn't take any more. She stopped sweeping and turned to Alex. "So, you're set?"

"I guess. I'll be back to sleep tonight, but it will be late. Then I'll spend the day with the girls tomorrow. That should help."

"Bunches," Madge said.

"Right." Alex straightened up and reached for the garment bag, but she stopped before lifting it. "It's just that I didn't expect it to be like this, you know? We were supposed to all move out at the same time. Sell the house. Pack up our stuff. Go off on our new adventures. I didn't expect to leave alone."

She said the last part just as Mara Lynn walked back into the kitchen, and Aspen stepped in from the family room. Mara Lynn spoke first. She put a hand on Alex's shoulder and gave a slight squeeze, "Don't worry, Lex, you're taking all the important things with you."

"Excuse me?" Aspen spoke with more sass than Madge knew a child should use with an adult, but she hoped no one would scold her. She rather agreed with the sentiment.

"I didn't mean you guys," Mara Lynn said. "When people sell a house they love, I always tell them they are taking the most important things with them. The memories. You know?"

Madge knew. She blinked hard and concentrated on the broom.

"I know," Alex said. She walked over and gave Aspen a side-hug even though the girl didn't respond. "Let's just pretend I'm going on another business trip, okay. It's really not much different. I'll be back later tonight. And I left more than half my stuff upstairs anyway."

"Sure," Aspen said. "It will be just like that." She walked across the room and stood beside Madge.

Madge had no idea what to do. She supposed someone like Catherine would have put an arm around the girl or offered a word of wisdom or a cookie or something. All Madge knew to do was say, "Get me the dustpan, will you?"

So, Aspen fetched the dustpan while her mother and Mara Lynn finished loading the car. Once Aspen had dumped the sweepings into the trashcan, she and Madge stood staring at the floor. Finally, Aspen said, "I wish I could be somewhere else right now."

Madge looked out the window. Blue sky, white clouds. The weatherman had said it would be a high of seventy-five today. Practically perfect.

"I have an idea," she said.

A few minutes later, Alex came in to fetch her purse and take a last look around. "I don't want to bother the little girls," she said. "I think they're all settled, and I don't want to stir them up again." She looked around the kitchen and leaned toward the staircase. "But I might say one more thing to Aspen; do you know where she is?"

"Oh, I'm afraid she's gone for a while," Madge said.

"Gone? Gone where?"

Madge looked out the window toward the wooden swing set. "Most of the way to China by now."

Chapter Seventeen

Sunday, September 25th
Forty-nine Days to Go

Sunday brought rain. The kind of dark, chilly rain that reminded Madge September would turn into true fall one of these days. Then winter. She always dreaded winter.

The house felt cold and empty when Madge shuffled into the kitchen for coffee. She turned on a light over the sink but didn't bother with anything else. Let the house stay as dark as the day felt.

She didn't know why a house feeling empty should bother her. She had always been perfectly content on her own. She wondered if that would still be true when she went home. Would she sigh with gratitude when she finally crossed her threshold? Or, would she feel like this, sad and empty?

"Get a grip," she told herself.

She expected the family to sleep even later than usual without any sunshine to wake them, so she took her coffee and her new calendar to the bar. She pulled an ink pen from a nearby cup and started flipping pages. On the square for October fourteenth, she wrote, "Thirty Days. Half-Way There!"

She flipped on to the middle of November and found the final day of her employment. "Day Sixty," she wrote. But she couldn't think of what else to say, so she just put a little dollar sign on either side to remind herself why she was here. November. She would be all done at the Marvel house before Thanksgiving. She could get her Oldsmobile out of the shop, get her driver's license back, and go home to her regular life in time for the holidays. Maybe she would drive out to Colorado and see her nephew Clyde this year.

"What's the saying today?"

Madge snapped back from her road trip and found the two little girls standing at the end of the bar. Quinn pointed at the calendar and asked again. "What does it say for today?"

"Oh, I don't know. Let's look." Madge flipped back to September and found the twenty-fifth. "It says, 'the first ones awake get to pick what we have for breakfast.'"

"Cinnamon toast," Peyton said as she climbed on a stool.

"Waffles," Quinn said. "But what does it really say?"

Madge pushed the calendar toward Quinn. She squinted at the words twirled around a steeple and read slowly, "I was glad when they said to me let us go into the house of the Lord."

Quinn looked up. "Where's that?"

"Church," Madge said, "This is Sunday, so the calendar people talked about going to church. That's what people do."

"We don't."

"I know."

"Do you go?"

"Mostly. When I'm not here."

"Why don't you go when you are here?'"

"Because I don't have my car, and it is too far to walk."

"You could ask my mom to take you."

Madge almost laughed at that idea. Instead, she got up and pulled bread from the pantry. "Don't get any ideas, Kiddo. The church carpool isn't on your mother's to-do list today."

Evidently, Alex didn't have a to-do list for Sunday. She had come back to the house long after the girls fell asleep Saturday night, and she slept until almost noon on Sunday. When she finally came downstairs, the others had wandered off to their own rooms again. Even Madge decided she would give herself a Half-Day as they called it on those old television shows. She put her feet up on the ottoman, flipped on the television, and started looking for something entertaining. Which could be tricky.

She didn't get far before Alex knocked on the door. "I hate to bother you, but could I ask a favor?"

"Sure."

"I just got a call from my boss. We have a big meeting in St. Louis Monday, and he wants me to put together an extra presentation. All my stuff is at the apartment now. I called Luke, and he can be here tonight to make the switch early. Could you go back on active duty with the girls until he arrives?"

Madge thought for one second about the scripture quote Quinn had just read, and then she said, "Sure. I'm not going anywhere."

The girls made it all the way through lunch before the grumbles set in. Madge had been expecting it all day. The mood fit the dark day. She wanted to put the entire clan down for a nap with Grace, and maybe take one herself, but that seemed like a battle too big to fight.

So, instead, she tried offering suggestions. "Don't you have any games in this house? Like Monopoly?"

"That's boring."

"I bet you have homework."

"That's more boring."

"I'm going to do re-do my nails," Aspen eventually said with a long sigh. "I don't like this color at all."

"Will you do mine?" Peyton asked.

"Sure, come on. We'll do rainbow colors for you."

Madge hadn't heard the final verdict on nail polish. Right now, she really didn't care. She watched the two sisters bounce up the staircase and hoped the polish would all end up on fingernails and not the floor.

When she turned back toward the kitchen, Madge found Quinn waiting as if Madge had some kind of magic trick up her other sleeve. "What?"

"I want to do words."

"What do you mean words?"

"Your words book. I want to circle words."

So, Madge gave up her latest volume of *Easy Word Searches* and watched. She wondered why Quinn could find and spell all these hard words, but she couldn't manage her own spelling list. What went on inside that little head? Did the challenge of the puzzle make it more fun? Or did Quinn actually do better when she could see the words this way? Maybe like wearing glasses or something.

While Madge watched, she felt the mustard-grain of an idea forming. She let the thought simmer all afternoon, and by the time she closed the final bedroom door Sunday night, Madge had made a plan.

On Monday morning, she waited until all the girls were loaded into Luke's big car before she wandered into the garage with her purse slung over her arm. "I wonder if you could drop me off at the bakery," she said. "We need bread."

Luke motioned toward the car parked beside him and said to Madge. "You don't want to take the car?"

"Not today. I'm meeting someone after I shop."

"Okay by me. Which bakery?"

Madge gave him the name of the intersection she had been

practicing all morning. Then she climbed into the monstrous vehicle beside Quinn. "Big as a bus," she said.

"It's an SUV," Quinn told her.

Madge stretched her neck to look over the seat. "I've been on smaller buses," she said.

Once Luke dropped her in front of the bakery, Madge made a show of looking in the windows and wandering toward the door. She watched Luke's vehicle as it left the parking lot. Once she saw Luke round the corner and disappear out of sight, she turned and high-tailed it across the street to the building that had been her destination all along. She appeared at the Oakley Law Office in a few minutes.

"I need a ride tomorrow morning at nine," she said without any small talk.

"Mr. Oakley isn't in the office just yet," Paige said. "If you would like to wait, I can offer you coffee, tea, spring water."

"I'm not thirsty," Madge said, "and I didn't figure he was out of bed yet. I want you to drive me, anyway. He'd be a nuisance where we are going."

"You know we've arranged transportation for just about anything you might need. All the children's after-school events, the grocery store. Is there something else you want to do? I could call for a cab if you'd like to go downtown and get your hair done. I just found the best salon."

Madge patted her temple. "Mine's all natural," she said. "I don't need the hairdresser for that, thank you very much."

"Oh, wow." Paige leaned in closer and examined Madge's hair. "I've never seen anyone with that particular shade of red. It's amazing how it grows like that, just a teensy bit darker at the roots. Isn't that amazing?"

"Amazing," Madge said. "Been that way all my life. Now, as I was saying, I need to get somewhere tomorrow morning, and I want you to take me."

"Where?"

"Mount Zion Church. Forty-second and Maple. It's easy to find."

Paige squinted and stared at the ceiling for a minute. "Forty-second Street? That will take almost an hour."

"Fifty minutes, probably. So, we need to leave at nine. Circle starts at ten, and I don't aim to be late. Wear a skirt. The girls are kind of old-fashioned."

Chapter Eighteen

Tuesday, September 27th
Forty-seven Days to Go

Paige wore a skirt. It was a skimpy little thing, and Madge worried that Grace Colby would find a way to comment on the inappropriateness of a miniskirt in the House of God. They didn't have time for Paige to go home and change. Madge's clothes would wrap around her three times. Finally, Madge gave up. She folded her body and her purse into the tiny car and hoped the room would be chilly so she could offer to drape her jacket over Paige's lap.

They listened to music on the ride, which prevented the need for conversation. Madge had never cared much for the longhaired stuff, but today it settled her raging thoughts. She didn't like asking favors, and she couldn't remember the last time she had done so. Plus, she had no idea how to describe to the other ladies what she needed. Madge chewed on the problem throughout the long ride. By the time they pulled up at the front steps of the church, she knew what she would say.

Unfortunately, climbing the front steps and being greeting by Pastor Cleveland in the vestibule caused every thought to flee her mind.

"Well, look who's here," Pastor Cleveland yelled as he

climbed down from the ladder where he had been attempting to change a light bulb. "Man-oh-man, we have been missing you around here."

He wiped his hands on a hanky and reached out to give Madge a quick hug. She allowed the embrace since he was the pastor, but she pulled back quickly. "This is my employer's assistant," she said, "Miss Paige Rosedale."

"Welcome to our little community," Pastor Cleveland said. "Come right on in and meet the ladies." He led the way down the hall and threw open a door. "Ladies, I'd like to present a guest this morning, Miss Paige Rosedale."

He bowed, swept his arm wide and said, "Miss Rosedale, the Glory Circle Sisters."

"Every one of 'em," Madge announced as she stepped around Paige and entered the room.

The noise that followed sounded like geese rising on a fall morning. So much honking, shouting, and calling back and forth to one another that no one could really hear anyone else. Finally, Evelyn banged her gavel and ordered the geese back into formation.

"Madge," she said, "this is a wonderful surprise. Why didn't you tell us you were home? Someone could have picked you up this morning."

"I'm not home yet," Madge said. "This is just an emergency visit." She reached into her mammoth bag and pulled out a *Word Search*. From another pocket, she retrieved Quinn's wadded up spelling list. "I need to turn this list into one of these puzzles, and I need your help to do it."

"You've lost it," Grace said. "Completely addled. I always knew it would happen."

"What exactly do you mean, Madge?" Evelyn came closer and picked up the magazine, trying to get a better look.

Two or three other ladies crowded around, and soon the entire Glory Circle began reading Quinn's spelling words.

"We need to mix them up," Madge said. "The poor girl can't spell 'cat' to save her soul. But, she can do one of my *Word Searches* faster than I can. And, you know I'm good."

"She is good." The voice came from a tiny lady with fluffy, white hair. Madge turned and smiled. "Bessie, it's good to see you. How's life on the golf course?"

"Oh, it's fine," she said. "I have to keep the shades drawn, of course. Men wandering about at all hours of the day and night. But the food is decent."

"Bess, those men are staff," Evelyn said. "They mow the lawn, take out the trash, and help with laundry."

"My laundry?" Bess' eyes widened. "I certainly hope they don't allow men to handle ladies' laundry. What kind of place did you move me into? Maybe I should go back to Boston."

Madge laughed. "It's okay, Bess. I'm sure the men just take care of the machines. They don't actually touch your clothes. Why don't you come over here and see if you can help me mix up some of these words?"

"Oh, I can do that. I'm very good at mixing."

Paige leaned toward Madge. "She lives on a golf course?"

"Well, she thinks so. Assisted Living, they call it. But the golf course is next door, so there's no harm in her thinking she's got a luxury apartment."

Madge leaned back and watched Bess study the spelling words. Bess had been the first to welcome Madge to the Glory Circle Sisters, back in the days when Bess knew up from down. She hadn't said a word that first Sunday when a pack of Camels fell out of Madge's purse. Bess just scooted over to make room for Madge and patted the pew beside her.

Madge had tossed her last pack of Camels about the same time Bess started losing her mind. Their friendship had weathered both storms.

Now, she turned back to Bess. "How are the roses doing?"

"Splendid. It's the largest garden I've ever had. I've been sharing it with some of the neighbors, of course. I don't want to be stingy."

"No, of course." Madge gave Paige an exaggerated wink and then spoke to the rest of the ladies. "Okay, girls, let's see what we can do with this spelling list."

The ladies pulled their chairs around one table and started talking. Eventually, Evelyn straightened up. "I think what we need is a simple grid," she said. "If we make a grid of random letters, we can just erase the ones where we need to insert spelling words. After that, Madge can use the same grid every week. Who has a pencil? Grace, can you go down to the Sunday school rooms and see if you can find a ruler?"

"I'll go to the secretary's office," Grace said. "Elmer Grigsby is painting the Sunday school rooms, and he is rather persnickety about the wet paint."

Evelyn laughed. "He just wants to do a good job, Grace. Don't let him get your goat."

"He'll think goat if he waves that yellow paintbrush at me again," Grace said. "I'm going to the office." She marched out of the room while everyone else kept laughing.

"Who is Elmer Grigsby?" Paige whispered, but Madge answered out loud.

"He is Catherine's answered prayer."

"We did a project a few years ago," Evelyn said, "of praying through the phone book. We cut up an old phone book, drew names at random, and prayed for people anonymously one week at a time."

"Catherine drew Elmer Grigsby the first week," Bess said, "And she never put him down."

Sometimes, Bess could surprise a person. Several ladies nodded, and the room grew quiet until Paige said, "And what happened?"

"Oh, Catherine died," Bess said.

Madge broke in when she heard Paige gasp. "Well, not right away. She prayed for a long time. Never knowing who Elmer was or what became of him. She just kept right on praying. She had the strongest feeling he was in some kind of trouble and needed help. So, she prayed."

"And, was he in trouble?" Paige asked.

She looked at Madge for some reason. Madge really didn't want to be the keeper of Elmer Grigsby's story. Not even the part where Catherine prayed him through as the old-timers would say. She certainly wasn't going to add the secret. The bit where Catherine spilled the whole story on her deathbed and made Madge promise to keep praying for the mysterious Elmer Grigsby. Nobody knew that part, and nobody ever would.

Grace had walked back into the room by that time, and she must have heard Paige's question.

"He was a falling down drunk," Grace said.

Madge sat straighter in her chair and looked Grace in the eye. "He never fell down," she said. "He managed pretty well for an old man with no help from anybody, thank you very much." She looked at Paige to finish the story. "The liquor had got him, though."

"Oh, I'm sorry to hear that," Paige said. "Alcoholism is a terrible disease."

"Well, I don't know whether it's a sickness or a curse, but it had him," Madge said. "And little by little, it let him go. It took us a while to patch it all together later. But we finally figured out that the more Catherine prayed, the less Elmer had been able to drink."

"Until he showed up on the church steps one glorious day and suddenly became found," Bess said, and she flung out her hands as if singing a song.

"That must have been a beautiful day," Paige said as she smiled at Madge.

"It was Catherine's funeral."

"Oh, I'm so sorry."

Evelyn picked up the story in her usual manner of trying to smooth over an awkward moment. "But the good part came from the big surprise. Tell her the surprise, Madge."

Madge wanted to stop talking about that day. She wanted to move back to Quinn and spelling and forget about things like funerals. She did have to admit the next part of the story would have made Catherine smile.

"We were standing on the steps," she said, "waiting to go in, when we heard Pastor Cleveland introduce himself to the man who turned out to be Elmer Grigsby. So we were the first ones to find out that the man Catherine had been praying for, the man who showed up by chance at her funeral, was the pastor's own dad."

"His father?" Paige looked from Madge to Evelyn and back again. "Did the pastor know him?"

"No," Evelyn said. "Pastor Cleveland had been just a child when his father disappeared. He didn't know the man was even alive. It is such a beautiful story of redemption and reconciliation."

"And now he is here at the church. Painting the Sunday School rooms." Paige smiled as she spoke as if the whole thing was some kind of wonderful fairy tale.

"Well, he's got to do something to earn the keep for him and that nuisance of a cat," Madge said. "Now could we please get back to the business at hand? We need some help with spelling over at our house." She hadn't meant to say "our," and she hoped nobody noticed.

Chapter Nineteen

Tuesday, September 27th
Forty-seven Days to Go

Before noon on Tuesday, Madge held a shining copy of *Quinn's Magic Word Search* in her hand. Grace Colby had objected to the use of the word "magic" coming from something connected to the church. While the ladies were arguing the point, Paige pulled Madge aside in one corner. "Grace seems a little, I don't know, less charitable than the rest of the ladies today. Does she have a sad life or something?"

Madge looked across the room where Grace was shaking her finger and her head at Evelyn. "Grace Colby is a grouch. I hate to say it. I probably shouldn't. Everybody tries to cover for her, but she's just a grouch and always has been."

Paige watched the conversation another few seconds. "Yes," she said. "But, why is she so grouchy? Haven't you ever wondered that?"

Madge drew back. "For Heaven's sake. It's none of my business what gets her drawers in a bunch. Maybe she's just naturally grouchy."

"Maybe," Paige said. "But people like that usually have a reason."

"All I know," Madge said, "is that her grouchiness tends to meddle in my business, which isn't very Christian of her if that's where you're headed with this line of questioning."

"I'm not heading anywhere. I just wondered."

Madge crossed her arms and waited for the argument on the other side of the room to finish. When it looked like it might end in a tie, she said, "Grace Colby once had the nerve to suggest to the Glory Circle Sisters that someone needed to take away my car keys."

"No," Paige drew the word out in horror, but she smiled.

"It wasn't a joke," Madge said. "The nephews had just swooped in and told poor Bess she couldn't drive anymore. They were one step away from a nursing home for her. That happened a few weeks later. It was a terrible time. And Grace Colby decided to make a crack like that about my driving in the middle of Bess breaking down in tears."

"I'm sorry," Paige said. "I didn't mean to make light of it. I just think she seems to be quite unhappy about something. I'd think the Glory Circle would be a safe place for her to express that."

"Oh, she expresses. Don't you worry. She expresses all over the place."

"I mean express as in talk about her feelings and work out her problems."

"Look, I've only been at this church a dozen years. I'm still an outsider. All I know is that Catherine Benson and Grace Colby were both born in church. Transplanted here as brides the same year, and they spent the rest of their lives together on the third pew. They both had their share of troubles, and they may or may not have talked about them. Somehow, the struggles made Catherine all roses and few thorns. Grace Colby grew in the other direction. That's all I know."

Paige might have gone on with her questions if Grace Colby hadn't chosen that moment to express her feelings rather loudly. Evelyn attempted to respond without raising her own voice, but the effort was useless. In the end, they called for Pastor Cleveland

and asked if he had any problem with the title.

"Well," he said, "I've always thought when a child learns to read it is rather a magical process. We can't really explain how it happens. When the light goes on in their eyes and the letters finally form words that tell stories, well, I've never seen anything much more magical than that. Yes, I think it's fine to use the word."

And so, it was titled. Grace Colby muttered about progressive pastors under her breath, but she agreed to run off the extra copies in the secretary's office. She knew how to do it without breaking the decrepit machine.

All the talk about magic made something else begin to rattle in Madge's mind. Once all the ladies had said their good-byes, which took much longer than it needed to, of course, she dawdled in the vestibule. Finally, she said to Paige. "I just want to stop in the office for one more thing."

"Sure, we have plenty of time," Paige said. "I'm going to peek into the sanctuary. This reminds me so much of my church back home. Makes me miss my mom." She smiled as she wandered away.

Madge actually knocked on the edge of the office door before she walked into the room. Not so much for permission as to announce her presence. Pastor Cleveland looked up from his desk and immediately stood and offered a chair. "Come in, Sister Madge. Have a seat."

"No need. Just a quick question."

"Okay."

"Talking about magic reminded me of a book I heard you read to the kids last summer during camp."

"Oh? I'd forgotten you helped out at camp."

"I worked in the kitchen, but I heard the story. Parts of it anyway."

Pastor Cleveland reached over and pulled a red-jacketed volume from a set of books on the shelf. "The Chronicles of Narnia," he said. "This is the first one. *The Lion, The Witch, and The Wardrobe*. Classics by C. S. Lewis."

Madge took the book and flipped through it, pleased to see a few pictures here and there. "Is it the kind of thing a dad could read to kids at bedtime? I've heard they do that kind of thing."

Pastor Cleveland put on his thoughtful look and said, "I've heard that, too. Having grown up with only a mother who had to work a lot, I don't have much experience with such things. I like the concept, though."

He leaned in and spoke in almost a whisper. "Want to know a secret? Now I'm reading them to my dad."

Madge raised her eyebrows. She could not imagine Elmer Grigsby sitting still for a child's storybook. As far as she knew, the man still preferred the company of his cat to humanity.

"Oh, I have to pretend I'm reading to the fifth grade Sunday school boys on Wednesday nights. But, we meet over at the house, and my dad always takes a chair in the far corner."

"Well, that beats all."

"Yes. Yes it does."

"We're on *The Horse and His Boy*," Pastor Cleveland said. "A personal favorite of mine. If you know someone who could use a little family interaction, you can certainly borrow this first one and give them a taste. I suspect every family could be helped and healed by going through the wardrobe into Narnia together."

Madge held the book and considered. She suspected the idea forming in her mind would qualify for Meddling in the First Degree, well beyond the job description of a short-timer. Yet, she could not resist the idea of Luke sitting in a rocking chair with those little girls instead of Julie Andrews hitting the high notes one more time.

"I'll take it," she said.

Paige navigated smoothly through traffic before either of them spoke again.

"The Glory Sisters are a sweet bunch."

"They put on their best faces for you. We aren't always sweet."

"I'm sure. None of us are. But you've obviously been friends a long time."

"We've known each other quite a while. Since before we started forgetting each other."

"You mean your friend Bess?"

"She seemed pretty good today."

"Yes, and happy."

"Bess is always happy. That's the beauty of not knowing what's really going on in the world."

"So, I was thinking," Paige glanced in her side mirror and stopped talking to make a lane change. "This is really kind of a nice drive. I'm not usually busy on Sundays, and I haven't found a church to attend in the city, so if you wanted me to drive you out here some week...." She stopped talking to make another lane change.

Madge suspected Paige was waiting for her to pick up on the offer, and she hesitated. Going to church on Sunday had been her habit for several decades. But she realized it had been that. A habit. The last few weeks she had done perfectly fine without the ritual. In fact, she rather enjoyed the idea of not putting on pantyhose and uncomfortable shoes and trying to stay awake through another sermon. She was about to say so when Paige spoke again.

"I know I should have gotten consistent about going to church. I got this idea that I shouldn't just go to church out of habit. That church should be about more than just meetings. I convinced myself that relationships with God and people were more important than attendance awards."

Paige hit the brakes a little hard when the light changed. "Sorry. Anyway, when I stopped attending church, I realized I didn't actually have relationships with many people either. I mean, not really. I have some acquaintances, but I don't have friends. Not the kind of friends you had in that room this morning. People who know your soul. Not friends like Emily who would drive over to check on me in a new position. Those are 'church friends', you know? I'm afraid skipping out on church is like being part of a family but never attending the family reunions or the Sunday dinners or the birthday parties or the weddings."

Paige kept talking as if Madge wasn't even in the car anymore. Madge kept feeling smaller and smaller in her corner. Every second made her feel like even more of a sinner for not wanting to put on her pantyhose and go to the family reunion every Sunday.

"Okay," she blurted. "You can take me to church."

The conversation died after that, and neither of them said much until Paige pulled into the driveway. "Did you need to run any errands today? I forgot to ask."

"Nope," Madge said. "Luke is bringing the girls home, so I've got a few hours of the place all to myself. I plan to enjoy it."

"Well, don't do anything crazy," Paige said with a grin.

"Oh, I may do it. You know me."

Chapter Twenty

Tuesday, September 27th
Forty-seven Days to Go

The craziest thing Madge did Tuesday afternoon was to add mustard to her sandwich. She normally stuck with mayo because mustard had too much zing. But, she tried a little zing on Tuesday. She decided to go back to mayo.

The mustard made her think of her nephew, Ben, though. He always liked brown mustard on his sandwiches. She supposed she ought to call and give him a report since she had said she would.

Madge waited until late in the day when she knew Nancy might be home from school. She dug the little phone out of her purse and scrambled around until she found the address book with Nancy's telephone number. While the phone rang, she thought of the last evening at their apartment.

Ben and Nancy had been in their traditional spot, curled up on the sofa. Nancy had her papers and red pen. Ben had his laptop and law journals. They both worked away as if no one else existed in the room. Every few minutes, someone reached out to squeeze a hand or rub a shoulder. Or even plant a kiss on a cheek before turning a page. Madge had never seen anything like it, and she wished she could rub some of that off on the couple in this house.

"Hightower residence. Nancy speaking."

"Marvel house, Madge the Housekeeper speaking."

"Aunt Madge! Thank goodness. We thought you'd lost our numbers or something. Ben will be so glad you called. I'm sorry he isn't here."

"Oh, I knew he'd be busy. I just grabbed a minute to tell you all's well, and I'm fine."

"Well, that's good news. They're treating you well? Not wearing you out?"

"Nah, this job's a piece of cake, just like I knew it would be."

"Uh huh, I'm sure. When is your next day off? I can run over and get you. We'll bring you over here for a rest."

"Oh, no need. These folks are providing me with a chauffeur."

"Really?"

"Yep. I went to Prayer & Share over at the church today."

"No kidding?"

"I'm not kidding. I saw all the girls and we had a big ole confab. It was great. So, I'm just staying busy as can be. I'll try to see you and Ben again before I go home, but it might be nearly Thanksgiving."

"Well, as long as you are doing okay."

"I'm fine. Perfectly fine. Say, you don't happen to know anything about my car, do you?"

Madge noticed that Nancy paused a little bit before she answered. "No, I think you'll have to talk to Ben about that. I'm not really involved in the car situation."

"I figured as much. That's okay. I'll call back some evening when he's home."

"Or, I can have him call you. I have your number now."

"You do? How did you get my number?"

"Well, you called me. So, your number showed up on my phone, and I can save it."

Madge pulled the phone away from her ear and looked at the screen. "Well, I'll be. Isn't that something?" She wasn't sure she liked having a telephone that gave her information away without her permission. "I better hang up now," she said. "The girls will be home soon, and they'll want a snack."

"Are you baking cookies?"

Madge laughed. "Oh, sure. That Little Debbie girl and me. Although she's too expensive. We go off brand around here."

"Well, you take care, Aunt Madge. Ben will call you later. I think he is trying to stay out of the situation as much as possible, so it doesn't cause any problems with the case. It's still so amazing, isn't it? That you ended up finding a job with people he's connected to in court?"

"It's a small world," Madge said. "Tell Ben not to worry about calling unless he's got some info to pass along," she said. "I'm busy and so is he. In fact, I think I hear the girls barging in the door now."

Madge found the little girls giggling in the kitchen as they dug into their snacks. Even Aspen was smiling because she didn't have any homework.

"Well," Madge said, "let me tell you something else that will trip your trigger." She looked at her watch and waited just a second until the doorbell rang. "I figured out how to order pizza."

The girls shouted and clapped while Aspen ran to answer the door. Madge looked at Luke with a shrug and said, "I didn't have time to cook today. I had some business to do."

"Cool by me." The minute the pizza boxes hit the counter, Luke grabbed a plate and started stacking slices for his escape to the family room.

"Just because it comes from a man in a funny hat doesn't mean we can't eat it at the table," Madge said as she reached for his plate.

Luke surrendered the plate and held up his hands. "Yes, ma'am." He made a funny face at the girls and waved his arms as if Madge had arrested him. Peyton and Grace giggled. Aspen rolled her eyes, but she added a tiny a smile at the end. Only Quinn held out with a stoic face.

"No grin from Quinn tonight?"

Quinn shook her head.

"She brought home a new spelling list yesterday," Aspen said. "And it's hard."

Before actual tears could fall on the pizza, Madge held up her hand. "I have a cure for Spelling Blues. First, we eat. Then, the magic."

She might as well have said Santa was coming. Madge wasn't accustomed to having secrets or playing games. She liked things straightforward, so it felt a little awkward for her to keep things going while the little girls threw questions like a badminton bird across the table. But, just like the game she played a few times in her school days, she did get better as they went along.

By the time the last bite of pepperoni had been devoured and the last smudge of sauce had been wiped from Grace's face, Madge was actually enjoying the espionage.

"Okay, I can't take the suspense any longer," Luke said, "By Jove, Woman, if you have bought us a puppy, you better bring it out and let it eat the scraps under the table."

"A puppy! A puppy! Madge bought a puppy!"

Madge looked at Luke in horror. The man was an imbecile. Why would he plant such an idea in the children's heads? Now they would beg for a puppy every day.

"It's not a puppy," she said with something similar to a growl. She attempted to sound more like Evelyn than like Grace Colby with her next statement. "It is something fun, created especially for Quinn by some of my friends."

She reached into her purse and pulled out the *Magic Spelling Word Search* for the week. Quinn stared at the paper and then looked at Madge with a small frown.

"It's your spelling words. All scrambled up in the search." She handed Quinn a pencil. "If you find them, I bet you can learn to spell them."

Quinn accepted the pencil and bent her head over the paper.

For several seconds, she didn't move. Slowly, she lowered the point of the pencil, contacted the paper, and drew a long, slow oval around the word "perfume."

She looked up at Madge with solemn eyes. Madge took in a deep breath and said, "Ahhhhh, smells good."

Everyone at the table broke into applause, and Quinn smiled. Then she went back to work. Her pencil moved quickly through the page, circling word after word. When she finished, Madge pulled a second sheet from her bag. "Okay, do it again. And this time, say the letters out loud as you circle."

No one left the table while Quinn worked. The entire family seemed caught in the magic. The second sheet went even faster. When she finished, Madge said, "Now, Aspen, you quiz her."

Aspen pulled the list from the refrigerator and said, "Perfume."

Quinn closed her eyes, held the pencil over the table as if she could see the paper in front of her and said, "p-e-r-f-u-m... Silent 'e'."

Aspen evidently forgot to be a sullen adolescent for a few moments while she grabbed her little sister in a bear hug and danced around the kitchen. "You did it," she shouted. "You did it. You learned spelling."

"Madge did it," Quinn said when she stopped giggling.

"What Madge did was make a mess in the kitchen. You girls had better help me get these pizza boxes to the trash, and then everybody get on about their business. Gracie needs a bath."

"I'll give her a bath," Luke said. "You look a little tired."

Madge didn't argue. Her trip across town had taken more gumption than she realized. She thought about the Narnia book waiting in her room, but she didn't think she had any strength left to bring up the subject tonight. Instead, she retreated to her room and managed to get into her nightgown without groaning. She took some Tylenol and even thought about rubbing on a little of the Icy Hot that she kept in her medicine bag. She had never actually used the stuff, but Catherine had loaned it to her, so she kept it around.

She rolled into the big bed and bunched the pillows up into a puffy mountain. With the covers pulled up around her shoulders, Madge felt entirely too much like royalty. She should probably toss all the extra pillows on the floor so she didn't get used to this kind of luxury. She'd be going home to her second-hand box springs and mattress soon.

Maybe she would have enough cash left over after fixing up the Oldsmobile to buy some new bed pillows. She couldn't remember when she had done such a thing. She should. She would. She would just drive herself right downtown, go to the big J.C. Penney's outlet store, and get gigantic pillows like these for her own bed.

Madge had just started to fall asleep in the middle of her fluffy mountain of pillows when she heard *The Sound of Music* floating down from upstairs. "Adieu, adieu, to you and you and you..."

Chapter Twenty-One

Friday, September 30th
Forty-four Days to Go

Madge took her time getting dressed on Friday because the girls had a no-school day. Something about teachers needing extra training. Madge wondered what the families without housekeepers did on such a day. Then she realized they probably left children like Aspen in charge of things. "Lord help us," she said. "You better figure out some other solution by the time I leave here. Those girls need a full-time grown-up in the house."

She muttered to herself about the problem of children left unattended on Teacher Friday as she started for the kitchen. The thought kept her so distracted she took several steps into the room before she spotted Aspen standing in a pool of blood. Madge grabbed the counter to steady herself. She couldn't see an obvious wound, and Aspen wasn't crying. She just stood there with an open can in her hand and a look of terror on her face.

"Where are you cut?" Madge grabbed a towel from the counter and stepped toward Aspen who drew back and shook her head.

"Nowhere."

"What?"

"It's not blood."

Madge leaned closer.

"It's paint." Aspen held out the now-empty can of red paint. "The lid was stuck."

Madge edged around the mess and looked at the open can, then at the blank canvas leaning against a bar stool in front of the windows. "So, you're a painter."

"Not really. It's a school project."

"Uh-huh."

"It's a stupid project. And choosing a painting instead of all the other options was even more stupid."

"That's a lot of stupid."

"Whatever."

Madge took the can with two fingers and studied the label. "I don't think this is the kind of paint you use on one of those picture things. This is what you use for crafty stuff. Painting trinkets and beads and boxes." She fluttered her hand as if that kind of stuff might be in Alex's streamlined kitchen. Which, of course, it was not.

"I got it out of one of Mom's boxes," Aspen said. "I figured she was just going to throw it all away, so she wouldn't miss it."

"Maybe." Madge didn't intend to discuss Alex's state of mind. Instead, she reached back for a vague memory. "I used to watch this fluffy-haired fellow on the PBS station while I had my lunch," she said. "I didn't have cable, and the other channels had trashy soap operas. Anyway, he used the kind of paint that comes in little tubes, I think. Did you see any of that in the boxes upstairs?"

Aspen squinted for a second and then said, "I think I did."

"Well, as soon as we use every paper towel in the pantry to sop up this mess, you go find that paint and see what you can do with it."

The sopping almost succeeded. Eventually, a red stain on the tile floor was the only evidence. They were staring at it when Luke wandered into the kitchen looking for coffee. He came and stood beside them.

"Bleach," he said. "The detective shows say bleach takes out all traces of blood."

"It's not blood," Madge and Aspen said at the same time. Despite her best efforts, Aspen smiled.

"Why aren't you at work?" Madge shoved the last paper towel at Luke and turned toward the laundry room for bleach.

"I'm going in late. Had to pack my stuff." He reached over and attempted to dab away the red paint on Aspen's hand. "Painting a masterpiece?"

"It won't be as good as any of Mom's."

Luke stopped dabbing. "You remember when your mom painted?"

Madge stopped on her way back from the laundry room, half-afraid that her entry into the room would stop Aspen from talking.

"Yeah. A million years ago. I mostly remember when she took it all off the walls and said it had just, 'been a stage.'"

"Well, your mom has gone through a few stages in her life. But she's a great painter. I hope she picks it up again someday." He walked to the counter and started making coffee, so Madge took that as permission to re-enter the room.

"Do you think it's okay if I use some of her stuff?"

"Sure. It may be all dried up by now. If you need more, we can get it."

"It's for a school project. I mean, I'm not just painting for fun or something. I'm not trying to waste money."

Luke turned from the coffee pot. "It's okay. I'd buy you paint just for fun if you wanted it. We aren't that hard up."

Madge reached over to the counter and picked up a stack of mail. She tossed it toward the man of the house. "Maybe you better look at the electric bill before you brag."

Luke frowned and picked up the mail. Aspen dropped the paint can in the trash and escaped up the stairs. Luke watched her as if he might speak. Instead, he turned back to Madge and held up the electric bill with "Third Notice" stamped in red.

"When did this come?"

"I don't know. The mail isn't my job. But that one kind of caught my attention yesterday what with the red-letter edition and all."

"Alex is supposed to pay the household bills from a fund we both contribute to."

"I don't know about that."

"It's the same fund you get groceries from."

"I get groceries with my card."

"Right. And Alex pays the card from the fund. If she is falling behind on this stuff, you'll find yourself standing in line with your Ben & Jerry's oozing into a puddle while the checker keeps telling you your card has been declined."

"I only bought Ben & Jerry's once."

"I wasn't complaining." Luke rubbed a hand across his forehead. "Do you have any idea if she is paying bills at all? Like the mortgage?"

Madge held up her hands. "Don't ask me. She sits over there at the computer some nights and moans. But I have no idea what she's doing. I thought it was work."

"No. She does work on her laptop. Usually in bed."

Madge raised her eyebrows, but Luke didn't respond. She thought about telling him a thing or two about how she thought a marriage ought to work and about giving him her opinion on laptops, telephones, and other third wheels in the marriage bed. She decided to refrain. This time.

"I'm going to have to ask her," he finally said. "I hate this. We always fight about money. Why should we still be fighting about money now that we're separated? Wasn't that the point? Separate and stop fighting? But if she isn't paying the bills, they'll start shutting things off. I can't have the kids living in a house with no electricity." He grabbed his keys from where he had dropped them on the counter.

"I don't have the money in the bank for all of this," he said. "I'll need to go handle some things to get it covered. I'll be back for supper tonight. Alex is coming in late, so I'm going to stay until bedtime."

He stopped for a moment with his hand on the door and turned. "Thanks, Madge, for being here. This feels insane, right?"

"Certifiable."

The little girls weren't as much of a handful as Madge expected the rest of the day. Quinn and Peyton accepted Madge's challenge to take advantage of what she called "fine weather." They discovered the backyard could provide actual fun despite their fear that they might die for lack of screen time before lunch.

After lunch, she persuaded them to take Grace along and take turns swinging her. Madge stood at the sink washing dishes. She had listened to Alex explain all about the automatic dishwasher one evening, but she still preferred to wash by hand. She had always found the suds and the silence to be soothing. But she had never experienced what she felt today. This kitchen window, over this sink, with this view of three little girls flying high on their swings in a backyard glowing with maple trees. Madge wondered if Catherine could see anything more beautiful in Heaven today.

"Good grief, Woman, get a grip." She attacked the frying pan with zeal. "Pay attention to your job. You've been watching too many Hallmark movies. Just be glad the little rascals have decided to give you a few minutes of peace and quiet."

By the time Madge went out to retrieve Grace for a nap, Quinn and Peyton actually turned down her offer of a cartoon break.

"We're going to have an adventure," Peyton said. "Hunting for doodlebugs under the rocks."

"Sounds like a good idea. I've heard doodlebugs are good if you fry them up with a few onions."

"Noooooo! We're going to put them in a circus!"

"Oh, my mistake." Madge brushed leaves from Grace's hair and turned toward the house. "Happy hunting."

The hunters finally came in two hours later. They accepted a snack after reluctantly returning all their well-trained bugs to the yard. Then they collapsed on the sofa to watch cartoons.

Aspen had spent most of the day concentrating on her project in the corner of the kitchen. She had turned the makeshift easel at an angle so the light fell well for her. The positioning would block the view of anyone wandering through the kitchen, though.

The autumn sun dipped low by the time Madge heard Luke's car. "Time to start cleaning up for supper," she said to Aspen.

"Good, I haven't made much progress. I may trash the whole thing."

"Oh, I wouldn't make that decision till I'd slept on it," Madge said. "They say artists are temperamental beings. They tend to hate their work one minute and love it the next."

"Really?"

"That's what I've heard. 'Course, I can't do a color-by-number myself, but I've heard it."

Aspen started gathering brushes and tubes without saying anything more. Madge pretended not to watch as Aspen tipped her head at different angles to study whatever she had taken the entire day to produce. Finally, she pulled another bar stool over and carefully arranged an old sheet over both stools to hide the project.

After Aspen left the room, Madge stood in the kitchen and thought about her day. "This is one for the books, Lord. I don't know what You are up to, but I don't plan to get attached to this clan. You got that? I just need to earn my money and get out the door. So, just because I had a few suggestions for a school project and taught some kids to play outside, don't You go getting any ideas about tricking me into a longer stay. I'm not doing it."

Of course, Madge did plan to stick her nose into one more part of the day. Then she would be done interfering. She waited until after supper and then said to Luke. "Could you tuck Gracie in while I finish up down here?"

He hedged just a second and then said, "Sure. I think I can accomplish that task."

Madge crept up the staircase once she heard the sound of the nursery door opening and closing. She stepped into the Green Room and waited.

When Luke left the nursery, he paused at the little girls' room and said, "Teeth brushed, jammies on, movie ready?"

Before the girls could answer, Madge popped into the hallway and held out the Narnia book she had borrowed from Pastor Cleveland. "I had an idea," she said. "Probably silly, but I heard once that some kids like to be read to at bedtime. They say this one is good."

She shoved the book at Luke and scurried away. Then, she paused at the top of the stairs. She waited, not even knowing what she hoped to accomplish or why she had done something so nosy. Why she had butted herself into something so completely none of her business. She, who was nothing more than temporary help, for goodness sake.

The day she wandered into the wrong room at the courthouse, she should have done exactly what that man in the uniform said. She should have moved on down the hall instead of slipping into the last pew and listening to Jack Oakley get his ears pinned back by the judge.

Maybe she ought to just turn in her notice and give this whole thing up. She had surely earned a little bit of money by now. Maybe she could cut back on some expenses and save up to get the Olds out of hock. Maybe if...

Just then, she heard Luke's voice from the little girls' room. "Once there were four children whose names were Peter, Susan, Edmund, and Lucy."

Something warm and strong shot through Madge's chest. At first, she didn't understand the strange feelings. Eventually, she realized she was simply responding to the universally comforting sound of a father's voice at bedtime. Madge recognized the sound, even though she'd never heard it for herself.

Chapter Twenty-Two

Saturday, October 1st
Forty-three Days to Go

Madge didn't stay to listen to the whole chapter of Narnia Friday night. Instead, she went downstairs and finished a few chores. Then, she thought she would check the weather on the local channel if she could find it. Instead, she found reruns of *I Love Lucy*.

She must have dozed off in her chair after that because she woke up much later to the sound of voices in the kitchen. Luke and Alex were discussing the bills. From the volume and tone-of-voice, Madge felt glad she couldn't actually hear the words.

She squinted at the clock on her side table and realized Alex had come home closer to morning than to bedtime. Madge listened long enough to start feeling anxious. Her plan depended on those two getting along just enough to finish out her sixty days. And they needed to keep the house and the utilities going that long.

They hadn't even reached the half-way mark yet, and the ninnies were about to blow the whole project. Madge felt her Oldsmobile slipping away. She thought about stomping right out to the kitchen and telling them to straighten up. Instead, she unhinged her stiff knees and shuffled to the bedroom. Kneeling at the side of the bed had become impossible a few years ago. Instead, Madge clasped her hands, bowed her head and said, "Lord, this is serious business tonight. I don't like the sounds of things in there. Now, You need to keep those two together at least to the end of my stint. I don't care what You do after that, but don't let them blow it tonight."

She had crawled under the covers and almost dozed off before she realized how hard-hearted she might have sounded. "P.S. Lord," she said. "If You want to keep them together forever, that would probably be the best thing. I just mean, don't let them figure that out till I'm done."

Just after daylight, Madge felt something soft on her face. She opened one eye enough to see Peyton and Quinn standing beside the bed. Peyton tapped a finger against Madge's cheek again.

"Daddy's asleep on the sofa," she said. "Can we watch cartoons in your room?"

"Sure. Might as well. But I'm not serving you breakfast on a tray." Madge opened both eyes and heaved herself into a sitting position. "You want pancakes, you'll have to scurry your little selves out to the kitchen in fifteen minutes."

"We'll scurry," Quinn said. "S-k-u-r-e, scurry." She and Peyton ran toward the television.

Madge reached for her housecoat and yawned. "Nice try," she said to herself. "Still can't spell, but at least she gives it a whirl."

The smell of pancakes evidently roused Luke. He joined Quinn and Peyton at the bar a few minutes later. Aspen carried Grace down the stairs before anyone had time for seconds.

"Mom's still sleeping," she said as she plopped Grace into her high chair.

Luke swallowed a mouthful of pancakes before speaking, "Well, it is pretty early for a Saturday morning. And your mom got in really late. Or early, actually, this morning. You girls should stay quiet and let her sleep this morning. Turn the volume way down on the TV."

"Or, we could go outside," Peyton said. "And have another adventure."

Quinn nodded and both girls continued focusing on their pancakes. Luke stopped eating and looked at Aspen.

She shrugged and poured syrup in a flower pattern on her pancake. "Do we have any bacon?"

"I don't think we have bacon," Luke made his voice sound lighthearted. "Probably bad for your cholesterol anyway."

"Pancakes need bacon."

"Well, your arteries will thank you for not clogging them."

"You could eat a hotdog," Madge said. "They both come from a pig."

Peyton grabbed her throat. "Bacon comes from a pig. I'm never eating bacon again. Poor little pigs."

"All meat comes from animals," Aspen said. "Do you want to know how they actually make hotdogs? I saw it on Discovery Channel. I promise you will never eat another one if I tell you."

"Okay, that's enough." Luke poked a fork in Aspen's pancake. "I like this design. Does it represent what you're hiding from us under the sheet? And when do we get to see your masterpiece?"

"I don't know. I wish I'd picked something else."

"What do you mean?"

"It's this awful project in history. Mrs. Scivens is making us research our family, and we had to pick a way to report on it. She's into 'creative expression', so we could write a story, or make a video, or a sculpture."

"Or paint a coat of arms." Luke finished the sentence.

"No, that would have been easier. It isn't like a family tree kind of history." Aspen put her fork down and folded her hands into a triangle. "We had to research the meaning of our names. At least the first names of each person in our immediate family.

You couldn't have given any of us a normal name like Tiffany."

Madge gave up any pretense of making breakfast. She had never heard of a school project like this; and, she was quite interested in where a couple of idiots came up with a name like Aspen.

"I'm sorry," Luke said. "Your mom and I didn't mean to give you an embarrassing name. It was special to us. It still is. And, for the record, Tiffany is the name of a store."

"Dad."

"So, tell the rest of us." Madge hadn't meant to butt in, but she couldn't stop herself. Once she had started, she couldn't seem to stop. "Where did you get a name like Aspen?"

"From a ski resort in Colorado," Aspen said. "It's where I came from."

Now Madge wished she had stayed out of the conversation. She started cutting up another pancake for Grace and hoped Aspen would drop the subject. But, no. Instead, she got up and walked toward her painting corner as she kept talking.

"Yeah. My parents spent their honeymoon in Aspen. I arrived nine months later."

"Oh." Madge suddenly wished she had asked a question about math class or the price of eggs in China.

"They used to go back there every year. So romantic." Madge wanted to get a dishrag and wash the syrup off Grace's face and the tone out of Aspen's voice, but she seemed paralyzed in the moment.

"Once the three of us went at Christmas."

"You remember going to the lodge?" Luke asked.

"I remember that time at Christmas." Aspen's tone softened. "And I remember you guys talking about it. I remember pictures. But you stopped going after Quinn."

Luke scooted back his chair and folded his arms. "That's right. I lost my job, and we didn't have the money that year. Then we just never went again."

Madge remembered her prayer from the night before and

wished she could tack on another postscript. Maybe God could figure out a way to restore the Oldsmobile and this family at the same time. Maybe.

"Anyway," Aspen said, "I picked painting a picture to tell the story of our family names, but it's going to be terrible." Aspen pulled away the sheet and revealed the beginning of a mountain scene with one medium sized aspen tree. A girl with blonde hair stood beside the tree. It wasn't great, by Madge's estimation, but she never tried to judge art.

"Wow." Luke got up and walked across the room. "This is going to be fantastic. Look how you captured the light on the leaves. They look just like that in the fall."

"They do? I looked at pictures on the Internet."

"Yeah, exactly. They shine sometimes when the wind blows. It's beautiful."

They stood for a few minutes staring at the painting. Obviously, Luke saw something Madge could not see. She squinted from across the room, but the leaves didn't move or shimmer as far as she could tell.

"Yep. Beautiful," he said again. He reached over and pulled Aspen under his arm and against his chest. "We named you exactly right. One Who Shines When the Wind Blows. Don't forget that."

He kissed the top of her head and gave her one more hug before he turned away. "I gotta go, kiddos. Remember to stay quiet this morning and let your mom sleep. Have a great week, and call me on Aspen's phone if you need anything. I'll see you Friday."

The little girls ran for kisses and Grace reached up her hands. Aspen just kept standing and staring at her painting. Madge stared, too. She couldn't see much promise in the painting, but so much promise in the girl. The thought surprised her.

Luke turned from the final hugs, grabbed his bag, and walked toward the door. He paused for a moment, though, and looked back.

"This stinks," he said to no one in particular.

Madge had already finished three loads of laundry when Alex finally made an appearance on Saturday afternoon. Her eyes were puffy, and her hair was knotted up into some kind of bun on top of her head. She wore a big shirt again over a pair of tight stretch pants. She looked like a college student after a night of parties. Madge had the idea she hadn't been partying.

"Rough week?"

"The worst. But, I think it will pay off. Hopefully, I've convinced them I can work the additional territory. It will mean a nice bonus and a raise. We could use it." She sorted through the accumulation of mail on the counter as she spoke.

A few seconds later, she tossed it all aside and picked up a plastic grocery bag she had brought downstairs with her. "Could you please tell the girls' father next week to stop leaving his trash in my bathroom?"

Madge retrieved the bag Alex dumped into the kitchen trashcan. "I don't think that's trash," she said. "I think it's his shaving kit. He must have forgotten it this morning."

Alex stopped thumbing through the magazine she had picked up and took the sack from Madge. She peeked inside and pulled out a razor and a toothbrush. She rustled around the remaining contents.

"He carries his stuff back and forth like this all the time?"

"Think so."

"In a grocery sack?"

"Looks like it."

"Well, I'm going to send him a text to tell him he left it. He'll need to shave on Monday if he hasn't lost his job again."

Madge raised one eyebrow. "You might want to leave that last part off."

Alex skimmed her fingers across the phone screen and paid no attention to Madge. When she finished, she looked up and said, "Oh shoot! I forgot to tell you I have to go meet some people tomorrow for brunch. It's a work thing. I know you should probably have the whole day off, but could you hang with the girls until I get back?"

Madge thought about saying, "No," but her plans with Paige weren't really settled. Their little trip to church could wait another week. "Sure," she said. "I'll hang." She said the last word with an exaggerated voice, which Alex ignored.

"Great." Alex turned back to the stack of mail again. "I thought sure we had an electric bill here that needed paid, but I can't find it. Have you seen it?"

Madge turned around and pretended to be busy at the sink, "Oh, I think maybe I heard Luke say something about paying an electric bill yesterday."

"Ha. That will be the day. Luke doesn't have a clue about the bills. He wouldn't even know where to go to pay the electric. Nor does he have that much money in the bank."

Madge turned around and cocked her head. Alex raised her hands and acted innocent. "He's using all the same passwords. If he doesn't want me checking things, he should change passwords. I just wanted to make sure he was telling the truth when he reported his income on the child support forms. I know it was disgraceful of me, but I got suspicious."

"And?"

"He told the truth. He's as broke as ever. He couldn't have paid the electric bill."

"Well, I think he did."

"How could he have done that?"

"I don't know how he managed it, but I know he left here yesterday morning with the bill in his hand."

"Well, I better follow up on it Monday. That bill might stay clipped to his visor for a month while we eat by candlelight around here. I'm going to take a shower. Do you have things covered down here?"

Madge looked out the window at the little girls and Grace playing on the swings. Aspen sat on the grass twirling a leaf, obviously in deep thought. "Yeah, we're covered," Madge said.

Chapter Twenty-Three

Tuesday, October 4th
Forty Days to Go

The doorbell rang early on Tuesday morning. When Madge opened it, she found Paige standing on the step. This time, she wore a longer skirt. "Hi, ready to go?"

"Go where?"

"To Circle. It's every Tuesday, right?"

"Right."

"You aren't doing anything else are you?"

"Well, I kind of have a job."

"But the kids are at school. Your boss is at work, and my boss is in court. And I told him we needed to run some errands, and he said that was fine as long as I made it back by three to pick up the kids."

Paige laughed when she said the last sentence. "Not 'our kids', you know. The Marvel kids. I didn't mean to make that sound like..."

"I knew what you meant. Come in and shut the door." Madge limped toward a chair and eased into it. "I'm not up to a trip to-day. My knees are just as stiff as can be. I think the weather is about to change."

"Oh, I'm sorry." Paige pulled off her jacket and dropped her bag. "Have you taken any Tylenol? I probably have some. What else can I do?"

"Well, I was trying to move a couple of boxes that The Lady of the House left in the middle of the floor this morning. You might help me with those." Madge pointed toward two plastic totes. "She said she wanted to put them in the laundry room until she decided what to do with them. They're heavy suckers."

Paige went over and tried to shove one of the tubs with her foot. "Good grief, what is in these? Gold bars?"

"Books, I think. She said mostly books."

"We might have to unpack them, move the totes half-full, and then repack. Do you think that would be an invasion of her privacy?"

"Do you think I care?"

Paige giggled and popped the lid off the first tub. She pulled out several volumes of college textbooks. "No wonder these were so heavy."

Further down, she lifted out a green volume with an elaborate cover. It wasn't old, but it was designed to look that way. "*Peter Pan*," she said, "I loved this story. Oh, you have to hear my favorite part. This is the part that always makes me want to get married and have children."

Paige settled down on the floor, crossed her legs, and leaned back against the box. After she flipped a few pages, she read in her best imitation of a British accent:

"It is the nightly custom of every good mother after her children are asleep to rummage in their minds and put things straight for next morning, repacking into their proper places the many articles that have wandered during the day. If you could keep awake (but of course you can't) you would see your own mother doing this, and you would find it very interesting to watch her. It is quite like tidying up drawers. You would see her on her knees, I expect..."

"Where did you find that?"

Paige stopped reading and looked at Alex, who stood in the

doorway. "I'm so sorry. I was trying to help, but we couldn't move this one without unloading it."

"I asked her to help," Madge said, though she didn't think their actions needed a defense.

"Was it in that box?" Alex stepped closer.

"Yes." Paige held out the book. The room grew so quiet Madge could hear the scuff of Alex's bare feet as she walked across the floor.

"I thought I lost it." Alex took the book, still open where Paige had been reading. She stood for a few moments looking at the words. Then she closed the book and dropped it into the athletic bag slung over her shoulder. "Did you need me to sign something?" she asked Paige.

"No, I'm sorry, I dropped by to check on Madge, see if she wanted to go to Circle at her church this morning since I was going to be out and about. She isn't feeling up to it, so I'll just be on my way. I'm sorry to have bothered you." With that, she leaped to her feet, grabbed her bag, and bopped out the door before Madge could speak.

"Well, my goodness," Alex said. "I hope they aren't charging me by the hour for that kind of thing. I don't have Mr. Oakley on retainer, you know."

"Oh, I'm sure they aren't. I think she's just young and looking for ways to stand out in business. You know, some people give away calendars at the end of the year, and the Oakley Law Firm gives rides to church. Same difference."

"Whatever you say." Alex obviously wasn't interested in pursuing the conversation, which relieved Madge. "I'm going to hit the shower. Afterwards, we can talk about the schedule for the rest of the week if that's okay."

"Sure. I'll be here." Madge started picking up books two at a time to carry them to the laundry room.

Alex pulled *Peter Pan* from her bag and started to hand it to Madge, but then she said, "Oh, I might as well hang onto this one, I guess. The girls might want it someday."

"Present from somebody?"

"Their dad. When I graduated from college and got my first teaching job." She ran her hand over the raised lettering. "I didn't know it would turn out to be his autobiography."

Madge frowned. "I've never read it myself, but from that bit I just heard, I think you might need to read it again. I think you missed something."

She turned and walked toward the kitchen without waiting for Alex to answer. If Alex decided to fire her, Madge thought she'd prefer to hear about it in the kitchen. Instead, she heard Alex go upstairs and turn on the shower. The water ran for a long time.

The next twenty-four hours passed without any major incidents. After supper on Wednesday, the little girls and Grace took long baths. Alex got home in time to kiss baby Grace and tuck her into bed. Then, she stuck her head in the doorway of the little girls' room just before the last "adieu" played on *Sound of Music*.

Madge could hear the conversation from the foot of the staircase. She kept sweeping up crumbs from bedtime snacks, and she took her time with the crevices around the stairs. She knew the girls would ask for another drink or a hug, and Alex would beg off because she had work to do. Instead, Peyton said, "I hope Mr. Tumnus will be all right."

"Mr. Who?"

"Mr. Tumnus. The White Witch got him because he helped Lucy. But we have to wait until Daddy is here again to know if he will be all right."

Madge stopped sweeping and leaned against the newel post.

"Are you talking about Narnia, Peyton? Is your daddy reading Narnia with you?"

"Yes."

"One chapter at bedtime," Quinn said. "Sometimes two if we promise to go right to sleep after."

The room stayed quiet for a long moment. "Well, that's good. That's very good. I'm sure Mr. Tumnus will be just fine eventually. Now, go to sleep."

Madge hustled toward the kitchen so she wouldn't be caught eavesdropping, and so she wouldn't have to answer any questions about the new bedtime ritual.

Chapter Twenty-Four

Thursday, October 6th
Thirty-eight Days to Go

No one mentioned Narnia or *Peter Pan* the next morning. On Thursday afternoon, Paige had barely pulled away from the house after dropping off Madge and the girls when Alex returned home. The exchange was a little too close for Madge's comfort, but the little girls were thrilled to see their mother home before supper. They smothered her with hugs and information about their day.

Finally, when things grew quiet and Madge had passed around snacks, Quinn pulled a sheet of paper from her bag. "Mama," she said, "I passed spelling."

Aspen stopped munching on her apple, and Madge watched Alex for the appropriate response. Alex obviously had no idea of the importance of this announcement. "That's great, Lovie. Spelling is an important foundation."

"No, Mom. It isn't great," Aspen said. "It's historic. Quinn has never passed a spelling pre-test."

"Never?"

"Never," Aspen and Quinn said at the same time.

Alex reached for the paper and looked at it more closely. "Well-done, Quinn."

Madge reached into the pantry and grabbed a bag of chocolate donuts she had been hiding behind the bran cereal. "This calls for a celebration," she said. "Miss Quinn has done the miraculous. Nothing but chocolate donuts can mark the occasion. We might have to call up the Glory Circle Sisters and brag just a little bit, what do you think?"

"Let's do it," Quinn yelled. "Let's call 'em."

"Who on earth are the Glory Circle Sisters?" Alex asked.

"They are the ones who made *Quinn's Magic Word Search*," Aspen told her. "That's how she learned to spell."

Aspen pulled the latest *Word Search* off the refrigerator and showed it to her mother while Madge got the little telephone from her purse and carefully dialed a number. Then they all waited.

"Evelyn? This is Madge. No, I'm perfectly fine. Yes, I'm sure. No, I'm not in any trouble. Of course. No. I'm just calling because I have someone here who wants to tell the girls something. Can you take down a message? Do you have a pencil? Okay. Here she is."

Madge put the phone against Quinn's ear. "Now, tell Evelyn who you are and what you've done."

"Hello? This is Quinn Marvel. I'm in the third grade, and you made the *Magic Word Search* for me, and today I passed spelling for the first time in my whole, entire life. Yep. Thank you very much, too. Okay, bye."

Quinn stuffed a donut into her mouth and managed to grin at the same time. At least it looked like a grin. Madge could see it in her eyes.

"So, what now?" Madge asked.

Once Quinn swallowed the donut, she answered. "No spelling test tomorrow. I get to do art while the losers do retakes."

"Quinn," Alex said, but her scolding was lost on the room because Aspen, Madge, and even Peyton were giving high fives and laughing at the thought of Quinn graduating from the losers' circle.

Alex shook her head, walked over to the desk, and flipped on the computer. "Madge," she said. "Do you know before I get back to the house next time, we will hit thirty days? We'll be half-way there."

The girls stopped laughing and slapping palms. Quinn wiped a crumb of donut from the edge of her mouth, her eyes suddenly solemn.

"Well, I guess time flies and all that." Madge tried to sound light-hearted. She had wanted the time to go fast after all. This was just a gig she picked up to earn a little money so she could fix her car. She never intended to stay. She was a short-timer by nature. She thought this last thought just as Baby Grace toddled over and threw both chubby hands around her leg. She squeezed the sore knee and planted a kiss right on it as if she had understood the conversation. That kiss did more good than Icy Hot.

"Which reminds me," Alex picked up the conversation, "the law firm emailed over some forms to fill out so they can issue your first paycheck at the end of the month." She sat down and clicked to another screen as she spoke. "Evidently, the agency failed to send over your resume, and now they are claiming to have lost the file or something. Sloppy details."

"Imagine that." Madge picked up Grace and handed her another donut.

"Here it is. Shall we get this done while we're thinking about it? I think it's simple. Social Security number, home address, date of birth, that kind of thing. Would you rather type it in so I don't know all that?"

Madge looked at Alex whose fingers were poised over the keyboard like she was ready to play a piano concert. She was obviously eager to hear all the information she'd just described. Although for the life of her, Madge couldn't figure out why. She had nothing to hide, though. "Go ahead," she said. "You'll be faster.

What do you want first?"

"Let's start with your full name. Isn't Madge short for something?"

Madge hesitated. Maybe she should fill out the forms by herself after all. The little girls were all waiting, staring at her as if she had grown an extra eye in the middle of her forehead. Even Aspen had gotten suddenly interested in the conversation.

"Your name isn't Madge?" Peyton said.

"It's what people call her," Aspen said. "But she probably has another name. A longer name. Just like Mom does."

Alex turned toward Aspen with a surprised expression. Aspen kept talking as she walked toward the corner where her painting stood. "Everybody calls mom 'Alex' which kind of sounds like a boy's name if you think about it. And that makes sense, because she acts like the man of the family lots of times. She makes the most money. She travels all the time. She makes the big decisions."

"Aspen, that's not true."

"Yes, it is. I hear you say so all the time." Madge could tell Aspen was trying to sound grown-up and sassy. She thought tears were more likely.

"So, everybody calls her Alex like she is a boy. Her real name, though, is Alexandra. A long, beautiful, woman's name."

Aspen pulled the sheet off her painting and revealed a new figure. A woman wearing a suit of armor and carrying a sword pointed at the sky. "And do you know what 'Alexandra' means? 'Protector of Man.' Not kicker-out-of-man."

"Margaret." Madge blurted out the name as if she were shouting a Jeopardy answer for Alex Trebek. "Madge is short for 'Margaret.' Nobody has called me that since my mother died about a hundred years ago. So, don't go trying it on for size. But you better fill it in on that paperwork, because the Social Security has it down that way, so the bank won't cash my check unless you make it out to Margaret Adeline DuPree. I'd appreciate it if you don't spread that around to the whole world."

She turned to the bar where the little girls had taken advantage of the tension in the room to devour a few more donuts. "And you, Miss Queen of the Spelling Bee, don't be bragging about it to the Glory Circle Sisters if you call them up again. Some things remain private even in church."

The diversion had worked. At least for the moment. Madge had fallen on the hand grenade of her given name and stopped the battle of Aspen Hill. She had no idea if the girl was right about Alex's name. But, it seemed to hit a nerve.

"That looks like a Halloween costume," Peyton said as she stood beside Aspen and looked at the painting. "But I'd rather be a princess. Can I be a princess this year, Mama?"

Alex rubbed her forehead and closed her eyes for a moment. "Oh, I'm not sure what we are doing about Halloween this year, Peyton. Your dad and I haven't discussed it yet."

"I just want to be a princess," Peyton said again. "My friend, Kaylee, is going to be a princess and her crown has real jewels in it because her mother was a homecoming queen."

"Well, that is nice for Kaylee," Alex said. Her voice sounded just a little harder than it had a few seconds before, and Madge thought a meltdown might be coming for the entire household.

"But your mother wasn't a homecoming queen, and she doesn't have all kinds of spare time these days, so we are going to have to wait and see how things go, okay?"

"Hey," Madge said, "We could stop at that thrift store on the corner by Toodle Time. I bet they have a bunch of old jewelry, and you could make all kinds of crowns."

"Toddle Time!" Aspen and Quinn said at the same time. Quinn laughed and Peyton smiled when she said, "Do you know how to make a crown, Madge?"

Madge felt the trap spring shut. A trap she had set and then stumbled upon. Foolish woman.

"Well, no," she said. "But they say you can learn anything on that Internet. I bet Aspen could do it."

Aspen replied with something like a huff. Madge decided the lack of an outright refusal meant they had a chance at a crown. She counted the battle as won.

Madge had packed the last lunch Friday morning when Quinn came over and pulled the calendar down from the window ledge. She looked at the words twirled into the leaves of a vine. Flowers burst out all over the archway.

"I can't read it," Quinn said. "Too many flowers. What does it say?" She handed it to Alex, who was pouring coffee into her travel mug.

Alex took the calendar and read with an absent-minded tone, "I and the children whom the Lord has given me are for signs and wonders in Israel from the Lord of hosts, who dwells on Mount Zion."

"Whoa," Quinn said. "That is cool. Read it again."

Alex put her mug down and pulled the calendar closer. This time she read slowly, "I, and the children whom the Lord has given me, are for signs and wonders." She stopped and looked up at the girls. They were all watching her.

Madge lifted a napkin to her lips and whispered, "Don't blow it, Lady. You got a chance here."

"That's us," Alex said. "I don't know what kind of a sign we are, but it is certainly a wonder we've made it this far, don't you think?"

Aspen pulled her backpack across the bar and onto her shoulder. "A sign and a wonder. Isn't that kind of the same thing as a marvel?"

Alex reached out and snapped the lid on her coffee mug. "Why, yes, it is, Aspen Alexandra Marvel. How astute of you."

Chapter Twenty-Five

Sunday, October 9th
Thirty-five Days to Go

Paige wore pants on Sunday. Madge thought about telling her to go home and change, but they would be late for church. Depending on traffic, they might be late anyway. They were cutting it close. It wasn't that women never wore slacks to Mt. Zion. Of course, they did. The younger, modern women all wore pants. Some of them even wore blue jeans on Wednesday nights. However, the ladies were staunch about pantyhose and pumps in the third pew.

Why was the girl wearing pants anyway? She had worn a skirt every single time Madge had ever seen her. As if reading her mind, Paige brought up the subject while Madge was getting her purse. "I hope this outfit is okay. The laundry room in my building is on the fritz. Again. I couldn't believe it when I went down yesterday. I had stuffed everything I own into my laundry bag, a crumpled mess. Everything but this outfit and my favorite jeans, of course. I figured this would be the better choice."

"Good thought."

"I know your church is pretty traditional; but ladies do wear pants, don't they? I'd hate to embarrass you or the other Glory Circle Sisters."

Madge stopped stuffing extra Kleenex into her purse. She looked at Paige in her snazzy green jacket and black pants. Both her eyes and her necklace shining. She could pass for a younger version of Evelyn. "Give me a minute," Madge said. She marched back to the bedroom and pulled her own navy pants out of the closet. Might as well start a revolution today.

Of course, no one even noticed the revolt. Madge and her guest slid into their seats with only minutes to spare. Evelyn smiled from her end of the pew, and Grace Colby passed down an extra bulletin. Bess scooted closer to Madge and whispered, "I didn't know you had a daughter, Madge. It's nice you brought her today. She doesn't look much like you, though. Does she take after her father?"

Madge patted Bess's hand. "Just a friend, Bessie. I don't have any kids of my own." She wasn't sure why she tucked on that phrase at the end. "Of my own." Why not just say, "I don't have any kids"? She always said it that way when she answered the question. "I don't have any kids." It was a simple answer. Where did "of my own" come from? Did she suddenly have some borrowed kids from somewhere? Madge wiggled in her seat. The pew suddenly felt more uncomfortable than usual.

The choir stood and started the opening hymn before she had time to examine the thought further, thank goodness. Paige slid the open hymnal toward Madge as an offer to share, which Madge accepted. But, she didn't sing. She knew every word, though, and she followed along in her mind.

Once the service ended, the ladies swarmed around Madge to hear all about Quinn's spelling test. Pastor Cleveland interrupted them. "Well, look who's here this morning. Are you home for good, Sister Madge?"

"Nope. Just out on good behavior. Paige offered to bring me over for church."

"Miss Rosedale, isn't it? We met on Circle day."

"Yes, thanks for remembering me. I just thought Madge

would enjoy a taste of home. Those little girls are working her pretty hard. Especially Aspen, the oldest one. She can get a 'tude. Which I remember well from being that age. It wasn't so long ago, to be honest."

Pastor Cleveland laughed. "I'm glad Madge has you on her side. I'll confess we were all a smidgen surprised to hear our Madge had taken on a nanny job."

"It's a temp job," Madge said. "Short-term. Just another month."

"Right. Because last I heard, you were just going across town to visit your nephew. Was I right about that?"

"Yes. Ben and his wife Nancy." Madge hesitated. She wasn't sure how much she wanted to say. "I had a little car trouble," she finally said, "and needed to make a few dollars to get it worked on before I came home. This job came up, and it was temporary, so it was a good fit."

Paige jumped into the conversation. "She is doing a great job. The little girls just love her. And the stability is so good for them in this situation."

Madge could tell Grace Colby was less than convinced about her credentials as a nanny, but Evelyn smiled. "That's good to hear," she said. "So many troubled families these days. I blame the economy for one thing. Families have a hard time making it with all that stress and strain. What about you, dear, where is your family from?"

With that, Evelyn steered the conversation away from Madge. It might not have been on purpose, but Madge felt grateful anyway. She leaned against the side of the pew and watched people talking in little groups around the room. Eventually, she felt someone move up next to her and bump against her elbow. She turned her head just enough to see Elmer Grigsby standing with his hat in his hands.

He wore a spotless white shirt, a plaid bow tie, and the kind of sweater Madge thought of for a professor. Quite a change from the homeless attire he had on when he made his first appearance at the church. He still stood with the slight hunch of a man who feels he might not be completely welcome in the conversation.

"How's your cat?" Madge asked.

"Tolerable. Overfed now that we're livin' in the parsonage, of course."

"That happens to the best of us. I've put on a few pounds myself over in Cherry Hills."

"I heard you was livin' big in the snobby part of town."

"Not too snobby. But a little fancy for my taste."

"You'll be comin' back home then?"

"Sure. Just another month. It's a short-time thing."

"Well, that's good. A body can't take too much of that high livin'."

"No. But I could get used to some of the conveniences," Madge said. She nodded in Paige's direction. "Like having my own, personal chauffeur."

"I reckon so. She looks like a good one. I better get on home myself. The cat's likely beggin' for dinner. Now that we both get fed on a regular schedule, we've got used to it."

"Well, that becomes a problem, doesn't it? You take care of yourself." Madge watched him walk away. She thought he stood a little straighter than when he first came up to her, but it might have been her imagination.

"Tom and I are having lunch at Grandby's." Evelyn stood beside Paige with an expectant look on her face, and Madge swore the two women had the exact tilt of the head. She wondered if they taught that in some ladies' finishing school somewhere. "Why don't you and Paige join us before your drive?"

"That's up to Paige," Madge said. "But I am famished."

"Is everything covered at the Marvel house?"

"I wasn't hired as the weekend cook." Madge didn't mean to answer quite so gruffly. She probably did it because she had an immediate mental image of Aspen doling out cold hotdogs to the girls while their mother ate yogurt over the sink and stared at her laptop. Sunday lunch at the Marvel house.

"Grandby's it is." Page gave Evelyn her perfect smile and reached for her purse.

Evelyn turned to Bess, who was still sitting in the pew. "Will you have lunch with us before we take you home, Bess? It's adding up to be something of a party."

"Oh, that would be nice. Of course, I eat out for lunch nearly every day. They have a lovely little place just down the way from my apartment. The service is slow. And the menu is terribly limited."

"Well, you'll like this place. It's a full menu," Evelyn said.

Madge leaned over and whispered to Paige, "Sometimes Bess forgets that she lives in a home."

"Yes. Assisted living, right?"

"More like lock-down these days. She's slipped over the edge of assistance. But she's still happy, so we try to keep it that way. If she says something goofy at lunch, just try to go with it. And, by the way, she thinks you're my daughter. I told her you weren't, but she's liable to forget that part."

Paige put her hand on Madge's shoulder. "I'll just adopt you for the day, how's that?"

Madge pulled back automatically. "It may not even come up. She usually hops from one thought to another. She may think you are Jackie Kennedy by the time we get to the restaurant. You look a little like her, you know. Similar style. Same hair. If she asks you where the President is today, don't assume she is in this century. Tell her he's with the family at the Cape or something."

Madge hadn't really expected to predict the conversation, but she could often read Bess in advance. Sure enough, things went as she had expected. They had just given the elegant waiter their drink order when Bess spoke to Paige. "Do you drink diet soda in the White House, too? For some reason I expected it to be more iced tea and coffee with state dinners. Maybe even some hard liquor since you're Catholic. Of course, you couldn't get that on a Sunday."

Paige appeared to choke slightly on the water she had just sipped. Evelyn breezed in and took control. "I think you've mistaken Paige for Mrs. Kennedy, Bess. They do look something alike. But this is Madge's friend, Paige Rosedale."

They seldom corrected Bess. Madge hated for Evelyn to do it today because it usually made Bess get sad and weepy. Sometimes, Madge thought they covered for Bess because they wanted to cover for themselves. For the little slip-ups, the failed memories, the signs of aging nobody wanted to admit.

"Oh, silly me," Bess grinned. "The resemblance is amazing. You are such a stunning beauty. I bet you get mistaken for her all the time. She's so constantly in the news. People must stop you on the street and ask for your autograph."

Paige smiled and touched Bess's small hand. "You know," Paige said, "I expect I could pick up a side job doing impersonations of the first lady. I saw that in a movie once, and I thought that would be a fun job if I ever needed to make some extra money."

Madge coughed and reached for her water. She wanted to stop this conversation about side jobs and mistaken identity. Paige was not Jackie Kennedy, and Madge bore no resemblance to Mary Poppins.

Bess, of course, remained oblivious to Madge's discomfort. "Oh, what a lovely idea," she said. "We have a little community social every Thursday night, and people are always performing. I could put you in touch with the organization. I don't know that it pays much, but it might get you started."

"Well, I'm sort of tied up with my current job right now, but Madge can put us in touch if my schedule changes. Would that be okay?"

Bess looked at Madge and smiled. "Of course it would. Madge can always be trusted to take care of things."

Chapter Twenty-Six

Monday, October 10th
Thirty-four Days to Go

Taking care of things was not Madge's specialty. On Monday, the whole family left the breakfast table with grouchy faces. Including Alex. She called Madge ten minutes later because she had forgotten to leave a list of things Luke needed to do at the house during the week.

The house itself was a wreck. The girls hadn't done their regular chores for some reason over the weekend. Madge stood in the middle of the upstairs hallway. She tried to decide if it was her job to clean it up before Luke arrived so the evening could be peaceful or if she should butt out, and let him come home and restore order.

In the end, she didn't have time to take care of it. They had run completely out of groceries again, and it took most of the morning to place the order. After that, the kitchen needed a good scrub from Alex's attempt to cook on Sunday. Evidently, they had something more than cold hotdogs. Madge couldn't even see the floor of the laundry room for the pile of dirty clothes and towels. She wondered how things could get so out-of-control in two days. Hadn't she been paying attention on Saturday?

Luke brought the girls home on Monday evening, and Madge

knew they were in for an emotional circus the minute they walked through the door. "Grace is fussy," he said to Madge. "The daycare people say she's cutting molars."

Madge took the crying baby and shooed Luke toward the other room. As she patted the little back, Madge wondered why everyone blamed teeth for this meltdown.

"The poor child never knows which parent will be in the house morning or night," she said to herself. Then, she decided to pull the Almighty in on the problem.

"You know, Lord, this week-on, week-off schedule has gone off the tracks. I never know who's going to be here, either. Alex gets called out of town, or Luke has extra work. And nobody bothers to tell the nanny. Or the baby." She reached for the Cheerios, and Grace immediately stopped crying.

"You know those two don't have the sense You gave a goose," Madge said. "Can't You do something about it?"

Madge's prayer was interrupted by Peyton shouting at Quinn for taking the last chocolate donut. Quinn responded by shouting at Peyton for hogging the remote. And so the evening went. Aspen stood in the corner frowning at her painting for what felt like hours.

Finally, Luke addressed the silent one. "How's the masterpiece going?"

"I'm blocked."

"I think writers have dibs on that one. Painters have a different excuse, but I'm not sure what it is."

"Well, whatever it is, I have it."

Luke crossed the room and peeked over Aspen's shoulder. Madge turned slightly while she scrubbed a pan, trying not to make it obvious that she was watching. She couldn't believe Aspen would allow an art critic to observe.

"I know I want to put Quinn in that spot beside the boulder. But I have no idea how to represent her. Her name is Gaelic and means "counsel." How do I show that?"

"Ah," Luke put his chin in one hand like a professor. "Well, there is your problem. You don't know about Quinn's name."

Quinn stopped in the process of dividing her donut and looked up. Aspen turned from the painting to her dad. "What does it mean?"

Madge poured more Cheerios into Grace's hand and pulled up a stool to listen.

"Well, for the full story we would have to ask the great Nobel Peace Prize winner Bob Dylan."

Aspen waved her paintbrush in the air and said, "Dad, get real."

"I am real. Dylan won the Peace Prize for his lifetime contribution of lyrics. He's a national icon. And he wrote this amazing song about Quinn the Mighty Eskimo. Although, your mom and I actually liked the Manfred Mann version best, but don't tell Dylan."

"Oh, don't worry, I won't."

Madge thought Luke might be speaking a foreign language, but she kept listening.

"We never heard Dylan sing it in person," he said. "But we did go to one of his concerts when you were about four. We bought an album. The actual vinyl kind. And Quinn the Eskimo was on it."

Luke stopped trying to be funny then. He looked over the top of the painting and out the window toward the backyard. Madge thought that maybe he could see as far as China while he talked.

"Things had been kind of tough for us for a while, but that song did something. We kept singing it to one another for weeks, like a promise that things were going to get better."

"In the song, everyone is doing what they can to make life better. They built ships, took notes, and fed pigeons. I'm not sure how the pigeons fit in, but nothing was working. Yet, they have this beautiful hope about a mysterious person named Quinn the Eskimo who is going to set everything right."

"He was kind of like Aslan in Narnia, you know? A Jesus figure. One line in the song said that when the Mighty Quinn arrived, everyone would jump for joy. Your mom and I loved that line. We said it to each other all the time. And then, we found out your mom was pregnant, which we had wanted for a long time. We took it as a sign."

"But it wasn't a sign," Aspen said.

"Of course it was a sign." Luke suddenly seemed to remember his daughters. He turned toward the little girls and then swooped over to the table and grabbed Quinn up in a hug. "Just look at this girl," he said. "The Mighty Quinn. Everybody jumped for joy when she came to town. We're still jumping. Now, I hear she is acing her spelling tests. Who couldn't jump for joy? Let's all jump!"

And the game was on. The little girls started jumping, even Grace. Aspen managed a smile before she turned back to her painting with a look of determination.

Luke did a side jump over to Madge and said, "Of course, I lost my job just before she was born and didn't find another one for more than a year, but who's counting that, right?"

"Right."

The jolly attitude lasted right through supper and bedtime and even into breakfast the next day. Madge had to give the guy some credit. He had managed to cheer the whole place up a notch. On the way home from school Tuesday, Quinn and Peyton were complete chatterboxes. Suddenly, Quinn said, "We should stop and get Peyton's jewels today."

"What?" Paige pulled to the curb at Toddle Time and looked over her shoulder at Quinn.

"Madge and Aspen are making a Halloween costume for Peyton," Quinn said. "She wants to be a princess."

Paige raised her eyebrows and looked at Madge. "A princess costume, I assume?"

"Well, I might have mentioned something."

"And Aspen is in on this?"

"Aspen has dance today," Quinn said. "So, we'll have to pick out the jewels without her."

"For the crown," Peyton said, "I want real jewels."

"I see." Paige leaned back and folded her arms as if she was enjoying this project Madge had gotten herself into. "And what about you, Quinn, what do you want to be for Halloween?"

"Oh, I don't know for sure. Maybe an Eskimo."

Madge groaned. She knew she should have kept her big mouth shut. She had never helped make a costume of any sort in her entire life, and now was not the time to start. She looked at Paige with what she hoped was pleading, but Paige shook her head. "I can't sew. And I have a class tonight. You are on your own for this one, Sista."

They stopped at the thrift store even though Madge expected it would be a bad idea. Paige promised she had enough time to spare, and she even offered to wait in the car with Grace and read books. So, Madge and the little girls traipsed into the store looking to outfit a princess and an Eskimo.

A clerk wearing a red apron with lots of pockets greeted them the minute the bell rang on the door. "May I help you and your lovely granddaughters?" she asked.

Madge didn't bother with introductions. She said, "We are looking for some gear to turn into Halloween costumes. Something with jewels for a princess and fur for an Eskimo."

The woman drew back and put one hand on her heart. The other hand covered her mouth. But that didn't stop the words from coming out clearly. "Oh, my. Surely you know Halloween is of the devil. You don't mean you are going to let these precious, little girls worship the devil on his holiday, do you?"

Madge felt Peyton press against her thigh so hard she thought they both might tumble into the Five-for-a-Dollar bin of scarves beside them. She reached out to steady herself and said, "We're just looking for some dress-up clothes to play in. That's all. No devil worship."

"Well, but Halloween. Are you fully aware of the roots of paganism this fiendish tradition springs from? I have some literature." She waved toward a desk behind her and looked as if she might walk toward it.

"Do you have a furry coat that might fit this one?" Madge said as she patted Quinn on the head. "She needs a good, furry, winter coat. With a hood. And some fur boots. Got anything like that?"

"Well," the woman turned toward a far corner and spoke slowly as if she regretted even giving up the information.

"How about if we just look around a bit?" Madge said. "We'll let you know if we need anything." She took both girls by the hand and marched off toward the corner where she could see coats piled on a table.

"What did she mean about the devil?" Quinn asked.

"Never mind," Madge said. "She was just being silly. We'll find our stuff and get out of here." She knew Quinn wouldn't be satisfied with that answer, but she hoped to distract her long enough to get the shopping done and get home where Luke or Alex could answer such questions.

As they walked across the store, Madge mumbled, "Lord, this is the strangest prayer You've ever heard from me, but could You please find us some Eskimo and princess clothes before the zealous one pounces again?"

Suddenly, Madge felt as if Narnia's Father Christmas himself had been dispatched with an answer. Fuzzy boots, a hooded coat, and thick mittens all appeared in the same corner. The coat had probably been white fake-fur at one time but it had mellowed now to a creamy color. Madge thought it looked more authentic that way. The boots were a little big, but they would do.

"What about the mittens?" Quinn said. "How do I get the

candy with mittens on my hands?"

"We'll figure that out," Madge said. "But you've got to have the mittens. They match the coat, and every Eskimo wears 'em."

"Oh. How do you know so much about it?"

"I've seen lots of pictures," Madge said. When, in truth, she thought this Eskimo get-up came straight from the Sears catalog at some point and had never seen an igloo.

The princess outfit proved harder to come by. The dress was easy. Any number of silky nightgowns from the lingerie section would do. A few tucks here and there with safety pins. Peyton chose pink, of course. Madge had figured for the headpiece they could use a window curtain as a veil and pin on some kind of fake jewelry to make a crown.

They found a nice, flowy curtain for the veil. Peyton swished around the store with it, trying out her princess moves. The jewelry department turned out to be rather low on perfect pieces for a headdress.

Finally, just when she was about to give up and say they had to get home to make supper, Madge saw a handbag across the room. She led the girls over to take a closer look. The clasp of the bag was made from a beaded peacock with little feathers fanning out all around it.

"Rather gaudy, isn't it?" The saleslady had returned.

"Oh, I like it," Madge said.

"Oh? Would you carry something like that?"

"Never," Madge said. "But I'd cut it off the bag in a minute and turn it into a crown for a princess. Here you go. Ring these up and add the bag. We're kind of in a hurry."

While the saleslady took her sweet time adding up the purchases by hand and recording them on a tablet, Madge tried to distract the girls by asking about school. The last thing she wanted was for one of them to mention Halloween and get that conversation started again.

Finally, the lady handed over a recycled grocery bag with the furry coat peeking out. Peyton became suddenly friendly and said, "And we are having a costume day at school, too, so I'll get to wear my princess crown twice for Halloween."

"Oh, my!" the saleslady said. "Did you ever hear of such a thing?"

"Never," Madge said as she scurried the girls toward the door. She was telling the absolute truth because she had never helped a child come up with a Halloween costume for one event, let alone two.

Chapter Twenty-Seven

Thursday, October 13th
Thirty-one Days to Go

On Thursday afternoon, Paige was late. Not by much. But enough that Madge started to worry something had gone wrong. When Jack's sporty car whipped into the driveway, she decided something had gone badly wrong.

"Paige got stuck at the courthouse," he said while he and Madge climbed into Alex's car.

"Doing what?"

"Administrative Assistant work."

Madge squinted at him. "She's doing your work, isn't she?"

"No." Jack hit the gas a little hard as he backed out of the drive. "She is doing some paperwork for the office so I can concentrate on other matters."

"Did you make a new level?"

Jack looked at Madge as he made the turn at the corner. "How do you know about levels?"

"I've lived in this house for a month. You don't think I've heard people playing video games? So, did you make a new level?"

"It's not that kind of game." He made another turn and switched lanes smoothly. "But, yeah, I made a level."

Madge pulled her handbag closer on her lap and nodded. "I figured so."

"I don't really owe you an explanation," Jack said, "but what I'm working on is important. At least to some people."

"Why don't you stop doing divorce court and help these little girls keep their house instead? That seems like something important for a lawyer to do."

"I can't do anything about that. I just file the paperwork. Their problems are not mine."

"But you're glad to take the money for their problems. How can you do that? How can you look those little girls in the face and take their mother's money knowing it is wrecking their lives?"

Madge couldn't seem to stop her mouth from yammering on. She knew reconciling the Marvels would be the end of her job. She hadn't earned enough money yet. But, she couldn't seem to silence herself.

"I'm not wrecking their lives," Jack said. "The wreck happened a long time ago. I'm just the tow truck driver." He zipped into another lane with that statement, and Madge grabbed the door handle to keep from sliding across the seat and banging into him.

"Look," he said, as he slowed the car and his voice, "could we call a truce on this? I'm just doing a job. The Marvel divorce is a job. And you're just doing a job. We both need to earn some money, get our checks, and move on. Those people are going to have to work out their own lives. Don't you think?"

Madge folded her arms over her purse and settled down into her seat. She didn't want to admit how right Jack's words sounded. She needed to quit meddling.

She remained unusually silent during the remaining pickup routine, but Jack didn't seem to notice. The little girls chattered enough to cover any awkward silences anyway. The girls were competing to see who would spy the mailbox on their corner first when Peyton shouted, "Daddy's home."

Sure enough, Luke's vehicle pulled into the driveway just ahead of them. Peyton left her backpack on the seat and popped out of the car with a cheer.

Aspen slid out of the other side and looked at Madge. "Well, this could get awkward," she said.

Madge swung her legs out of the car and turned toward Grace's car seat. She pushed the button, pulled the strap, and lifted Grace out in a couple of smooth moves. Unfortunately, she didn't feel like celebrating her growth in the toddler-car-seat department. Instead, she looked at all their books and bags in the back seat.

"Bring the luggage, will ya, Jack?"

Jack brought the luggage; but he came through the garage slowly and crept into the kitchen like someone who didn't want to wake the dragon. Too late, of course. Steam was already rising.

Madge stepped through the doorway only seconds ahead of Jack, but Luke ignored her. He stepped straight in front of Jack.

"Why is my wife's lawyer driving our children home from school?"

"Your wife's lawyer isn't doing anything." Madge shoved herself between the men.

"Excuse me?"

"Your wife's lawyer is that squirrely Charles Oakley with the nice secretary..."

"Administrative assistant," Aspen broke in. Madge scowled, but Aspen shrugged and stood her ground near the fridge.

"Anyway," Madge said, "that Mr. Oakley is your wife's lawyer. This guy's name is Jack. And he was just helping out a friend."

"You are friends with my wife's lawyer?"

"They aren't friends," Aspen said again. "He hardly ever comes to get us."

Madge gave Aspen another warning glare, which Aspen ignored.

"What do you mean 'hardly ever' comes to get you? Get you from where? And why?" Luke's voice grew even louder.

"She means," Jack stepped around Madge and put himself in front of Luke, "normally, my administrative assistant helps Madge with after-school pick-up, but I couldn't spare her this afternoon, so I came instead."

Everyone stood still and waited to see who would speak next. Luke frowned with obvious confusion. Finally, Madge gave up. She might as well put an end to the mystery and take her lumps. She walked toward the sink and fiddled with an empty coffee cup.

"Turns out," she said, "that somebody failed to mention this job required chauffer services. Childcare, light housekeeping, some cooking. No one mentioned driving twice a day to pick up kids."

She kept her eyes on the cup. "And, it turns out I have a small issue with my driver's license."

Luke took the cup from Madge's hand. "What kind of problem with your license?"

"Well, I don't exactly have one. A license, I mean. Not one that works, anyway." Madge crossed her arms and tried to sound confident, as if losing her license was a mere inconvenience like misplacing her purse. "I'll get it back. The judge said so. But right now, it is sort of suspended."

"Oh, my Lord in Heaven," Luke said. "Why is your license suspended?"

"She hit an ice cream truck," Aspen said from the corner. Then despite the tension in the air, she grinned. "I'm sorry," she said, "but you have to admit that's kind of hilarious."

Luke stared at Aspen for a second, shook his head, and then turned to Jack.

"So, you drive her," Luke said. "To cover up the fact that you hired someone with a record, you've been doing Madge's driving for the past month."

"It isn't much of a record," Jack said. "She isn't a felon or anything. And, I'm pretty sure we can work something out with the court. But, yeah, this seemed like the best solution in the moment. As I mentioned, my assistant does most of the actual driving. And it is temporary."

Madge bristled. It was fine for her to remind folks she was temporary help around the place. Jack didn't need to say it so boldly. Like he would be glad to get rid of her. Before she could voice a protest, though, Madge suddenly remembered the other thing he had said. He might be able to work something out with the court. Bless his heart. Jack might get her license back.

Luke didn't appear to share her gratitude. "This is totally insane," he said. "First, the judge gives the house to four little girls. Then, the nanny hires my opposing lawyer to do her job. That seems to fit about right."

He walked to the refrigerator and reached inside for a Pepsi. "My life is unbelievable. If they made this into a movie, nobody would believe it."

"Well," Jack said, "I've seen worse. I mean, you do have a nice set-up here, minus the license issue. Which, again, I think we can solve."

Luke flipped open his Pepsi, stared at Jack for a moment, and then shook his head again. He reached into the fridge for a second Pepsi and held it out to Jack.

Madge had to remind herself to close her mouth, which had dropped open about three sentences ago.

"Thanks," Jack said as he took the drink. "By the way, she isn't paying me for driving. That would be a conflict of interest. Or something."

Luke leaned against the bar and kept talking. "You do a lot of this kind of stuff?"

"Drive my client's kids around?"

"No. Divorces."

Jack took a long drink and shook his head.

Madge dared to speak. "We're his first one. Aren't we lucky?"

"You gotta be kidding me." Luke grinned the way he did when his team was winning on television. For the first time in the conversation, Madge thought her job might survive.

"We're your first divorce case? And you got a ruling they're gonna write about in books. No wonder you're working so hard to keep it together."

"No, that's not it."

"Oh, yeah, that's it." Luke nodded slowly and leaned back, grinning even more. "You are in so much trouble, Man. People are going to point to this one for years to come. Marvel vs. Marvel. The case that set the precedent for Nest Homes. That's what they're calling it on the Internet, you know. It's already a thing. And people are going to say, 'Who's the lawyer who handled that deal and made everything work out so smoothly?'"

He reached for his soda and took a long swig. Then he finished his thought. "Or, they'll say, 'who was the schmuck who messed that deal up because he hired a nanny with a rap sheet?'"

"I don't rap," Madge said. "I know about that stuff. It's just an excuse to cuss real fast so maybe people won't hear all the bad words."

Neither of the men paid any attention to Madge. Jack crossed his arms, puffed out his chest, and started nodding his head like a big time lawyer on one of those TV shows.

"Uh, huh," he said, "I hear that. And who is the poor schmuck who got stuck paying for his kids' health insurance even though his wife makes three times his salary just because she has a brilliant attorney, huh? Who is that guy?"

Luke leaned forward and shoved his finger into Jack's chest. "Hey, buddy. These are my kids, and I'm gonna pay for their health insurance. Where I come from, a man takes care of his family, and that includes things like health insurance and braces and ballet class and rides home from school. So, you can just butt out."

Madge felt her sliver of hope evaporate.

Jack set down his Pepsi and raised both hands. "Fine by me. I don't have time for charity work, anyway. You take care of your own carpools. And you can drive Madge all over town for her errands, too. I'll notify Miss Rosedale that her chauffeur services are no longer needed at the Marvel house. See you in court next month." He turned and marched toward the door.

The little girls stared at their dad. Even Aspen seemed short on snide comments. Madge waited a full beat before she played her only card. "You plan to tell the Lady of the House she has to drive on her days?"

Luke dropped his head into his hands. "What happened to your license?" he asked.

"Aspen told you. A little traffic accident."

"How long is it suspended?"

"Another thirty days, at least."

"And Alex doesn't know?"

Madge shook her head. Even though Luke didn't look up, she could tell he guessed the answer. She wondered if she would get sacked right along with Jack, and she started trying to count up how short her funds would be.

Luke lifted his head and tilted it all the way back to stare at the ceiling. "Aaargh! Who hates me up there?" He slammed his stool away from the bar and stomped out of the room.

Madge heard him swing the back door open.

"Hey," he yelled at Jack, "hold up a minute."

Chapter Twenty-Eight

Thursday, October 13th
Thirty-one Days to Go

And, so, Luke joined the conspiracy. Against his will, of course. Paige ended up being busy all week, and Jack made all the runs. Madge had no idea if Jack was keeping her busy with office work or if she was busy with homework from her night classes. Or maybe she was out applying for a new job. The mystery nagged at her, but it seemed like a good idea to keep quiet and not ask too many questions just now. Not Madge's best trait.

Normally, Jack just gave a salute as the girls jumped out of the car, and then he drove away. On Thursday, he got out and started unsnapping Grace's seatbelt. She reached for him once the restraints dropped away, so he picked her up and carried her inside. And, of course, Luke came home early again. Madge sucked in a breath and waited for the explosion.

Instead, Luke looked around the room, shook his head, and then pulled a Pepsi out of the fridge. He tossed it toward Jack without even asking. Jack accepted the offering, nodded, and popped the tab. Luke nodded back.

Everyone stood silently while the two men each took a swig from their cans. Then, Jack asked what Luke thought of the Cubs. Luke said, "Well, let me tell you."

With that, the two men walked together toward the family room, talking baseball, while Madge stood in the middle of the kitchen staring.

She had always heard men did that. That they could swing hard punches at each other in a brawl and then turn around and act like best friends. She had never witnessed such a thing.

Aspen walked up beside her, staring at the doorway where they could both hear the men laughing. "The wide world of sports," she said, "bringing enemies together since the dawn of time."

"Your dad's a fanatic."

"Yeah, pretty much." Aspen turned toward her painting where another figure was beginning to form beside Quinn. "That's how Peyton got her name."

"Her name?" Madge said.

"Peyton, as in Manning. As in one of the greatest quarterbacks ever."

"Oh. That's good," Madge said. "I thought it was from that old soap opera, *Peyton Place*. This is much better."

"Whatever. Dad couldn't find a job after Quinn came, so he stayed home with us. Did you know that?"

"No. But I've heard men sometimes do." Once again, Madge wished this child didn't know so many personal details. Yet, she kind of hoped the full story would spill out. The thought made her a little ashamed of herself. But only a little.

"I don't think he was so good at it," Aspen said. "I remember eating lots of peanut butter. And they yelled. When I started first grade, he got a new job at a sports store at the mall."

"I bet he was good at that." Madge started cleaning up from snack while she listened to the story. She didn't want her employer to think she stood around being a gossip all day. This background information could be called research, though. To help her do her job better.

"Yeah, I think so. They didn't yell as much. And, they had Peyton."

Madge turned around and got busy scrubbing the counter-top. Aspen said the last phrase so easily, Madge was afraid the girl might start explaining the facts of life to her next. Fortunately, Aspen spared her that embarrassment.

"The store closed when Peyton turned two," Aspen said. Dad brought home a football for her birthday and told us it would be special because nobody else could ever buy one there. He had a fancy cake from the bakery and a whole tub of chocolate ice cream. Quinn and I dug in with spoons and no bowls. Mom locked herself in the bathroom."

Grace interrupted the story by wandering into the kitchen and reaching up for Madge to lift her. Madge had almost forgotten that holding a toddler didn't come naturally to her. Instead, she leaned down and lifted the child despite the scream it gave her arthritis.

"Well, here's little Miss Gracie," she said. "Her name didn't come from some old ball player. Grace comes from the Bible, doesn't it?" She smiled with satisfaction.

Aspen looked confused. "No. It comes from *Little House on the Prairie*. Quinn named her."

"What?"

"Mom said she didn't have any creativity left for baby names. So, Dad said we should name it Our Little Bonus, and Mom said we should name it Lapse in Judgment."

"Do you ever think you might listen in on too many adult conversations?" Madge asked.

"No," Aspen said. "Anyway, Quinn said they should let her name it, and my mom said, 'Fine, go ahead.' Quinn watched a lot of *Little House* in those days. They had a baby named Grace. So, we did, too."

Madge didn't have time to reply to that outrageous idea, because she heard a shout from the entryway. Quinn stood between the kitchen and the living room, still wearing her backpack from school and holding a sheet of paper up in the air. She shouted above the racket of the television in the next room.

"Isn't anybody going to ask me about my spelling?"

Madge heard the volume go down on the television, followed by Luke and Jack both appearing in the doorway. "I'm asking," Luke said. "I'm asking right now. How did The Mighty Quinn do on this week's spelling pretest?"

"The words were hard," Quinn said. "You know they were hard." She worked the room like the host on a game show. "Double consonants and silent 'e' sneaking all around the place."

"They were hard," Luke said. "We know they were."

"But we had the *Magic Word Search*," Quinn said.

"Let's hear it for the *Word Search*," Aspen said. Madge felt a surge of warmth, as if she had personally received some kind of award.

"Now stop teasing us," Aspen said. "Tell us how you did on spelling."

"May I have the envelope please," Quinn said in a fake voice. She pretended to adjust a pair of glasses on her nose, stretched the paper out at arm's length and studied it for a minute. Finally, Quinn threw her arms up in the air and shouted, "One-hundred percent! I got one-hundred percent!"

The kitchen erupted with joy to equal the streets of Chicago the night the Cubs won the Series. Everybody hugged everybody and congratulated everybody else. Even Jack got in on the fun, although he probably had no idea why spelling deserved this much applause. Madge found herself whirling, clapping, and shouting right along with Luke and the girls, even though she had never been either a sports fan or a Pentecostal.

"We have to call the Glory Sisters," Quinn finally said over the ruckus.

"Yep, we better call them," Madge said. She looked at the clock. "Evelyn should be home from her volunteer spot at the hospital by now. Let's ring her up, and everybody can just shout out the news at once. Are you ready?"

And so, they did. Madge wasn't sure Evelyn had ever received such a phone call. She wondered if it rattled the bric-a-brac in her stately living room. She hoped so. She'd secretly wanted to rattle something in that magazine perfect home for years.

Madge looked around the kitchen. Grace had peanut butter on her face and her fingers. Aspen was dotted with blue paint. Peyton wore mismatched socks. On purpose. And Quinn had gotten one-hundred percent on spelling. Nothing picture perfect about this lot. Madge suddenly felt for the first time in her life that she kind of wished she had brought a bigger suitcase.

Chapter Twenty-Nine

Friday, October 14th
Thirty Days to Go

The house still had a party feel on Friday afternoon, and Madge thought that gave quite a bit of credit to a spelling test. Aspen set her straight. "This is High Holy Night," she said as she pulled a box from the pantry. "Mara Lynn and her husband come over to watch football and celebrate her birthday. It's how we start the holiday season. Next will come Halloween and then Thanksgiving and Christmas."

While she talked, Aspen pulled a bag of balloons and crepe paper from the box.

"Am I expected to cook for this party?" Madge asked.

"I don't think so. My mom usually orders pizza and stuff."

"Will your mom be here?"

Aspen stopped exploring the box and looked up in surprise. "Why wouldn't she be? It's a tradition."

"Well, I've heard traditions change sometimes. You know, sometimes when two married people aren't married anymore."

"You mean because my parents say they are getting a divorce we can't have the Football Festival anymore?"

"That's what I'm thinking."

"Well, that's just wrong. They aren't fighting half as much as they did when they both lived here. So, they'll be fine. And didn't the judge say this is my house?"

"Well, that's kind of a stretch."

"That's pretty much what he said. So, I can invite over anyone. I want my mom. And my dad. I want everybody at Mara Lynn's party having fun, just like always."

Aspen went back to work on decorations, and Madge gave up. Somebody needed to talk to this girl and bring a little reality into her world. But it wasn't going to be her. No sir, nobody hired her to be a shrink for the kid. She was just here to do the laundry and wash the dishes. Why, if Madge stuck her nose into this thing now...

"So, here's the thing," Madge said, "I think you should ask your mom or your dad for some clear guidelines."

"What do you mean?"

"Well, normal people don't have Christmas together once they stop being married."

Aspen let her hands droop on top of the open box. "I'm not sure if you've noticed, but our family isn't all that normal."

The sound of the garage door rising interrupted the conversation. Aspen's eyebrows perked up and she swung her hair away from her face. "One of them is home," she said.

It turned out to be Luke, who sauntered through the door with a case of soda under each arm and grocery bags in his hands. "Hello the house," he yelled. "I've brought party food."

"So, we're still having the party?" Aspen asked the question in Luke's direction, but she looked at Madge.

"Of course we're having the party. It's tradition isn't it?

"And Mom is coming?"

Luke buried his head in the refrigerator as he stashed sodas. "Yeah, well, I guess she will be here. I mean we're switching places sometime tonight, so she'll be coming in at some point."

"So, you aren't both coming to the party. Not really. Not together."

Luke pulled back from the safety of the appliance and looked at Aspen. "I'm sorry, kiddo. I know this is confusing and not even fair. I have no idea how tonight will go. I sent your mom a text and asked if she wanted me to cancel or move the party to my place or anything. She told me to go ahead with plans as usual. I don't really know what that means."

"Great." Aspen slammed flat balloons back into the box. "This should be just great."

"Look," Luke pulled more balloons from the box. "We all love Mara Lynn, and she deserves a great birthday from this family even if we are a mess. I have a ginormous cake in the back seat of my car. Besides, ice cream is melting as we speak. I say we party on and let life work itself out. What do you say?"

"Is it chocolate mint?"

"Of course."

"Let's get it."

The pizza arrived as predicted. Along with cheesy bread, four liters of soda, and various dunking sauces. Madge pulled Grace out of the food frenzy long enough to secure her in the high chair and add a banana to the tray. "Eat some fruit," Madge said, "to balance out the grease."

She heard the doorbell, but the little girls squealed and dropped their pizza to go running and answer it before Madge could respond.

"Happy birthday," they shouted.

Madge leaned forward and caught a glimpse of Mara Lynn over the banister in the entryway. The girls were swarming her with hugs, and Aspen stood nearby with a real smile. Grace shouted for her own equal time just then, so Madge missed the entrance of Mara Lynn's husband. From the sounds of the girls' greetings, they obviously liked the man.

Madge held Grace over the sink and rinsed off as much mess as she could while the adults disappeared into the family room. Luke carried a box of pizza with him, and Aspen came back for drinks. She had just stepped out of the kitchen when the garage door went up again. Aspen turned and stared at Madge. They both waited without speaking until the door opened and Alex walked through with her briefcase, overnight bag, and a giant pink gift bag with frilly paper sticking out the top.

"I heard we were having a party."

"It's tradition."

"So it is."

"Want some pizza? Or a soda?" Aspen held up a bottle of diet soda and a paper plate.

"No, thanks. I'll just put my things down and change, I think. Get into some comfy clothes. Tell Mar, I'm here, though, okay?"

"Sure." Aspen slipped into the family room but Alex didn't move. Finally, she looked at Madge.

"This is so weird."

"You said it."

"I don't know how to do this exactly. I mean, am I the hostess? Is Luke the host? Are we co-hosting? I wanted it to feel normal for Mara Lynn, but it isn't normal, and we can't make it feel that way, and I don't know what to do."

Madge wanted to escape to her soft chair in her blue room and put her feet up on the ottoman. She definitely wanted to close her door. Instead, she said, "Well, you can start by putting that present on the table. Then, change your clothes and come back down. Aspen announced this afternoon that this is her house, and she is throwing the party. So, I say you let her do it. Just sit back and be a guest."

"Okay. That might work." Alex moved like a child whose parent had just sent her to do homework. She followed Madge's suggestions and trudged up the stairs. When she came down in her comfy clothes, Madge had restored order in the kitchen.

"You coming in?" Alex asked.

Madge stopped with a dishrag in her hand. Was this an invitation to go to the zoo? Had Alex suddenly forgotten that Madge just worked for her?

"I'm about ready to turn in," Madge said. "I don't think I need a party tonight."

"But the girls might need something."

Ah, there it was. The nanny again. Not a guest at the party, just somebody who worked for the family. She thought about refusing, but Grace should probably go to bed soon, and nobody would think of it once the game started. She'd learned that much. Grumbling under her breath, she walked toward the family room.

The television greeted Madge at just one level below blaring. She didn't know why people even bothered inviting friends over when they were going to blast the TV at each other that way. Mara Lynn sat on one end of the sofa with Aspen tucked in beside her. The little girls were snuggled on her lap, and Grace played with toys at her feet.

The men sat in matching recliners opposite the television. "Madge," Luke said, "I don't think you've met Mara Lynn's husband. Joe, this is our nanny, Madge DuPree."

"Pleased to meet you." He stood so tall Madge had to tilt her head back to make eye contact. She accepted his giant hand and strong handshake.

"Glad to meet you, too," she said.

"Mar told me about your situation here, and I could hardly believe it. That judge was feeling his power, wasn't he?"

"I'd say he was exercising his best judgment," Madge said. "From what I've heard, of course. I mean, how could I know? It wasn't like I could have been in the courtroom or anything. Those are closed cases when they talk about custody issues, you know."

"Yes, I know," Joe said. "I do some work in the courthouse myself."

"Oh." Madge didn't ask it as a question. She waited for someone to give more information, and the birthday guest finally did.

"Joe is a cop," she said. "He has to go testify in court all the time."

"Worst part of the job," Joe said. "I hate court."

Madge wanted very much to change this conversation about court and about cops. They weren't her favorite subject either. "Well, it's nice to meet you," she finally said. "I didn't realize Mara Lynn had a mixed marriage."

The room grew so quiet even Grace looked up from her toys. Madge shrugged. "What? He's a Kansas fan. Mara Lynn has the good sense to wear a Mizzou shirt to the party, but this guy walked in wearing a blue cap. What's that all about?"

"Ah, man, I like this lady." Joe reached out and grabbed Madge in a hug with his giant arm. "I'm gonna call you Aunt Madge. Is that all right with you? Anybody call you Aunt Madge? I'm gonna do it, anyway." He kept hugging her and laughing while he talked. "And you're right. This is one mixed up marriage. That is for sure, Aunt Madge. That good-looking Mizzou girl married a linebacker from KU. How do you like that? Not only do I cheer for the Jayhawks, I tackled for them."

Madge managed to pull herself free and shake her head at the same time. "I guess it takes all kinds," she said. "If Luke says it's okay for you to eat his pizza and drink his precious soda, I guess it's okay by me."

Joe laughed a huge laugh again. By now, everyone in the room had loosened up. Even Alex seemed to be a little less stiff. Aspen met Madge's eyes from across the room, and Madge could not stop herself. She gave the girl a huge wink, as if she had designed the whole escapade to break the ice at the awkward party.

The evening went on with lots of noise and plenty of food. Madge had never watched football, and she had no idea what was happening, but the picture was sure pretty on that giant television. She nodded off now and then, but the shouting always brought her around again.

Two hours later, when everyone was full of pizza and cake, the game ended with what was evidently an amazing play. Madge had dozed off again, but the cheering roused her, and she managed to lift a hand for the high-five Joe sent all around the room.

Alex picked up the sleeping Grace from Madge's lap, and carried her toward the staircase with the little girls traipsing behind. Aspen begged to stay behind for coffee and conversation, but Luke vetoed.

Once the girls had all left the room, the tone turned more solemn.

"You're doing a good job with them," Mara Lynn said.

"You think? It seems pretty patched together."

Madge wanted to leave the room and get out of this private conversation, but she knew her legs were still asleep.

"They seem fine," Mara Lynn said. "And you guys were really getting along tonight. Doesn't it ever make you think maybe you could give it another chance, work things out?"

Madge wiggled her toes to test things and felt pins and needles shoot straight up to her knees. It was no good. She was stuck here in the corner of spill-your-heart.

"I mean, what happened between you two?" Mara Lynn had leaned forward and looked at Luke as if she could pull the answer out of him with her huge, sad eyes.

Luke leaned forward, too, and said, "I have no idea."

"Balderdash," Madge spoke before she remembered she wasn't in this conversation. All three of the others turned toward her. "Well, if you don't know what went wrong, that's probably what went wrong," she said.

Mara Lynn leaned back with a little smile and raised her eyebrows at Luke.

"I'll tell you what happened," Joe said. "Alex finally got her way."

"What do you mean?" Mara Lynn asked.

"Child support."

"What on earth?"

"Isn't that the whole point of this divorce? Hasn't she always said she can't trust Luke to hold down a job, and she'd be better off if she divorced him and got the court to force him to pay child support?"

"Joe, that was a joke. She was kidding when she said that."

Luke grabbed a pizza box and started stacking plastic cups. "That's cold man." He smiled, but Madge didn't think he used his real smile. "Probably true, but cold."

"No, I mean, really. I've heard her say it. More than once. I know she tries to play it off as a joke, but I think she meant it. I think that's what this whole thing is all about. She's trying to court-order you to be a man. It pretty sick when you think about it."

"What's sick?" Alex stood in the doorway holding a fresh bottle of soda. Everyone stopped as if they had been caught in a game of freeze-tag.

"All this food we ate." Mara Lynn recovered first. She jumped off the sofa and grabbed an empty plate. "Don't you have some veggies in this house? Or coffee? How about coffee to finish up?" Mara Lynn walked out of the room as she spoke and grabbed Alex by the elbow, turning her back toward the kitchen.

Luke continued picking up trash, but he didn't say anything more. Finally, Joe walked across the room and held out his hand. "Come on, Aunt Madge," he said. "Let me help you outta that chair. I better do some kind of good deed tonight after I've managed to open my big mouth and make everybody miserable."

Madge accepted the help. Even after she felt almost steady, she still held onto to Joe's hand. Leaning in, she said, "You didn't make them miserable, Joe. They did that all by themselves."

Chapter Thirty

Sunday, October 16th
Twenty-eight Days to Go

Madge wasn't sure Paige intended to make church-going a Sunday ritual, especially since she had been too busy for school runs. Just in case, she put on her good pants Sunday morning and sat down in the kitchen to wait. She was surprised to see a small head appear around the corner.

"Well, if it isn't the Mighty Quinn," she said. "Pretty early for a Sunday. You want breakfast?"

Quinn walked the rest of the way into the room, and Madge realized she was fully dressed. Pink sweater, grey skirt, tights, and black shoes with little bows and a sparkle in the middle. "Well, you are all dolled up, aren't you?"

"I'm going to church with you."

"Oh?"

"I want to sit with the Glory Circle. Will they let me? Or do kids have to sit in a separate room or something?"

Madge coughed. "No. Kids can sit anywhere they want, I expect." She waited another second, trying to figure out how to handle this unexpected intrusion into her private life.

"If you come with me," she said, "you can sit right there on the third row between Grace Colby and Bess, and nobody will say a word." She leaned forward and squinted at Quinn. "But church is long. More than three pony cartoons put together. Can you sit that long?"

"I think so."

"And it's far away. Can you ride in the car without talking my head off or getting carsick or something?"

"Yes."

"Okay. It's fine with me." Madge hoped the Almighty would forgive that little lie about this being fine. "You want breakfast?"

The Mighty Quinn had half a Pop Tart, but she only ate a few bites. Madge felt a little sorry for the kid. She hadn't meant to make church sound quite so bad. It was nice of her to want to go. She probably wanted to thank the ladies in person. Or brag about her spelling. Madge thought maybe she shouldn't have mentioned the carsick part.

Paige rang the doorbell just as Madge started to soften things up by telling Quinn about Elmer Grigsby's cat, which they might get to see if they peeked over the parsonage fence when they left. Today, Paige wore a skirt.

Madge knew she didn't have time to change, so she climbed into the little car being the only one of their party inappropriately dressed for a morning at Mt. Zion. It ate at her for the first few minutes of the trip. Then she realized Quinn was telling Paige about the spelling test, so she attempted to pull herself into the conversation.

"Your mom must be so proud," Paige said.

"Oh, look at the price of gas," Madge yelled and waved her arm practically in front of Page's face. "Remember that place, and I'll fill you up when we come back. That's the cheapest I've seen it yet. Have you seen it lower anywhere else?"

Paige gave her a confused look. "I probably won't need to fill up today, but thanks anyway. You don't have to pay for the gas."

"Well, this isn't part of your job description, driving me all the way across town to church."

"I know. I'm not doing it as part of my job." She paused and drove a few seconds without speaking. "I may not be doing anything as part of my job much longer."

"You're quitting?" Madge felt a smidgen of panic over the thought. She didn't want to depend on Jack for school drop-off and pick-up the next few weeks.

"Probably not. Although, I think about it. This is such a dead-end. I don't see it going anywhere."

"The job?"

Paige shrugged. "Of course, the job. What else would I mean besides the job? It's the job."

Madge was not convinced.

"Maaaaaadge?" a voice from the backseat spoke in the tone Madge had been expecting since five minutes after they pulled out of the driveway.

"Let me guess, you need to go to the bathroom?"

"No."

"You want to know if we are almost there."

"No."

"What then?"

"Is my mom proud of me?"

Suddenly, Madge wanted more than anything in the world to go to the bathroom herself. Or to be almost there. Or to be on the planet Pluto. Why had she ever tricked Jack into getting her this job as a nanny in the first place? It was supposed to be some easy money. A few weeks of sitting around in a fancy house, washing a few dishes, fixing a few meals, maybe telling the kids "yes," "no," or "maybe" until their parents got home from work some nights.

Nobody ever hinted to her that she would be riding in a car one day with The Mighty Quinn feeling her insides ripping out while she tried to figure out how to answer the biggest question in the universe for one of the littlest people it had ever hatched.

"Of course your mom is proud," Paige said. She said it as easy as breathing. Just spit it out there on the wind without a second thought. Because in her world, moms were always proud of their kids. That's what they did. Paige's mom was proud of her. If Paige ever had kids, she would be proud of them, too. So, of course, she assumed maternal pride in Alex. Madge wasn't so sure. She didn't know how a woman could be proud of anyone else when all she ever thought of was herself.

"I thought so," Quinn said. "She didn't say it, but that is because she had to go to a meeting and didn't have time right that minute."

"Exactly," Paige said. "Sometimes moms have to store up everything they feel and save it for times when they can sit down and just pour it all out in big hugs and kisses."

"Yeah. That will be nice. I'm looking forward to that," Quinn said.

Madge felt carsick.

"I see the steeple," Paige said. "That's the game my brother and I used to play. We had to drive a long way from our house to town on Sundays, so we always played 'who could spy the steeple first.' I just won."

Quinn laughed. "You won this time. But I'll know how to play next week."

When they pulled up to the long, stone steps of the church, Madge felt almost too tired to make the climb. This job and Friday night's party were taking more out of her than she realized. When she hesitated, Paige said, "You want me to pull around back?"

"Absolutely not." Madge grabbed her purse and heaved the door open with her shoulder. She struggled out and up the first three steps. On the fourth step, she felt Quinn take her hand. Paige moved around on the other side and put a hand lightly under the elbow that held Madge's heavy purse in its crook. She felt the weight of the purse lift under Paige's assistance, and her aching shoulder relaxed.

Okay. Just this once. She walked up the steps breathing a little easier.

"Well, would you look who is here," Pastor Cleveland said when they walked into the vestibule. "The ladies of the Marvel house."

"This is The Mighty Quinn," Madge said.

"I do spelling." Quinn held out her hand and gave Pastor Cleveland a firm shake.

"Good for you," he said. "I always found spelling to be quite a challenge."

"Well," Paige said, "you didn't have the Glory Circle Sisters helping you, obviously."

"Obviously."

With that, Madge led the way into the sanctuary where every head turned. Or so it seemed. Madge DuPree had brought a child to church. She might have imagined the whispers up and down the aisles, but she had a strong inclination to stand up in the pulpit and announce to the crowd that she had not stolen the child, and she had perfect authority to carry her about and bring her to church. Instead, she ushered Quinn into a seat in the third pew, right beside Bess as promised.

"Well, hello dear. Aren't you sweet? Are you Beth's baby Kate grown so big already?"

"No, I'm Quinn."

"Kate is just a toddler," Grace Colby said. "You saw her at Easter when they came for the party at your apartment."

"Oh, yes. She looks like Catherine, don't you think?"

"I do. It's in the eyes. And the smile."

Bess patted Quinn's hand. "So, you are Quinn. And you belong to Madge. I didn't remember that Madge had children."

Quinn answered before anyone else could speak. "Oh yes, she has four of us. But she just got us this year, so you probably didn't know about us yet."

"Probably not. Well, that's nice for her."

"It's nice for us."

"Yes. For both of you."

Madge turned and looked straight ahead at the choir loft. She blinked several times and tried to think about anything except Quinn's description. "She has four of us." Four children. She didn't have them, of course. This was just a job. Just temporary.

The choir stood and started the first song just as Madge turned back toward Quinn. She and Bess were sharing a song-book, and Bess pointed to the words so Quinn could follow along. Madge knew all the words, but she couldn't manage to look up from the lines. They were blurry anyway.

After church, Madge turned down all offers for lunch dates. Quinn had gotten a chance to thank all the Glory Circle Sisters in person, and they had all pawed over her plenty enough by the time Paige got them herded back to the car.

"Want to stop and grab something on the way home?"

"I don't think so," Madge said. "I figure this one will be asleep before we make the highway. Do you mind just heading home?"

"Not at all. I have errands to run anyway. I can eat while I'm out and about."

Madge ended up being the one who fell asleep before the highway. She jerked awake when she felt Paige shaking her, and she realized they were home.

"Did I snore?"

"Not much," Paige grinned. "Okay, like a freight train running through town at high speed, but I figured that meant you were worn out and needing a good rest. Are these girls being too much for you?"

"Not a bit. We just stayed up too late Friday night, and I'm slow to recover from a party." But even as she said it, Madge realized she was having trouble again making her legs work to get her out of the car. Paige came around and helped her navigate.

"They make these new models too low to the ground," Madge said. "You can't get any leverage to heave yourself out."

"Exactly. Someone in engineering should have thought of that. Go get a bite to eat and then finish your nap, okay? You deserve the rest of the day off."

"I'll do it. You, too."

Once inside the house, though, Madge doubted a nap or an afternoon off were in store. No one had bothered to finish cleaning up from the party, and it was obvious the family was just now arriving in the kitchen, looking for food.

"Do we have any pizza left?" Aspen said.

"We ate every bite," Madge told her, "but I think we've got some hotdogs. Maybe some macaroni."

"Any fruit or vegetables?" Alex asked as she entered the room.

"Possibly." Madge opened the freezer and surveyed the contents. "I could put together a casserole."

"That sounds yummy," Alex said. "Hide the vegetables under some cheese and the little girls will never know."

Madge tried to forget about being tired and set to work. Alex, meanwhile, dropped a shopping bag on the counter.

Madge thought that maybe she had something to contribute to the spread. Instead, Alex pulled out a brown, leather case and started snipping off the price tags.

Aspen pulled up a stool. "What's that?"

"Nothing much. I noticed your dad still carries all his toiletries back and forth in a plastic grocery bag, and this shaving kit was on sale the other day."

"It's nice. Distressed leather."

"How do you know about distressed leather?"

"I know. It's nice."

"Yes. It is nice."

"It looks like Dad."

Alex stopped snipping tags and let her hands run over the

leather. "Yes, I suppose it does." She stood still for a moment, and Madge thought something softened in her face. The moment passed, and Alex said, "It was on sale. That's all. I thought he could use it." She tucked the kit under her arm and bopped up the staircase, taking the stairs two at a time.

Chapter Thirty-One

Monday, October 17th
Twenty-seven Days to Go

"I'll pick the kids up after school today," Alex said at breakfast on Monday.

"Oh?" Madge didn't turn around from the sink where she was already stacking dishes. The announcement surprised her, though. Mondays were usually late days for Alex.

"They've called a meeting of all the district managers and team leaders, so I'll be downtown instead of out on the road. It's an early meeting, so I should be done by two o'clock, I think. I'll run a few errands and then get the girls."

"That sounds peachy." Madge's tone didn't quite match her word choice, and she knew it. The idea of having Alex underfoot all afternoon didn't sound peachy at all. Now she would have to call Paige and rearrange her own plans, which had included a trip to the pharmacy to get a refill on her blood pressure medicine. She would have to do that tomorrow. Or maybe later in the week. She hated taking the stuff anyway. Maybe she'd just skip a couple of pills. She thought the doctors and the drug companies were in cahoots on that stuff. She probably didn't need it.

Alex pulled a pile of mail from her shoulder bag. "Maybe we'll celebrate with ice cream or something tonight. I think they're announcing promotions this afternoon. Oh, Madge, I forgot to bring this in Friday night. It's mostly bills, of course. But you have a letter. Sorry."

Madge looked at the envelope and recognized Emily's handwriting. She tucked it into her pocket. "Thanks. I'll read it when I get these chores done."

The chores didn't take long, of course. Madge called Paige and settled their plans for the week. "I'll see you on Tuesday," Paige said.

"Sure. Unless Her Highness comes up with a different idea," Madge said.

Finally, around ten, Madge sat down in her room and pulled Emily's letter from her pocket. It started with the usual pleasantries about weather and health, which were both fine for this time of year and season of life. Then, Emily turned to meddling:

"As you know, I would never dream of meddling in your affairs if it were just up to you and me. As far as I'm concerned, you are a grown woman and can flit about the city doing as you please. But, I feel like Catherine rather left you in my care. And, I don't believe she would have approved of this arrangement. You aren't driving a car over there in Cherry Hills are you? You know I always warned Catherine not to ride with you. I never said it in front of you, but I know you knew. It's time somebody came out and said it for your own good."

Madge flipped the letter over. "For my own good, is it? Have you been taking to Grace Colby?" She thought about tossing the letter in the trash before she finished it, because Emily had filled every line on both sides. She decided to keep reading.

I know when I kept house for Catherine, you drove fairly often over in that direction. But they have added a lot to the city in the last few years. That part of town is too busy, too full of traffic, too many one-way streets. You really should

not drive there. Please, for the sake of Catherine's memory,
consider using public transit.
   Sincerely,
   Emily

Madge laid her head back against the chair and belted out a laugh. "Good for you, Emily. Good for you. Public transit. That is rich. Yes, ma'am, I'll look into public transit just as soon as I can. That is perfect. I can't wait to tell Paige her new name is Public Transit."

Madge laughed so hard she barely heard the sound coming from the kitchen. What was it? She stopped laughing and listened to see if someone had come into the house. Sure enough, the door to the laundry room opened, and she heard the shuffling sound of feet.

It couldn't be Alex. That would have been the clipping sound of heels. Fast, determined, knowing exactly where they were headed and not having time for any detours or distractions. And it wasn't Luke. His tennis shoes would have been a slow squeak. More of a dance than a walk, although Madge would never have described him that way. It just came to her now as she was sitting there thinking about the two of them. And, it was true. Luke danced his way into the kitchen every night. Like he was preparing to entertain the kids rather than parent them.

Of course, if it wasn't Alex or Luke, it must be a burglar. Madge realized she had taken a long time to come to that conclusion. He'd probably stolen the television or the computer by now. She didn't bother trying to figure out how he got the garage door open. She just started thinking of options.

"Oh Lord," she whispered, "I left my telephone in the kitchen. Looks like You're going to have to get me out of this scrape."

She looked around the room for a weapon. The lamp looked heavy, but she could probably lift it. Or, maybe not.

She heaved herself out of the chair and ignored the complaints of both her knees and her hips. Nothing in the sitting room looked promising, so she checked the bedroom. No weapons at first glance, but then she saw the giant can of Aqua Net the grocery boy had delivered last week.

"Hairspray to the eyes," she said. "Better than pepper spray." Madge knew from experience that a squirt of hairspray in the face could blind a soul for a few seconds. If she could spray him just right, she should have time to grab her purse and get out the back door. Then she could call for help.

"Let's do this," she whispered again.

She grabbed the hairspray and tried to tiptoe toward the kitchen, although her feet didn't achieve the full tipping-toe position anymore. She leaned against the wall and extended her arm with the hairspray pointed to aim and fire. She waited a few seconds, trying to hear if the burglar had stayed in the kitchen. And, trying to get her breathing back down to a normal rate.

Finally, she heard another sound from the kitchen. Madge took one giant breath and hoped it wouldn't be her last. Then she whipped around and faced the intruder with both feet planted wide. One hand held the Aqua Net and the other hand gripped the doorframe for support.

Alex stood at the end of the bar in her sock feet. "Sorry, Madge, I thought you might be napping."

"Exercising." Madge attempted a shallow knee bend and hoisted the hairspray can in the air. "Saw it on the television."

"Oh."

They stood for several seconds without talking. Madge noticed the absence of a coffee cup in Alex's hand. Unusual for this time of day. And the absence of her bag or laptop, which was serious neglect.

"Meeting over?"

Alex looked at Madge as if she had forgotten anyone else was in the room. "Yes. Over. Completely, officially, irrevocably over."

"That's good."

"Not really. I'm fired."

Madge dropped her hairspray. She bent to pick it up and tried to think what to say at a time like this. Nothing appropriate came to mind, so she said what she was thinking, "Just like that?"

"Yep. Just. Like. That." Alex snapped her fingers and sat down on a barstool. "The company sold last week, and the new management is redesigning territories. That district I'd just worked so hard to earn? They merged it with one being run by the new company's top guy."

"Don't they have another spot somewhere you could take?"

"They don't." Alex sounded honestly surprised. "All those times when Luke came home trying to explain to me how they cut his job, and he didn't have any say in it, and there was nothing he could do, I never believed him. Not really. I thought he was weak. I secretly believed he could have stood up to them and explained that he had a family to feed, and he needed a job." She got up and started pacing the kitchen.

"I used to tell him he should look the boss in the eye and demand a transfer instead of a cut. That we could move anywhere. Surely they had jobs in other cities or something." She looked at Madge with a shocked expression on her face.

"But you don't get to do that. You don't get a chance to say those things. I always thought you could, but you can't. They just hand you this envelope, slap you on the back, and say, 'Thanks for playing, here are your parting gifts.'"

She sat down again and dropped her head into her hands. "That's the worst part. Not only have I lost the job that is holding us together and paying for this house, but now I have to admit I've been wrong. I don't think I can do that."

Madge sat on a stool, too. They would lose the house. She wondered how long it took to foreclose on a place. Maybe she could finish out the month. Of course, if the Marvels couldn't pay her, what good would that do?

Suddenly, like morning light filtering in through her curtains, Madge saw the truth. She would finish the month at no charge. If they asked her, she would stay just to help the girls through the transition of moving to Mara Lynn's guesthouse or Luke's studio apartment. If they asked her, she would probably even go along to one of those places.

Madge shook herself back to the moment. They wouldn't ask her to move into a cramped apartment. They would fire her just as surely as the big company had fired Alex.

"I don't think I can do it," Alex suddenly said. "I can't tell anyone about this until I find a new job. And you can't tell anyone I said this stuff. I'm just ranting like a lunatic because this is making me crazy. I still think Luke could have done something in his situations. Mine is different. I'm certain about that."

She rubbed her hand across her forehead. "Do we have any coffee?"

Madge reached for the pot and started pouring. If Alex planned to fake it, she might also be saving Madge's job. For the moment.

"The thing is; we will have to make some changes while I look for a job. I have a great resume, so I'll find something pretty quickly. There are some great companies in this city. And, of course, I got severance. We will have to tighten up around here. Stop ordering so much pizza, for one thing. And, we have to sell this house."

Madge handed her a steaming mug of coffee without interrupting the flow of monologue. She would have to prevent the sale of the Marvel house, of course. That would ruin everything.

"And Luke will have to pitch in on this. He might have to sell his precious golf clubs or something."

"Too late. He did that last month."

Alex stopped with the coffee cup halfway to her lips. "What?"

Madge suddenly stood and got busy scrubbing the counter. "What?"

"What did you say about Luke's golf clubs?"

"Did I say something about golf? I don't play."

Alex got off her stool and walked over to stand next to Madge. "No, when I said Luke might have to sell his golf clubs, you said that it was too late because he already had. What did you mean?"

Madge stopped scrubbing. "I don't know for sure," she said. "But there was that day when they were about to shut off the electricity."

"What?"

"Third bill. You hadn't paid it."

"I kept meaning to do that..."

"Well, Luke found the bill on the counter. It said they were going to cut us off the next day, and he said would do something about it. He stomped around in the garage, mumbling for a while, and I saw him load up his golf clubs. I haven't seen them since. And, we still have electricity."

Alex looked out the window over the kitchen sink. Madge decided not to say anything more. In fact, she sidestepped out of the way and tried to become invisible while the information sunk down as deep as it possibly could go.

After a few seconds, Alex spoke again without taking her eyes from the window. "I don't know what to do."

Madge wanted to pretend she hadn't heard the words. They were quiet. Maybe they hadn't been meant for anyone else. Maybe they were more of a prayer than a conversation. Maybe answering would be like opening the door at the confession box. But, Madge wasn't Catholic. Neither was Alex.

So, like every good housekeeper, Madge did the obvious thing. She butted in. She walked back over to stand beside Alex and joined her in staring out the window into the backyard. Fall had come while they were busy having big jobs and wiping grimy faces. The swing set stood under a glorious maple tree, and a breeze stirred one of the swings.

"Well," Madge said, "you could fly to China."

Chapter Thirty-Two

Friday, October 21st
Twenty-three Days to Go

Alex didn't fly to China. She called Mara Lynn instead, and they met somewhere downtown to "build a strategy." When she returned from the school run in the afternoon, Alex pulled Madge aside in the laundry room.

"We aren't going to mention this job issue to Luke or the girls for a few more days," she said. "I'm working on some options."

Madge wanted to vote against this plan, but she didn't suppose the hired help got a voice. Instead, she nodded and went back into the kitchen to start supper.

Alex followed her and kept talking. "I have a meeting tonight so I need to go ahead and run. The girls' dad should be here in a couple of hours. He just sent a text saying he is running a little late. Are you okay to be here, Madge?"

Madge shrugged. Where did the woman think she would be on a Friday night besides right here ready to put on her bathrobe and slippers?

"Yeah. I'm fine with that."

She knew the meeting was a cover. Alex just didn't want to face Luke and hear him ask how her week had gone. She could act as if she were wearing her big girl pants all she wanted, but

Madge knew one question and the woman would break down and bawl like a baby. Madge could see it on her face.

"I'll just run up and kiss the girls goodnight," Alex said. But, she didn't run. She stood at the table and looked at the staircase for several seconds.

"The little girls will probably be down in a whip-stitch. I told 'em they could watch *Andy Griffith* in my room if they got their pajamas on in time."

"Huh. I didn't know they'd ever seen that show."

"I introduced them. Gracie's probably ready to go down. You could tuck her in and check on Aspen."

"Yes. I'll do that. I'll come in and say 'good-night' to the girls in your room before I go. If that's okay."

Madge wanted to say, "Hey, Lady, it's your house and your kids." Instead, she said, "Sure, whatever you want to do."

The tucking, checking, and kissing goodbye all went smoothly considering it would have to hold for another week. Madge stood in the kitchen and listened to Alex saying farewell to her children.

Nobody complained. Nobody cried. Madge couldn't even detect a change in the tone of voice as the little girls chattered about Halloween costumes.

"So, I'll see you in a week," Alex called down the hallway one more time. "Your dad will be here soon."

"Okay," the little girls shouted together. And then, from Peyton, "But Madge is still here, right? She'll take care of us?"

Madge turned and leaned against the wall. She didn't even hear Alex's reply, because her heart pounded too loudly in her ears. "Madge will take care of us." Such faith in that little voice. Such assurance. And truth? Madge stood straighter. Had she found a bit of Mary Poppins after all?

Madge didn't wait to say anything more to Alex. She escaped to her room and flipped on the television. She tried to process this new thought while she made room for two extra bodies in her chair.

Luke came home after the little girls had already climbed into bed, so Narnia would have to wait until tomorrow night. Aspen, though, had come down to the kitchen and taken up her painting corner. Madge could hear her talking with Luke even though their voices were quiet.

"You're making good process on the painting."

"It's more work than I expected."

"Yeah. Everything always is. The aspen tree is beautiful. Really well done."

"It's supposed to be a young tree. Like me."

"I can tell. You captured the light perfectly. It shines. There's only one thing about it I'd change."

"What's that?"

Madge could hear a change in Aspen's voice. She hoped Luke wasn't about to blow it.

"Let me show you. I think I can find it."

Madge heard the sound of the pantry door opening and someone pulling a stool across the floor. She couldn't stand the mystery any longer, so she got up and walked down the hall. She stood just at the edge of the kitchen where she could hear the conversation and see the interaction. She didn't even care if it was eavesdropping. She probably needed a glass of water to take her bedtime medicine if anybody asked.

Luke pulled a box down from the top shelf of the pantry and removed a square object. He carried it over and turned it toward Aspen. As it flashed by, Madge caught sight of a mountain scene with a grove of aspen trees in the fall.

"Your mom painted this from a picture she took on our honeymoon," he said, "before we even knew you were coming."

"Wow. It's beautiful." Aspen held the picture and turned it so light danced off the shimmering leaves. "You're right, mine is nothing like this."

"No, you're missing the point. Yours is very much like this. I'm not talking about the quality of your painting. Notice something about aspen trees. They never grow alone like the one in your painting. They always grow in groups. You always see at least three, usually many more. Aspens always grow in families."

Aspen looked at the painting again. She leaned in toward her dad, and he put an arm around her shoulder until she rested against him.

"She was a great painter, wasn't she?"

"She was," Luke said. "Probably still is. She even made her own frames, you know. She had her own miter saw and box. Which I also saved, because you never know when a person might need a miter box."

"And you saved this when she took all her paintings off the walls?"

"Yeah. I wasn't sure what she would do. I was afraid she might decide to burn them, so I put this one away. I knew you would want it someday."

"Thanks."

"You're welcome."

They stood that way for another few seconds. Then Luke kissed the top of Aspen's head and said, "Don't stay up too late, okay?"

"Okay."

Just before he left the room, Luke turned back and said, "Your mom is a strong woman, but that doesn't make her bad. It's a good thing to have your own tools. You just have to know how to use them."

Madge waited in the shadows of the hallway until Luke had gone to bed. She wanted to pull a chair from the dining room and sit up all night with the girl while she painted. If nobody else felt the need to sit by this child while she fought her way through the forest of family life in the Marvel house, Madge would do it. Wasn't growing up hard enough without these people adding their own mess to it?

Yet, Madge knew her body would rebel. She couldn't really sit up all night. Besides that, she didn't know anything about helping a girl grow up. She hadn't managed her own girlhood all that well, and she had certainly never helped anyone else since.

She stayed in the hallway as long as her arthritis would allow. Then, she asked the Almighty to take over, and she gave up and went to bed.

After her late-night snooping, Madge overslept. She didn't know when she had done such a thing. She heard rustling in the kitchen before she got out of bed. She tried to hurry getting dressed, but the faster she tried to go, the slower her hands and feet seemed to respond. Finally, she made it to the kitchen to find Quinn, Peyton, and Grace seated at the bar with empty plates.

"Expecting a delivery?"

"We thought you'd make pancakes," Peyton said.

"Or maybe French toast," Quinn added.

Grace just banged her plate and said, "Bite, bite."

"Well, the kitchen is now open," Madge said, "but the cook doesn't respond to banging plates. Somebody teach that baby to say 'please.'"

The little girls got busy trying to coax a "please" out of Grace while Madge started stirring up pancakes. They were all absorbed in their various duties when the sound of a vehicle interrupted them. "Mom's home again," Peyton yelled. She jumped off her stool and ran toward the door.

Sure enough, Alex came through the laundry room door in a few seconds, looking apologetic. "I'm sorry to barge in on a Saturday morning," she said. "I left in kind of a hurry last night and forgot my suitcase. I don't even have my toothbrush."

Aspen came around the corner of the kitchen bar, rubbing

sleep from her eyes, "Can't you buy a toothbrush downtown?"

"Well, I suppose. But I can't buy my favorite green shirt or the jeans that actually fit, and those are in my suitcase, too. Plus, my running shoes, which cost more than you want to know."

"I would like to know." Luke appeared behind Aspen. "I'd like to know several things, to be quite honest with you, Alexandra. I'm kind of glad you dropped in this morning."

Madge didn't like the sound of his voice. She had heard this kind of tension in him once or twice before, and she had a feeling he was about to say things he and Alex would both regret. She looked around for a way to clear the room, but she found nothing short of shouting fire. She looked at the stove and thought about dropping a tea towel on a burner.

"For instance," Luke went on, "how is it that you can afford to buy expensive running shoes, but you never pay the electric bill? And, I've yet to see you go running by the way. Why is it that when I come home on Friday nights, the upstairs is a wreck? You can't even bother to clean up behind yourself when you know I'm coming back from a hard week at work. Do you want me to spend all day Saturday cleaning up your messes? Do you get a kick out of that? And finally, but most importantly, is this." He held up the new shaving kit and dropped it on the bar with a thud.

"I think we can set some ground rules. If you are going to start having men over before we are even divorced, do it in your own place. Don't invite them to sleep here. This is the girls' house. Get rid of this before I get back. Because, unlike you, I do run for exercise."

With that, he slammed out the back door.

Alex stood perfectly still in the middle of the room. Quinn and Peyton stared at her, but Aspen looked at the floor. Finally, Madge took two steps across the room, retrieved the shaving kit, and retreated to her room. She didn't want anyone doing something stupid like throwing away an expensive gift just because of a misunderstanding. If these people would just talk to each other, they could straighten a few things out.

But, she didn't suppose they would.

When she got back to the kitchen, Alex was gone. The girls all looked at Madge with wide eyes, waiting for something that Madge felt totally ill equipped to provide. Finally, she said. "Pancakes?"

Aspen growled and whirled out of the room, which scared Grace so she started to cry. Peyton squeezed out a few tears, too. But Quinn saved the day.

"I'll have pancakes," she said. "We little children might as well not starve."

Chapter Thirty-Three

Saturday, October 22nd
Twenty-two Days to Go

Luke came home nearly an hour later. Madge had cleaned the kitchen, and the little girls were playing in the back yard. Aspen turned from her painting and said, "Dad, I think you should know something."

"I don't want to talk about it. This is grown-up business, Aspen, and no matter how mature you feel, no matter how much pressure your mom and I are putting on you right now, you are not old enough to be mixed up in this stuff. So just leave it."

Aspen looked at Madge as if asking for backup, but Madge had made up her mind to stay out of this one. If Luke wanted to be an idiot, she would let him. The truth always had a way of coming out, and when it did, he could feel like a jerk without any help from her.

"Don't drip your paint," Madge said. "We just got that floor cleaned up."

Aspen huffed her best teenage huff and went back to her masterpiece. Luke slugged down a Pepsi in a few big gulps and then said, "I'm going to help Joe with some stuff later. I'll be in the garage a while if you need anything."

Madge didn't know why that sentence sounded threatening

to her until a few seconds later when she heard Luke banging around in the garage.

"Aspen," he yelled. "Have you seen my red toolbox? The one where I keep..." He appeared in the kitchen within seconds. This time he spoke in a quiet voice. But it held the edge of an explosion inside. "Aspen, why is Mara Lynn's stolen *For Sale* sign hidden in the back of our garage?"

Aspen turned with a frown, "I don't know what you're talking about."

"How can you not know what I'm talking about? The *For Sale* sign Mara Lynn dropped off on our lawn weeks ago. Someone shoved it into the back of our garage and covered it with a beach towel. I don't think Grace and Peyton put it there."

"Maybe Mom did it. Maybe she changed her mind."

"Does that seem likely?"

Aspen sighed and leaned against the wall. "No, but I didn't do it, either. Although I'll admit I'm glad somebody did. I don't want to sell our house."

Luke walked into the kitchen, and he answered with a little less steel in his voice. "Nobody wants to sell the house. We just don't have much choice."

"Yes, we do. Well, we girls don't have any choices, but you and Mom do. You could choose to keep it. I'm not a baby. I know you aren't going to stay together. But why can't we keep living here like this?"

Luke folded his arms and leaned against the wall. "Well, because it's expensive. And exhausting. Besides, Madge is only going to be here three more weeks. After that, it won't work at all."

Madge felt something tight in her chest. Three more weeks. Only three more weeks of cooking breakfast for this demanding crew. Three more weeks of spelling tests and school pick up runs. Only three more weeks of sleeping in a strange bed and sharing her remote with a bunch of wiggly kids. Only three more weeks of Marvels.

Before the three weeks could entirely play themselves out in Madge's head, she heard Aspen become defensive.

"But this is my house."

"No," Luke said. "It's mine and your mom's."

"The judge gave it to us," Aspen said in a shaky voice.

"That's temporary," Luke said. "This house belongs to the grown-ups. The people who actually pay the mortgage."

"No, this is Catherine's house." Madge hadn't meant to speak out loud. She wasn't even sure she had until Luke responded.

"Madge? What did you say?"

The words had been rolling around in her head for so long. Since the day she took the long walk up to the front door and first met Alex Marvel. She had been beating them back and trying not to give them a voice. But they had been hovering, waiting, wanting to get out and tell somebody.

"What are you talking about?" Luke asked again.

Madge looked across the sparkling kitchen toward the rosebud wallpaper in the dining room. "This is Catherine's house," she said. "You've spiffed it up, that's all."

"Catherine," Aspen said, "like your friend who died?"

"Exactly like."

"Does my mom know?"

"She doesn't." Madge took a breath. "I didn't know when I signed on. Not until I saw the papers at Jack's office and they gave me the address. Kensington Avenue. That was a shocker. I didn't know her kids had sold the house. Of course, I should have expected that. They both live out of state, and Beth wouldn't want it. When I saw Catherine's address on the paper, though, I almost backed out. I guess I was so far into the forest by then, I didn't know how to turn back."

Luke dropped his arms and took a step toward Madge. "It must have seemed strange to find us living here."

"Oh, it's almost a whole other place," Madge told him. "The kitchen is so fancy, and the garage is so huge. I will admit I'm glad you haven't had time to tear off the wallpaper in the dining room. It was Catherine's favorite."

She blinked a few times and then went on. "My sitting room is a perfect addition, too. The family room, of course, is mostly the same as it was back in the day. Catherine used it as her parlor. She almost froze to death there one winter when the electricity went off. I'm glad you replaced the furnace."

"High efficiency," Luke said.

"I think the upstairs is a lot different, too," Madge said. "But I was never up there. Catherine was private in some ways. Emily kept house for Catherine for decades, and I think she only went upstairs half a dozen times." She stopped then. Because the last time Emily had gone upstairs, she had called the ambulance.

"So, you hid the sign?"

Madge nodded.

"Because you didn't want us to sell it?"

She sniffed, folded her arms, and said, "Well, I needed the job."

Luke smiled, "How did you drag that heavy thing all the way up from the street?"

"I'm tougher than I look."

"Yes, you are."

Luke stood for what felt like a long time and looked at Madge. Finally, he said, "I'm really sorry, Madge. I can't imagine all the memories this place brings up for you. I wish we'd have known. And, I'm also sorry we have to sell it, because we have some great memories here, too. But we really have no choice."

"Well," Madge reached for a tissue in her pocket and dabbed at her nose, "this place kicks up my allergies, that's for sure. As for selling, do whatever you please. I'll be headed out in a couple of weeks, so it won't matter either way to me."

"Okay. If you're sure it won't bother you, I'm going to put the sign in the yard."

"No business of mine."

"Okay." Luke looked at Aspen. "Want to help me?"

"No." She turned her back and stabbed her paintbrush into a can.

The two of them stayed that way until they heard the sound of Luke dragging the sign across the garage floor and out into the yard. Aspen turned to Madge with tears at the edges of her eyes.

"This stinks so much."

"Agreed."

"Did they tell you I have to change schools?"

"No." Madge tried to cram her own thoughts back into the untouchable place where she preferred to keep them. If Aspen felt a sudden need to unload a few emotions, somebody should listen. "Which school?"

"That's the worst part." Aspen flopped onto her painting chair. "I have no idea. I don't know if we will live with Dad mostly or with Mom. Or which one of them will pick the new school or where it will be."

"You could ask them." As soon as she said it, Madge knew the suggestion was useless. Alex had no clue about her future, and surely the girls would go with her. "Or, you could just hold on and trust that your folks will make things the best they can for you."

Aspen rolled her eyes. "Yeah. They are winning at that one right now, aren't they?"

"Okay. You're right. This stinks." Madge dabbed at a spot on the bar. "Lots of life stinks, if you want to know the truth."

"Tell me something stinkier than your parents getting a divorce."

"I could." Madge kept wiping the bar.

"So, do it." Aspen stopped messing with her paints and focused on Madge.

Madge kept busy at the counter. "I could tell you a story about a girl who thought her life was stinky, and so she got her head turned by the first slick-talking man who came through town after she turned seventeen."

"Was he handsome?"

"He was a salesman."

"What did he sell?"

"Vitamins, salve, furniture polish," Madge kept talking while she stacked dishes. "And smooth lines to country girls about an exciting future in sunny California."

"Did the girl run away with him?" Aspen said it like eloping was something romantic and exciting. Not the embarrassing and shameful thing Madge had kept mostly to herself the past fifty years.

"She did," Madge finally said. "They got all way to a Justice of the Peace in Reno, Nevada, before the money ran out." Madge had run out of dishes, so she turned to face Aspen. "This isn't one of those romance stories where the girl has stars in her eyes, and Cary Grant figures out he made a great deal after all, and they live happily ever after."

"No?"

"No. They stayed in Reno a week. Then, one morning, he left a note and enough nickels for her to call her dad."

Aspen stepped closer and looked straight into Madge's eyes. "Did your dad come and get you?"

"He did." Madge crossed her arms and leaned against the counter. "And he paid to get the marriage annulled. He told me that would be better for a girl's reputation than divorce. But he couldn't afford to get my name changed back. Besides, he thought it would be better to keep DuPree so folks would know I hadn't just run off and been wild. I'd been properly married. For a whole week."

Aspen stood staring at Madge for what seemed like a long time. Then she spoke in a quiet voice. "Sometimes life really stinks, doesn't it?"

"Sometimes," Madge said. "It really does. And, fussing over it doesn't change anything. So, you go clean up your paint stuff. I've got to call Paige about tomorrow."

Madge escaped into the family room and leaned against the window frame. It took several moments for her hands to stop shaking enough to punch the buttons on her phone. When she started telling Aspen the story, she hadn't expected it to take so much out of her. She just wanted to give the girl some hope that life could stink but a person could still move on. Of course, she hadn't told the story in a long time. And the last time had been in that same kitchen.

She stood in the family room and looked out the window as the phone rang. When Paige answered, Madge said, "I'm going to cancel out for church tomorrow."

"Are you sick?"

Madge watched Luke pounding the *For Sale* sign into the yard. She thought he might pound it all the way through the ground. "No, I just feel a little off," she said. "Allergies, probably. Maybe a cold. Things are kind of topsy-turvy here. Might be good if I stick around."

"You'll call me if you get a fever, won't you? I know a good doctor, and he can fix just about anything."

"I will," she said.

Chapter Thirty-Four

Sunday, October 23rd
Twenty-one Days to Go

Neither Luke nor Aspen appeared for Sunday morning breakfast. This did not surprise Madge. She kept the oven on warm after the little girls had devoured their cinnamon toast and scrambled eggs, just in case either party wandered in.

"Should I get dressed for church now?" Quinn asked as she dropped her cup and plate into the sink.

"Not today," Madge said. "I've got a cold."

"You aren't coughing."

"It's a silent cold. Worst kind."

"Bess will worry if we aren't there."

Madge looked down at the solemn eyes. Some kind of conspiracy, evidently, between this one and Paige. She looked at the clock on the microwave and calculated. "We don't have time to call Paige and get ourselves ready and be there on time. Worst thing in the world to walk in late."

"Daddy could take us."

"Daddy could take us where?" Luke stood at the counter picking at a leftover piece of toast.

"To church with the Glory Circle Sisters. It isn't far, and you would like it."

Luke grinned. "Oh, I would?"

"Yep. Pastor Cleveland tells jokes, and he talks about football. And," she leaned toward her dad as if telling a secret, "he knows about Narnia."

"Like he knows how to get there?"

Quinn giggled and ran toward the staircase. Madge heard her yelling up the stairs. "Everybody wake up. We're going to church."

Luke reached for the coffee pot and said, "I didn't hear me say 'yes.' Did you hear me say, 'yes'?"

"She's a quick one. You gotta pay attention."

If Madge had worried that taking one, small child to church might cause a stir, she had not prepared herself for the rumble of bringing in an entire family. Luke carried Grace, who was completely decked out in a frilly, white outfit Aspen had found in the back of the closet. Madge wondered if the child had ever worn a dress. She kept tapping her shiny, black shoes together and giggling at the sound.

Peyton and Quinn had matching plaid dresses with sparkly tights. They looked like models from a fancy catalog, and Madge felt a little in awe to walk beside them.

Luke wore a black suit. The modern, skinny kind like Jack had worn in court. He looked about ten years younger with his hair all slick and his shoes all shiny. He had asked Madge's opinion between the blue tie and the red, but she had no idea. Aspen came to the rescue and chose red.

Aspen wore violet. She corrected Luke when he said he liked her new purple dress. "It's violet," she said. "Mom says it complements my eyes."

"It makes them dazzling. Violet is perfect for you."

Once everyone's attire had been approved, Madge hustled the family toward Luke's big vehicle. On the way to church, Luke said, "By the way, Jack might be coming over some night in the next couple of weeks. Maybe more than once. Do you mind if we add him for dinner some time?"

"It's your table and your grocery bill," Madge said, but she did hope Luke would say more.

"This doesn't have anything to do with our case," Luke told her. "I know it might seem weird, but we actually found some common ground."

"None of my business," Madge said.

"Right. Well, it is about business, if you want to know."

"Oh?"

Luke smiled. "I know. Not what you expected, right? It turns out Jack wanted to become a software developer. Or some kind of cyber-engineer. He's created a couple of amazing apps that could revolutionize parts of the trucking industry. But, he needs connections. He needs help for marketing and investors. I happen to know those people. So, we are looking at teaming up."

"You work with trucks?" Madge said

"That's a pretty simplistic description of what I do," Luke said. "I work in the transportation industry. It's antiquated and vulnerable for disaster from all points, and yet our entire nation depends on it for survival. So, yeah, I work with trucks. But Jack's computers and my trucks could save the world someday. How do you like that?"

"I like it," Madge said. "Turn left up here."

"Oh, yeah, thanks."

A few minutes later, Madge found herself walking up the center aisle toward the third pew with Luke and the girls in tow. She did not imagine the stir their entrance made this time. People didn't just whisper. They actually stood and stopped the family in the aisle to introduce themselves and welcome the guests to church. Madge had no idea Mt. Zion was such a friendly place. She thought they would never make it to their seats.

Pastor Cleveland stopped them just before they sat down. "Sister Madge, are you trying to win the award for Pack-a-Pew Sunday? We aren't playing today, but we could probably stir something up."

Madge couldn't think what to say. In truth, the pew looked packed. Grace Colby had already scooted closer to Tom and Evelyn than she liked to sit. The little girls settled one on either side of Bess and started chatting away. Luke reached out to introduce himself and his family to Pastor Cleveland, saving Madge from any words at all.

"We are really grateful for all Madge is doing for our family," Luke said. "It's a privilege to be here with her today."

"She's a treasure, isn't she?"

"One of a kind," Luke said.

Both men laughed and shook hands again. Madge was not at all sure she had been complimented. She was, however, fairly sure she had been loved. She didn't know exactly what to do with that experience.

"Here," she said to Luke, "let me hold Grace while you get settled."

Madge had never held a toddler in church. It struck her as strange. She didn't know why she hadn't. She supposed there had been times in life when a cousin, a neighbor, or a nephew had been in need of holding. She had just never offered.

Even after Luke sat down, Madge didn't offer to hand Grace off. And, the most amazing thing happened. With Grace on her lap as a kind of frilly shield, Madge found herself humming along to *Amazing Grace*. Eventually, she mouthed a few of the words.

Grace snuggled deeper against Madge's bosom, as if the sound coming from there was a comfort. On the next song, Madge sang a snatch here and there until she eventually managed a full chorus. Finally, when the worship service closed with the first and last verse of *A Mighty Fortress is Our God*, Madge sang every word and wished they had included all the verses in the middle.

She didn't hear three words of the sermon, though. Madge felt overwhelmed by her victory and by the sensation of a little girl sleeping on her lap in church. She could not add anything more to the morning. She simply had to tune out Pastor Cleveland's voice and let her mind wander. She knew he would understand.

After church, Madge visited with the other ladies, as usual. They wanted to hear about Quinn's spelling, and they were happy to meet Peyton, Grace, and Aspen. Madge thought Aspen seemed suddenly grown up when she talked with Evelyn about school and art.

"And you know we live in Catherine Benson's house," Aspen said.

"Yes," Evelyn said. "We've all been a little concerned about how hard that might be for Madge, but she seems to be managing it well."

"Yes, she didn't even tell us until yesterday. I felt awful. I'm not sure what we would have done differently, but it seems sort of like we shouldn't be fighting and stuff there. Like it's holy ground. You know?"

Madge kept her back to the conversation and pretended to be listening to Bess and Peyton. But she turned her head to catch Evelyn's response.

"No, you can't worry about that. It is just a house. Just lumber, bricks, and nails. The thing that made the house special to all of us was Catherine. What makes it special to us now is you. What a wonderful thing, you know, to live in the Marvel house."

She said the last part with typical Evelyn-flair. Madge halfway expected to see banners fall from the ceiling and start waving around in a magical parade. This reminded her that they had to get home and make Halloween costumes. She looked around for Luke, to tell him they better get going.

Madge found Luke huddled in a far corner with Pastor Cleveland. She supposed they were talking sports. When she got close enough to hear, she caught the words "court" and "custody." So, she stopped. She dawdled around in the back for a while. Eventually, she sent all the girls for a second bathroom break.

Elmer Grigsby happened by while she stood alone, waiting.

"Quite a crowd you got with you today," he said.

"Yep. Five of 'em."

"Kinda hard to get used to a crowd when you've been on yer own so long, I've found."

"That's true." She didn't want to be rude, but she knew the little girls would be done any second.

"I've kind of taken to it, though," he said. "I 'spect you will, too." And he walked away.

Madge saw the girls running toward her from the bathroom. She looked back in the direction Elmer Grigsby had gone and saw the door swing shut behind him. Good grief. Now she was getting relationship advice from the man whose best friend was his cat.

"Come on girls," she said. "Let's sit over here and wait for your dad."

Eventually, the two men slapped shoulders, shook hands, and broke their huddle. Madge saw Luke reach into his pocket and pull out a business card, which he handed to Pastor Cleveland. The pastor nodded and kept talking as he tucked it into his own pocket. Then, they walked up the aisle toward Madge and the girls.

"Well, Sister Madge, it looks like you will be headed back our way pretty soon," Pastor Cleveland said as he walked the family toward the door.

"Yep. Before you know it."

"Madge can't leave before she makes my princess crown," Peyton said.

"Oh, no. That sounds important." Pastor Cleveland leaned down and came face to face with Peyton.

"It's for Halloween. I'm a princess. And it's for school and for fun and not for the devil."

"I'm certain you would never wear a princess crown for the devil. We are clear on that." Pastor Cleveland shook Peyton's hand as if she were a grown-up. He straightened up and raised his eyebrows at Luke. Luke shrugged and looked at Madge.

"We ran into a Bible-thumper at the store," she said. "I shouldn't have mentioned Halloween."

"I see." Pastor Cleveland rubbed his chin. "Well, I know some people get pretty worked up about it, worried about the pagan roots and all that. But over at the parsonage, my dad and I turn on the porch lights, bring out a big bowl of candy bars, and just get a kick out of all the neighborhood kids dressing up as Spider-man and stuff. I figure it's good for kids to see the preacher being a regular guy now and then. Maybe they'll feel like they can come talk to me when their super-powers fail them someday."

"Good thinking," Luke said. "For all of us. Thanks again for today. I'll probably give you a call next week."

"Great," Pastor Cleveland said. "I'll look forward to it. Lunch is on me the first time."

Chapter Thirty-Five

Monday, October 31st
Thirteen Days to Go

Madge thought several times during the next week that she might actually be working for the devil. Her arthritic fingers didn't bend well to a sewing needle, and she had underestimated the number of stitches required to turn a bangle into a crown.

The little girls begged at supper every night to see the costumes in progress, but Madge did not relent. She still knew in her deepest heart that she might need to call Paige on Sunday night and make a desperate run to the store. If she had to buy a couple of Halloween costumes at the last minute, she would punch a big hole in her car repair fund. So, she stitched. And tucked. And prayed.

On the big day, Madge tried to keep busy making breakfast. She had crept up the stairs near midnight and left two bundles outside the little girls' bedroom door. She had no real idea whether her project had succeeded or not.

"Here they come," Aspen said as she bounced down the stairs. "Make way for Quinn the Mighty Eskimo and Peyton the Peacock Princess."

Peyton tumbled down the staircase first. She had wanted to wear a pair of her mother's old heels, but Madge knew those would have to go. The nightgown made a good showing, though. Just silky enough to look regal. Madge had insisted on long sleeves underneath because the weatherman predicted chilly weather. The glitter from Peyton's Christmas tee shirt kept the theme working.

The crown dazzled. The peacock feathers flared out at a perfect angle, and all the little beads shimmered and glowed when Peyton moved her head. The window curtain floated around her shoulders just right. Madge felt sure there would not be a better princess in the parade, and she was slightly ashamed of herself for being so proud.

"I'm dying in here," Quinn said as she tromped into the kitchen. Madge pulled the hood down and fanned Quinn's face with a church bulletin from the counter.

"You'll have to put the hood up just in time for the parade," Madge said. "It's fake fur, but real weight. You could survive on the Tundra."

Quinn dropped the mittens on her backpack. "Maybe I should wear my bathing suit underneath."

"I don't think so," Madge said. "Normal clothes. You'll be fine."

Luke skipped breakfast and appeared just in time to rush the girls to the car for school. He paused to admire both costumes and said to Madge, "Can you and Jack do pick up this afternoon? I have to re-route some trucks from Dubuque, and it's going to make me pretty late, I think."

"Sure. I'll call the office. Jack or Paige can take me."

"It will have to be Jack. I talked to him last week, and he said Paige is taking some time off."

"Time off for what?"

"He didn't say." Luke kept stuffing things into his briefcase.

"Didn't say or didn't know? That boy better wake up one of these days or he is going to lose out on a good thing."

"I'm not sure I follow you," Luke said as he grabbed his brief-case. "But I think Paige is fine, don't worry."

Madge decided not to worry for the moment. Instead, she planned to take a well-earned rest for the whole day. She might have the sniffles, now that she thought about it. She retreated to her room, propped her feet on the ottoman, and contemplated what to do with her rest.

She could respond to Emily's letter. But her sixty days would be up soon so she might be home before it arrived. Two weeks. She hadn't heard Alex say how the appeal was going, but she supposed they would sell the house. She didn't see how they could keep this up now that Alex had lost her big paycheck.

No matter what the judge said, they wouldn't need a house-keeper. Madge looked around the room. She would miss these cushy digs. She'd gotten used to living in luxury. She sniffed. Drat that cold, it was getting to her. Probably kid germs. This time of year they brought in all kinds of things. Especially the baby. She always wanted picked up, crawling all over Madge's lap, rubbing her gooey hands over Madge's face, even kissing on her.

"No wonder I've got a cold. Good thing I'm getting out of here soon. I'd die of pneumonia if I stuck around all winter."

Winter brought up thoughts of the holidays, and Madge wondered how the mashed up family would handle those. Who would cook Thanksgiving dinner? Where would the children spend Christmas? Which parent would be alone?

None of those issues were her business, of course. She would be back home fixing up charity baskets with the Glory Circle Sisters by then. Not worrying about a bunch of little kids. Not a smidgen.

Maybe Paige could run Quinn out to church once in a blue moon, just so the ladies could check on her spelling. What a silly idea. Madge kicked it to the curb as soon as it crossed her mind. And what about Paige, anyway? She hadn't mentioned taking any time off. Was she sick? Had she decided to look for a new job? Madge thought maybe she would just call her up and find out. But her phone was clear across the room, and the soft chair felt pretty good to her weary back. So, maybe she would just sit here a tad bit longer. She could always call Paige after lunch.

Madge slept through lunch. She couldn't remember when she had done such a thing. She blamed the weather. Clouds had rolled in mid-morning, and the day felt almost like snow. It was nearly November, after all. Not too early for snow. She had hoped it might hold off until she got back home. Madge didn't really mind winter; she just liked to take it on her own terms.

Catherine had once suggested Madge might like to go south for the winter. What a preposterous idea. That's the kind of thing rich, old people did. Madge didn't fit either category. Today, though, she hoped to skip out on an early snow. She couldn't imagine the logistics of wrestling all those little girls around in boots, mittens, and scarves morning and night to go to and from school. The whole idea exhausted her.

It also got her up and out of her chair. She rummaged around in the laundry room until she found an unclaimed bag. Then she searched the hall closet for various stocking caps and gloves. She knew no one but Quinn had left the house with warm enough clothes this morning. She planned to meet them with the necessary items this afternoon. In the end, she couldn't find enough mates. Someone would just have to ride home in mismatched gloves.

Jack pulled up out front several minutes sooner than Madge would have expected. He hopped out of the car and sprinted toward the house, his heavy black dress coat and fancy, plaid scarf flapping in the breeze.

"No hat?" Madge said when she opened the door.

"I don't think I own one," Jack said. "At least not one distinguished enough to wear to court, which is where I've come from."

"Well, you better get one. The wooly worm says this is going to be a frigid winter."

Jack paused with his hands clasped together like a prayer. "Okay, I'll definitely look into that. Are you ready to go?"

Madge looked around the room. "I kind of dread getting out in this weather," she said. "Looks like it's going to get miserable."

"Yes, but not until later," Jack said. "We have plenty of time to pick up the girls and get you all back home before the blizzard sets in."

"Blizzard? Is it going to snow?"

Jack shook his head and grabbed a Mizzou jacket from a peg in the entryway. "No. Well, maybe. A wintry mix is what the weatherman said, I think. But I believe we can beat it if we get going."

"I hope so." Madge slid her arms into the jacket, grabbed Jack's extended arm, and ducked her head against the weather. "I can't imagine navigating that round-a-bout thing in icy weather."

"Well, all you have to do is ride along," Jack said. "So, let's do it."

As it turned out, Madge had to do more than ride along. The wind picked up, and the rain started before they reached the school where Quinn and Peyton stood in line waiting for pick up. The teachers had herded the children back inside, which meant someone had to go and personally fetch them rather than just wave from the car.

"I'll go," Jack said.

Madge wanted to let him. She wanted to sit tight with the heater blowing on her toes and let Jack take the weather. She had become something of an expert at pick-up lines, though. She knew the rules.

"That won't work," she said. "If the driver gets out, they consider it parking the car." Madge tried not to growl the words, but she felt rather growly. "They make you pull into the lot. I'll do it." She wrestled herself out of the car and fought the wind and rain to the front door of the school. Once inside, she fought the noise level of several hundred elementary students who were both ready to go home and excited about the first snow falling on the night they would bribe candy from all their neighbors.

"Marvel," she shouted to the teacher with the clipboard. "Quinn and Peyton Marvel."

"Marvel," the teacher shouted down the line.

Quinn emerged from the pack, her book bag dragging on the floor and her hood hanging down her back. Halfway to Madge, she reached into the crowd, grabbed the strap of Peyton's book bag, and pulled the princess along as well.

Madge handed Peyton a stocking cap and a pair of gloves from the bag over her own shoulder. "Here. It's freezing outside."

Quinn pulled up her hood and slipped on her mittens. Peyton waited for Madge's help. By the time they accomplished that chore, Madge knew she had been right about winter. It would be too much for her.

She grabbed both girls by their mittened hands and said, "Hold tight girls. We're in for it when the door opens." With that, they headed into the storm. It had picked up force in the few minutes Madge had been inside. Ice stung her face and the wind pulled at her breath. Jack had jumped out of the car and met them halfway.

"They can yell at me if they want," he said. He grabbed up Peyton and took Quinn's other hand. In a few seconds, he had both girls in the car. He turned around and took Madge by the arm. "Come on," he said. "Let me help."

Madge let him.

Chapter Thirty-Six

Monday, October 31st
Thirteen Days to Go

Traffic moved slowly on the way to Aspen's school, but the middle school teachers were less protective than the elementary. Although Aspen waited inside, she saw Jack's car before he pulled all the way up to the door, and she popped outside before Madge could move. Aspen hopped into the back seat and shook ice from her long hair.

Madge tossed a hat and gloves over the seat. "Well, I'm a little late with these, but hold onto them in case we land in a ditch."

"We aren't landing in a ditch," Jack said. He made eye contact with Aspen in the rearview mirror. "But you might want the gloves anyway. It's pretty cold."

"I'm fine." Aspen tucked the gloves inside the hat and dropped them on the seat beside her. Both Quinn and Peyton had started to look sleepy, all bundled up in their winter gear.

When Jack pulled up outside Toddle Time, he wrapped the scarf around his neck a second time. "I'll get Grace," he said.

"It's no good." Madge pulled up her collar. "You've gotta be on the list. With a picture." She looked at the door to the building, which seemed about a million miles away. She wished she had a rope to tie to the car in case she couldn't find her way back in the blizzard.

"Well, I'm going with you," Jack said. "I can carry Grace after you sign her out."

"Good plan."

"Aspen, I'm leaving the car running and locking you in so no one can carjack you. You're in charge of your sisters. Watch for us, and unlock the minute you see us coming out. Don't let us freeze to death out there."

"I wouldn't do that."

"I know you wouldn't. I just didn't want you to get side-tracked with an important text message or anything."

"Whatever."

Madge decided to ignore the comment. She pulled her coat as tight around her neck as she could and kind of rolled out of the car. The wind cut straight through. She felt Jack take her arm, and together they pushed toward the building.

In truth, she hated leaving the girls in the car. She would feel much better if they could all stick together right now. Hold tight to one another the way Jack held tight to her arm. The stormy day made her feel especially responsible for this crew. And, slightly useless.

After what seemed like an hour, Madge and Jack reached the building. Jack pulled hard to open the door, and he fought the wind to keep from having his arm jerked off in the process. Once inside, they took a moment to defrost before they asked for Grace. Madge couldn't remember how the baby had been dressed that morning, but she knew she wasn't prepared for this. "We should have brought a blanket," she said.

The staff seemed extra eager to get rid of their charges, so Grace appeared in record time. Jack helped pull on the hat and mittens Madge had brought. Then he tucked Grace inside his own coat and wrapped his scarf around her like a cape.

"I'll take her out and come back for you," he said.

"No, that will take too long. I don't want to leave them alone in the car."

"You'll have to hold onto my arm, then," he said. "Whatever you do, don't let go when the wind hits. It will be fierce, and the sidewalk is getting icy."

"I'll hold on," she said. They turned out to be vain words. The sidewalk was worse than icy. It was treacherous. The first step sent Madge sliding toward the parked car. She felt her shoulder wrench as her hand jerked loose from Jack's arm, and she heard him shout something. The words were lost in the wind.

She didn't really feel much pain when she hit the ground. Mostly she just felt cold. And embarrassed. And more helpless than she had ever been in her entire life. She watched as if in a dream while Aspen leaped out of the car and ran to her. She saw Jack toss Grace into the back seat and slam the door shut. Then he and Aspen were both kneeling beside her.

"Don't move," he shouted over the wind, "something may be broken."

No danger of moving. Possibly ever again. Madge thought she had broken something quite important when she sailed across the sidewalk.

"Get back in the car," she said toward Aspen, but the girl appeared not to hear.

Instead, Aspen shouted toward Jack. "What should we do?"

Madge struggled to reach out and wipe the tears slipping down Aspen's cheeks. She couldn't do it, though. She couldn't move no matter how desperately she wanted to help.

"Stop crying," she finally said. "Your face will freeze."

Aspen rubbed her sleeve across her face and sniffed. Jack looked at the daycare center and spoke while he removed his coat and scarf. "Go press the buzzer by the door. Tell them someone is injured. We need an ambulance."

He draped his coat over Madge and tucked the scarf around her head. "Be careful," he yelled after Aspen. "And we need blankets. Tell them to bring out all their blankets."

It seemed like only seconds before Thomas the Tank, Winnie

the Pooh, Mickey Mouse, and several characters she had never met covered Madge. Aspen held a giant red and white polka dot umbrella over all of them and fought valiantly to keep the wind from stealing it. Madge could still feel the icy sidewalk seeping into her bones, but she also felt a warmth that had nothing to do with the blankets.

"Go check on the girls," she said to Jack. "They must be scared."

"I can see them from here," he said. "They are fine."

Madge knew he was lying. From her vantage point, she could see two, terrified faces pressed against the car window. More than anything she had ever wanted in her whole life, Madge wanted to get up and go comfort those girls. She said a silent prayer that the Almighty would do it for her.

"I also grabbed these," Jack said. He pulled out the stocking cap and gloves Aspen had left on the back seat. He tucked the cap over Aspen's head and held the umbrella long enough for her to put on gloves.

Various parents came by to pick up children during the agonizing minutes that felt like hours while they waited for the ambulance. They all stopped and knelt down, offered advice, or help, or comfort. But, in the end, Jack and Aspen had done all that could be done.

Madge could see them shivering. Someone had draped a pink and fluffy blanket over Jack's shoulders. Madge wanted to laugh about it, but she knew his expensive dress coat was somewhere in the layers keeping her from frostbite, so she felt more like crying instead.

"You should wait in the car," she said to Aspen.

"You should save your strength," Aspen said. "Stop talking."

Madge stopped.

By the time the sound of sirens rose over the sound of the wind, Madge had begun to think she might die here on the sidewalk right in front of Toddle Time. Such a shame. Instead, two boys disguised as rescue workers scooted her onto a hard, yellow surfboard. She could have sworn they were young enough to have been at Aspen's school a few minutes earlier. These must be their Halloween costumes.

They slapped the surfboard onto a narrow cart, bundled her into warm blankets, and cinched the whole thing down with a bunch of straps. Madge felt as if they had wrapped her in a straightjacket and prepared her for the loony bin. She was so grateful to be off the pavement she didn't complain.

When one of the rescue boys climbed up front and prepared to drive, Madge tried to speak. She wanted to tell him to take her home. Although she didn't mean her home, exactly. She meant the Marvel house, which suddenly sounded like pure sanctuary to her. Before she could get any of those words out, though, Jack stuck his head inside the ambulance.

"We'll follow you," he said. "I've called Luke."

The doors closed before Madge could protest. All she needed was a parade in the waiting room while they dressed her up in one of those flimsy gowns. The rescue boy hit the sirens and started driving like a wild man. Madge opened her mouth to complain when the second boy said, "I can give you something to help with the pain while we ride. On a scale of one to ten, what level is your pain right now?"

Madge had been ignoring the pain, mostly due to the cold. Now that she felt some warmth, the pain started winning. "It's pretty bad," she said.

"Sorry, I need a number. If one is no pain at all, and ten is pain so bad it makes you want to cry and writhe on the floor, where is your pain now?"

Madge had never felt pain that made her want to writhe on the floor. She supposed women felt that kind of pain in childbirth. The picture of the little girls crying in the back of the car flashed through her mind, and Madge realized she had felt pain then. Not childbirth exactly, but something womanly and connected. Something new to her.

"Are you having pain?" the rescue boy asked.

"Not much," Madge said. "I'll wait." She wanted to have a clear head when they got to the hospital. She didn't want anyone making decisions on her behalf.

Chapter Thirty-Seven

Monday, October 31st
Thirteen Days to Go

Jack and the girls arrived shortly after Madge got shuffled into the emergency room. She was on her third round of "are you allergic to any medications" when Jack barged through the curtained cubicle and took up residence in the corner beside her bed. The young technician barely glanced up.

"And who should I put down as next of kin? Someone we should call in case of emergency?" She looked at Madge and then at Jack.

Madge hesitated. Finally, she took a deep breath and said, "Benjamin Hightower."

"Judge Hightower?" Jack put the emphasis on "Judge" as he leaned over Madge's bed. "Judge Hightower is your next of kin? I thought you worked for him?"

"I didn't exactly say that."

"Oh, you so exactly did. I asked if you had any references for employment, and you pulled out the business card of the judge who had just made this astounding ruling giving the little girls the Marvel house. The very judge who held my career in his hands. You threw his card at me and said he was your business reference. As if you had worked for him."

"Well, I've cooked him a few meals and washed his dishes, if that's what you mean. I've even changed his diapers back in the day. You didn't ask if we were related."

The nurse had been staring at the two of them through this exchange. Finally, she said, "Could I have this famous judge's phone number?"

"I don't know it," Madge said. "But it's in my purse."

"I'll get it," Jack said. He walked around the bed and grabbed the bag. "And while you're at it, you should put my name on the chart, too."

"Are you a relative?"

Jack looked at Madge. She waited for him to answer, but he just looked at her.

"Put him on the chart," Madge said. "He's pretty good in an emergency."

Jack finished up with the nurse, giving her all the pertinent information for himself, the judge, and even the address and phone numbers for Luke and Alex. He hadn't been done long when another young man came breezing into the room.

"Hello Miz DuPree," he said. "I'm your tour guide for the afternoon, and I'm about to give you the royal treatment. I understand they've given you a little something sweet for your pain, so this should be easy. We're gonna ride the elevator down to the radiology suite of this fine establishment where I believe they are going to take some beautiful pictures of your exquisite bones."

Madge rolled her eyes at Jack. "You might as well take the girls home," she said. "Hospitals take all night to get this stuff done."

"We've got things covered," he said.

An hour later, Madge would swear the hospital had a picture of every bone in her body. The table she'd waited on for the procedure had been almost as cold and hard as the sidewalk outside

Toddle Time. At one point, she had said so. The talkative tour guide appeared out of nowhere with a heated blanket which he tucked around her from her shoulders to her toes. Madge felt an insane desire to kiss the boy.

The desire vanished when he wheeled her back to her cubicle at ninety miles an hour, making her both dizzy and slightly carsick. He slid her into the bay with a flourish and announced, "If you have need of further assistance this evening, just ask your nurse to call for Lenny. No need for a tip. This service is provided free of charge courtesy of this fine establishment and your government insurance policy. Which we will bilk for thousands of dollars per hour, I am quite sure. Can I get you another blanket?"

"No," Madge said with something like a bark.

"Pretty painful?"

Madge turned her head to see Luke standing in the corner beside Jack.

"Who has the girls?" she said.

"They're in the waiting room," Luke said. "Mara Lynn is coming to take them home, but Quinn wants to tell you 'goodnight' first. Are you up for that?"

"Sure." She probably wasn't up for it, but she couldn't refuse those girls.

"Just Quinn and Aspen," Jack said. "Even Quinn is against regulations, but we're sneaking her anyway. I'll stay with Grace."

Madge almost smiled at the thought of The Mighty Quinn being smuggled. She would like that.

The girls appeared in the doorway within seconds. Aspen looked terrible. Neither girl spoke, and Madge searched her brain for something normal to say. Something that would let them off the hook for appropriate hospital talk.

"Who won the costume prize?" she finally asked.

"Robbie the Robot Johnson," Quinn said. "His dad works in computers. He lit up. It wasn't really fair."

"No kidding."

Madge struggled for another safe subject, but she came up empty. Fortunately, Alex broke the awkward silence when she blasted through the doorway.

"Oh, thank God you are okay," she said. "I had my phone shut off. Luke, I just got your messages. Oh, dear Lord, are the girls okay?"

"We're fine, Mom," Aspen said, although she looked about as fine as the guy at Quinn's school dressed as a mummy.

Alex bent down and grabbed Quinn in a giant hug. "Oh, look at you. Quinn the Mighty Eskimo. I'm so proud of you. Daddy told me on the phone how you stayed in the car and kept your sister calm and made Gracie happy. How you sang to her and read her books even though you were scared for Madge. He said you totally lived up to your name today. And just look, you even had the costume."

Quinn pulled back, smiled, and then looked up at Madge. "She's proud of me."

Madge nodded, even though it hurt to move.

Alex stood up and put her hand on Madge's arm. "I'm so sorry this happened. So sorry you were out in this weather. We should have covered you better today."

"What a lot of commotion over nothing," Madge said. But the pain growing in her back and leg argued otherwise. She hoped that nurse would be back pretty soon to ask about numbers.

"Come on girls," Luke said. "Tell Madge 'goodnight' and hustle back to the waiting room. Mara Lynn just sent a text from the elevator. She's on her way up to get you and your sister."

The girls each touched Madge's hand as they said farewells, and Aspen made her parents promise to call if anything changed before morning. The commotion settled once the girls left, and Madge looked around the room to see Jack, Luke, and Alex staring at her.

Madge had never been in the hospital. She had been born at home, like all babies in her day, and her childhood ailments had been the usual kind. Even as an adult she had avoided things like appendicitis and gallbladder. She didn't know how a person was supposed to behave. Did you have to make conversation with all these people huddled around your bed? She mostly wanted to close her eyes and try to block out the pain.

"Why don't you just close your eyes," Alex said. "Maybe you can sleep. Or at least block out the pain."

Madge turned to look at her. Who was this woman all wise and compassionate? Had they lived in the same house for the last sixty days?

Alex must have read the questions in Madge's face. "I broke my leg once. And, I hate hospitals. When I had the girls, I couldn't wait to go home. I loved having people take care of me, but I did not like the hospital. I told Luke they should let you have babies in hotel rooms. You could get the breakfast in bed without the sick smells."

Madge saw Luke and Alex exchange a smile. The first one she had seen in a long time. Maybe ever. That might be worth breaking a hip over. Maybe not.

"Good evening, Mrs. DuPree. I'm Doctor Dingle." The man who had walked into the room wore a white coat and was barely taller than Aspen. He had thick, black glasses and looked old enough to be retired.

"Not really," Madge said.

"Not really what?"

"That can't be your real name. Nobody could really be called Doctor Dingle. Sounds like it's out of a cartoon or something."

Alex squeezed Madge's arm and spoke to the doctor. "She's a little delirious from the pain medicine and the exposure to the cold, I think. We're happy to meet you and grateful to you for taking care of Madge. How did her x-rays look?"

Madge wanted to slap Alex's hand away, but that would have taken too much effort. Besides, she did want to hear about the x-rays, even from a cartoon doctor.

"Well, I think we all expected this outcome from such an accident for a woman of her age," the doctor said as if Madge weren't even in the room. He looked right over her head toward Jack, Alex, and Luke. "In laymen's terms, she has broken her hip and will require surgery. I think we can get her on the schedule first thing tomorrow. At her age, there are some pretty great risks, of course, especially if she has any co-morbidities."

"Hello, Dr. Dingleberry," Madge almost shouted. "Right here in the room with you. The patient isn't in a coma. I broke my hip, not my head."

"I'm sorry, Mrs...." he consulted his chart, "DuPree. Of course. Do you have any questions?"

Madge thought for a minute. She had a million questions. She knew about people who broke their hips. You might as well put them down afterwards in some cases. But she was still healthy in most other respects. She'd probably bounce right back. Probably have to do some of those exercises. It might put off her driving for a while. Could be a long winter. She would be herself again by spring. Certainly by spring.

"Nope. No questions."

"Fine. I'll go see if I can schedule an OR for first thing tomorrow. The nurse will be in with all the forms for you to sign. We'll get you something for the pain now, and then send you upstairs to a room."

When the doctor had left, no one spoke for a while. Finally, Madge said, "You should probably all go home. Put those girls to bed at a decent time. They've had a terrible day."

"Yeah. It was kind of scary," Jack said.

"I'm not sure what to do," Alex said. "I kind of hate to leave Madge alone tonight, but I do think the girls are upset."

"I'll stay." Madge turned her head just enough to see Paige standing in the doorway. She pulled off her hat and gloves and dropped a book bag on an empty chair. "How are things?"

"Let's get some coffee, and I'll fill you in." Jack slung his arm over Paige's shoulder and bent his head to talk as they left the room.

The moment they left, Alex laid her hand on Madge's shoulder. She turned slightly and spoke to Luke, "What do you think?"

"I think we should let Paige stay. She's the most obvious choice. No kids at home. Jack can let her take the time off work."

Madge saw the look that crossed Alex's face, and she felt another storm coming. When Alex spoke, she sounded like the woman who had tossed *Peter Pan* into storage.

"You sound terribly familiar with the lives of my lawyer and his administrative assistant."

"It's a long story," Luke said. "For another time."

"I'll be eager to hear it." Alex turned back toward Madge and seemed to soften a little as if she remembered where they were.

"Look," she said to Luke, "I know it's your week at the house, but maybe I should stay over tonight. The girls might need both of us. Plus, I'd be closer in case anything comes up here."

Madge hoped Luke wouldn't blow this moment. She wished she could signal him somehow to not be an idiot.

"That's a good idea," he said. "You should stay. It will help the girls."

The nurse came in before Madge could say anything, which was probably best.

Chapter Thirty-Eight

Monday, October 31st
Thirteen Days to Go

During the next half-hour, Madge needed Alex to help her with signatures. Not a situation she enjoyed. The nurse reeled off questions and information so fast that Madge found herself turning to Alex for suggestions on whether or not she should sign each form. Finally, the nurse said, "And this one is about end of life. If your heart should stop while you are here in the hospital, do you want us to try and revive you?"

Jack and Paige stepped through the door just in time to hear the question. Madge held the pen in mid-air. She stared at the nurse. "Is that the kind of question you ask like that? 'Do you want oatmeal for breakfast, are you allergic to penicillin, and if your heart stops do you want us to let you die?' Good grief, woman. Shouldn't you ask a question like that with a little tact? Or bring in a clergyman or something?"

The nurse took a step back. "I'm sorry." She held up the thick stack of papers. "It's just one of my forms."

"I'm sure it is. But you don't ask a person a question like that the same way you ask them if they want lime Jell-O, for Heaven's sake. You have to prepare them just a little bit. Give them some transition time."

Madge could feel Luke smiling in the corner, but she didn't care. Even Alex remained quiet. So, Madge plunged forward. "Let's try this again."

"Okay," the nurse hesitated. She looked at the form. Then she said, "Ms. DuPree, I'm going to switch things up now and ask you some personal questions."

"That's better."

"This one will take some thought, and you may want to talk to your children about it." She looked at Alex. "I can leave the room while you discuss it if you want."

Madge felt tears rushing to her eyes, and she suddenly regretted putting on this big show. She should have just signed the paper and moved on. Now she was going to make a big mess of the thing.

"No, I don't need..."

"That's a good idea," Jack said as he walked the rest of the way into the room. "I think we want to talk about that one. And, also, do you have a Power of Attorney for Healthcare Decisions on file anywhere? I'm sure she doesn't have one, and we could fill that out this evening while we are waiting."

"I'll check with the social worker," the nurse said. "I'm sure we can get one. I'll just finish with these other forms about family history, and then I'll come back for this other one in a while."

"Thank you," Alex said. "We appreciate it."

Madge didn't say anything. Even after the nurse left the room, she didn't trust herself to talk at first.

"So, that's a pretty big decision," Jack said. "But, to me, it is also pretty obvious."

"Oh?"

"Well, you are perfectly healthy. Strong. You have lots of years left. You obviously would want them to restart your heart if you had some kind of incident in surgery or something."

"Of course you would."

"Yes."

Murmurs of agreement from the unofficial children in the room.

"I don't want kept alive on machines," Madge said.

"No, no. Nothing like that," Jack said. "Not something long term. I'm just saying if some minor thing went wrong, and you sort of died a little, you would want to come back. That's all."

Madge thought about it for a few seconds. "Okay. I'll sign it that way. But no machines keeping me alive. You make sure it's written that way, Jack."

"I'll do it."

Everyone stayed quiet for a few minutes before Jack spoke again. "The other paper I mentioned gives someone the authority to make those kinds of decisions in the extremely rare chance that you, say, for instance, um, have a terrible head injury and wind up in a coma or something."

"Or don't wake up from this surgery."

"Right."

"So, I need to name somebody to speak for me if I can't talk."

"Yes."

"Somebody who would know exactly what I'd say if I could talk?"

"That's the idea."

Madge waited for one beat and then said, "Put yourself on the paper, Jack."

"Yes, ma'am."

After a few more seconds of silence, Paige spoke. "I think Jack and I should go get some food for all of us. Well, not for Madge. You probably won't get anything tonight. But the rest of us should probably eat."

"I'm not hungry," Alex said.

"But you should eat," Paige told her. "Just a bite of something."

"Great idea," Jack said. "We all need sustenance." He pulled back the curtain on the window beside Madge's bed. "And it looks like the storm has slowed down. We can probably make that café a couple of blocks away and find some decent sandwiches. We'll bring some back for you guys."

"Sounds good," Luke said.

"I'm going to tell you 'goodnight,'" Jack said as he leaned over the bed. "Just in case you are asleep when I get back. Because you should be."

Madge was feeling sleepy. It must be the pain medicine.

"Did you put your name on the paper, Jack? For in case I don't wake up?"

"I did. But you will."

"Or I'll wake up in Heaven. And that would be okay with me. If it happens, you tell the little girls I said so. You tell them I've gone to see Jesus and Catherine, and I'm happy about it."

"Yes, ma'am," Jack said again.

Chapter Thirty-Nine

Tuesday, November 1st
Twelve Days to Go

Madge did not wake up in Heaven. She knew she hadn't done so because everyone had always told her there would be no pain in Heaven, and by golly, she felt pain. Pretty much everywhere. She didn't know why her throat hurt so badly when she'd had hip surgery. What she wanted most in the world was to roll over on her right side and bunch the pillow up under her shoulder. But she couldn't seem to move.

And the noise. Heaven wouldn't be this kind of noise. It was supposed to be sublime. Madge felt like people were shouting at her in this place. Why were they shouting at her to breathe for them? Couldn't they breathe for themselves? Oh, wait, they wanted her to breathe. Of course, she could take a breath. There, one nice, deep breath, that seemed to be what they wanted. They stopped shouting, so maybe she could go back to sleep now. For a long time.

The next time Madge roused herself from sleep, she could hear machines beeping, but she was back in her own room. It seemed late in the day from the way the sunlight lay across the blanket on her bed. She couldn't focus well at first, but the room seemed crowded. She blinked hard, trying to clear her vision, and finally managed to say, "Water."

A crowd of people jumped at once to hand her the jug from a tray beside her bed. It was like a scene out of a sitcom as they stumbled all over each other trying to help. Jack and Paige, who looked exhausted and must have been there all day. Luke and Alex who looked only a little fresher. And Ben and Nancy who must have shown up sometime during the day. Madge wanted to tell them they shouldn't have come, but talking seemed like such hard work. Just as the water finally made it to her shaky hand, Tom and Evelyn walked into the room.

"Oh, my," Evelyn said, "we didn't expect such a crowd."

Paige stepped forward and made introductions. "The doctor was in a few minutes ago and said she came through surgery very well. They did a complete hip replacement so she will need several weeks of care and therapy, but she should make a complete recovery."

Madge came fully awake at those words. She kept sipping water, trying to soothe her dry throat because she felt words were about to be needed.

"There's a good facility near us," Ben said. "I know my brother, Clyde, has been trying to get her to move out near him for years, but I don't think she could travel that far. The place by us offers good rehab services, though."

"Or the facility where Bess lives," Evelyn said. "I know Madge would enjoy being near Bess and seeing her every day. They could even eat meals together. I think we should inquire about Green Hills." Everyone in the room seemed to like that idea. Everyone except a couple of people.

"Balderdash!" Madge and Alex spoke the word at exactly the same time. Madge thought Alex said it the loudest. In fact, Alex said it a second time. "Balderdash. Madge doesn't have to go to a facility. She can move downstairs to the rehab unit in the hospital for her early care. They have a wonderful staff. After that, she has a perfect set-up at our house. Her own suite on the ground floor. The bathroom already has grip bars, and we can install anything else we need."

"But Madge is going to need care," Evelyn said. She leaned closer to the bed and spoke over the top of Madge toward Alex. "With personal matters such as bathing, you know."

"Yes, I know." Alex reached down and pulled the covers up over Madge's shoulder. "As it happens, I'm rather available just now for that kind of thing. I used to sell pharmaceuticals so I'm familiar with the healthcare community in this area. I can set her up for therapy and so forth."

"What do you mean, you used to sell pharmaceuticals?" Luke came to the other side of the bed and stared at Alex.

"I, sort of lost my job a while ago."

Madge began to feel like she might need some oxygen. She had been waiting for this discovery, but she hadn't planned on being literally in the middle of it.

Luke spoke slowly. "So, you got fired?"

"Not fired. Down-sized."

"Yeah," he nodded and rubbed a hand across his head. "Yeah, I know what that means. I've been down-sized a few times." He paused for a moment and then looked up at the ceiling. "You. Got. Fired."

"I did." Alex's voice grew quiet, and Madge hoped she wouldn't start whispering. If they were going to duke it out right here, Madge at least wanted to hear the details. Especially the details that might pertain to the need of a housekeeper and nanny.

"We will be fine," Alex said. "I've been making inquiries, and Mara Lynn is helping me network. I'm just saying that I'll have some free time for a few weeks so I could help with Madge's care."

"You got fired, and you haven't found a job, and you've been hanging out with Mara Lynn trying to figure out what to do next because you didn't want to have to tell me."

Madge almost forgot about her own predicament as she listened to this soap opera taking place over her bed.

"I've sent out about a million resumes," Alex said. "Something will turn up soon. And, I got a good severance package."

"Wow," Luke said. "I've said those words to you so many times. Do you remember at all what the role is on my side of this conversation? Do you remember what you say to me now?"

"Luke, this probably isn't the time for us to work out our differences." She smoothed Madge's blanket again and tilted her head toward the side of the room that still held spectators.

Madge could tell everyone else had begun edging away from the bed toward the door as if they knew better than to eavesdrop on such a private conversation. Madge, on the other hand, was quite happy to be stuck in the middle of it. Evidently, Luke didn't mind, either, because he kept talking.

"No, I really want to know. Do you remember what you said to me every time I came home and told you I had been 'downsized?' Or that the store I worked for had closed. Or the company was going out of business. Do you remember?"

"I remember." She kept fiddling with Madge's blankets, and she spoke softly.

"What's that?" Luke leaned over the bed toward Alex.

"I remember." She spoke louder and looked up. "I accused you of refusing to grow up. Of living in Never-Never-Land and thinking we could survive on dreams and fairy-dust. I said if we were going to make it financially, I'd have to do it myself."

"Yes, you did." Luke leaned back and folded his arms. "I just wanted to make sure you still remember saying those things, because I remember them."

He walked in a tight circle for a moment and then looked at Alex again. "But, guess what? I'm not going to say mean things back. I could. I want to. It's not that I don't want to, or that I'm resisting because I'm a better person. It's just that I know it won't get us anywhere."

Luke gripped the rails on Madge's bed and rocked back and forth. Madge really wanted to tell him to stop moving the bed. It most definitely sent her pain from a zero to a five. Maybe a seven. She didn't want to risk interfering just as they were getting somewhere. So, she gritted her teeth. Finally, he let go of the bed and clasped his hands in front of him.

"You know what? I'm sorry," Luke said. "I'm sorry this happened to you, because I know exactly how it feels, and I don't want you to feel this way. I don't. I want you to be happy, fulfilled, and successful. Not because Pastor Cleveland told me to forgive and move on, either. I genuinely want you to be happy."

"Thank you," Alex said.

Luke nodded and folded his arms again. Madge thought he looked a little too pleased with himself, but she figured life would knock that down soon enough. Let him have his moment.

"So, what do you want? You didn't love selling arthritis pills, did you?"

Now Alex started rocking the bed. Madge didn't know how much more silent marriage counseling her post-surgery self could take.

"Well, no, not really. I mean I liked some of it. I liked the money. And the car. I really like the clothes. Except not the heels. I'd like a job where I didn't have to wear such high heels. I didn't like the stress. Or the travel. Or the constant need to be on."

"What about going back into teaching?"

"That's a dream, Luke. The girls and I can't live on a teacher's salary."

"I think you should re-visit that idea."

"What do you mean?"

"I mean I think you've spent your whole adult life feeling insecure about money. But, you've never been poor. Never even close to it. You just live in fear of running low on funds."

"I don't think that's true."

Jack suddenly spoke up from the corner he hadn't vacated. "It's true," he said. "I know I'm not in the conversation, and we should probably leave the room and let Madge get some rest."

"Oh, don't worry about me," Madge said. "Carry right on. I'm feeling lots better about my own misery."

"It's true then," Jack said. "I mean, have you seen your 401K? You are loaded for the future, yet you still wanted half of Luke's measly retirement fund in case yours ran short."

"Jack," Paige stepped up and grabbed his arm, "Let's go find some coffee before you get disbarred."

"Or busted in the nose," Luke said as Jack and Paige left the room.

Madge realized the other visitors had managed to leave during the drama. She was left on her own in the trenches of the Marvel War, and she didn't mind one bit. Luke picked up the conversation, but his tone changed. He sounded more like his best self.

"I may be guilty of hanging onto dreams, but I think Jack is right about your fear. Think back about our life. Even during the hard times, I always picked up enough odd jobs to fill in around the edges of your teaching salary. We never went hungry. But you were constantly fretting and scared and nagging about how we didn't have a stable income. You always worried, and yet we were always fine."

"We had to sell the golf clubs once," Alex said.

Luke looked up and narrowed his eyes. "Yeah, once, recently, we had to do that. When we were in a bad place. That wasn't normal, though. In our normal life, we were always pretty much fine."

"I guess we were."

"And now we own this great house. We have three cars."

"And a housekeeper," Madge said.

Alex smiled. "She seems rather laid up at the moment, plus I'm losing my company car at the end of the week."

"So, we might have to drive economy vehicles instead of luxury. Big deal. I'm just saying, I think we are in better shape than you realize." Luke stopped and looked straight at Alex.

"Are you still talking about money?" she asked.

"I don't know."

Alex stayed quiet long enough for Madge to think seriously about speaking up. She managed to resist.

"What about you?" Alex finally said. "Are you happy with your job?"

"Nope. Never have been," Luke said. "But I've been real happy providing a living for my family. That's what matters most for me."

"And, here are some other things that matter," Jack said as he barged back into the room. He waved a handful of papers at Luke and Alex. "I hate to interfere with this conversation which may or may not wreck my reputation as a divorce lawyer, but those people out at the desk are talking about kicking Madge out of here in a matter of days, and these are the rehab places you guys have been talking about. If we're going to use one, we better figure out the insurance issues and see if they have a room and start making arrangements."

Alex and Luke looked at each other over Madge's bed for another few seconds.

"We aren't going to use one, are we?" Alex said.

"It's going to be a lot of work," Luke said.

"I'm pretty tough," Alex answered.

"Does anybody give a hoot what the old woman in the bed has to say about any of this?" Madge finally asked.

With that, the tension in the room broke, and the entire crowd shoved through the door and flooded around the bed. They all started yakking at once. They talked mostly about things she didn't care about. Copays and deductibles. Home health and physical therapy. Retail pharmacy or mail order. Seriously, if she had known family life would be this noisy, she might have stayed on her own.

274

Chapter Forty

Saturday, November 12th
One Day to Go

Madge had spent ten days in the hospital rehab. She grouched a few times at the staff because they pushed her to the limit every day. Once she got back to the Marvel house, though, the hospital team suddenly felt like pansies.

Alex never let up. If the therapist told them Madge should take ten steps before lunch, they took ten steps. No sitting down at eight even if Madge's heart threatened to explode, and her knees wobbled.

"You've got the hip of a twenty-year-old. Press through," Alex would shout.

"I've got the lungs of ninety-year-old," Madge said. "I didn't give up smoking till I was in my fifties, and that ages you."

"I didn't know you'd been a smoker."

"It didn't seem pertinent."

"Well, it's a good thing you quit," Alex said, "because I wouldn't have hired a smoker. Now, two more steps."

Madge scooted a foot. "Is this how you plan to run that class-room they're giving you next month? Will you order those little third-graders around like a drill sergeant?"

Alex kept a grip on the belt around Madge's waist and didn't bother to slow down. "Yep, probably so. I'll have those rascals marching to a beat, jumping hurdles, and dropping to give me twenty if they offer any sass."

"Oh, I just bet you will." Madge tried to talk, walk, and breathe at the same time. "I've seen how you handle the third-grader in this house. Those kids are going to think they've got a marshmallow for a teacher."

"Probably, but right now you owe the marshmallow one last step. You can rest after lunch."

"I'll nap in my chair," Madge said. "Too much trouble to get to the bedroom."

"Well, you probably need the rest," Alex said. She helped Madge drop onto a chair and then walked to the counter and started making a sandwich.

"What day is it, anyway?" Madge asked. "I'm so mixed up from that hospital I can't get the week straight."

"It's Saturday," Alex said. Luke took the girls to an early movie, but they'll be back soon.

"Saturday? What day of the month?"

Alex paused and picked up Madge's calendar from the windowsill. "Today is Saturday, November first. Do you want to hear the verse?"

"No, not right now," Madge said. "I need to figure."

Alex waited a moment and then said, "If you are trying to figure where we are in the sixty-day agreement, I'll tell you."

Madge ran her hand along the edge of the table and thought for another second. "Okay, tell me."

"Tomorrow is Day Sixty," Alex said.

Madge heard nothing but the ticking clock for what seemed like a long time. Alex still held the calendar and looked out the window at a grey sky.

"Well," Madge said. "That's it, then."

"Not necessarily," Alex said. "We hired you for sixty days, but you've spent nearly three weeks on disability leave. So, technically, we could still hire you for another month or so when you get well."

"I suppose you could," Madge said. "I'm falling pretty short on my Oldsmobile money, I expect."

"Yes, I expect."

"The man at the garage would probably hold onto the car for me."

"Oh, yes. I think he would."

The ticking clock filled another block of silence. Finally, Alex came back to the table with the calendar in her hand. "Let me tell you what it says today."

"Okay. Fire away," Madge said as she pulled herself up and gave Alex her attention.

"From Psalm 68," Alex read. "God sets the solitary in families." She stopped and looked up. Madge wanted to deny the rush of emotion, but she couldn't stop the beating of her heart. She feared Alex might hear it thumping.

Madge had lived solitary for so many decades she couldn't imagine anything else. No, that wasn't true. She had begun to imagine it.

Embracing it, though, grabbing hold of that scripture and living it would cost her. She tried to count what the cost would be. Independence? Probably. Along with supper for one and control over her own TV remote.

"Shall I read the rest?" Alex asked.

"There's more?" Madge wasn't sure she could take another hit.

Alex kept reading with the same determination she used to keep Madge walking. "He brings out those who are bound into prosperity."

"Well, that sounds good," Madge said. "That could mean money for my Olds."

"I suppose," Alex said. "Here is the ending, 'But the rebellious dwell in a dry land.'"

"Well, that hurts," Madge said. She tried to sound flippant. As if she wasn't teetering right on the edge of rebellion in her decision about whether or not to stay on at the Marvel house. The tone of voice didn't manage to cover the truth, though. She suspected the Almighty had been up to something all along. Maybe she didn't trick Jack into giving her this job at all. Maybe Someone else had hoodwinked her solitary soul.

Alex stood and walked toward the sink. She stopped after a few steps, turned, and spoke again. "Seriously, though. No matter how things go for us here, for Luke and I and the girls, you will stay won't you?"

Madge considered the question one more time. She thought of her house across town with its peace and quiet and steady routine. She thought of the Oldsmobile sitting all busted up in the repair shop and of the Glory Circle Sisters waiting for her to come back and start volunteering again.

"Well," she said after a brief pause, "I did give up smoking."

Chapter Forty-One

Madge could not imagine eating a catered turkey at Thanks-giving. Not that she had ever been much of a cook herself. She normally ate her holiday meal at someone else's house. Either at Ben's or Clyde's. Or, if the weather was too nasty for a trip, she ended up getting an invite to one of the Glory Circle Sisters. She and Bess had tucked their knees under Catherine's table more than once. They had even gone to Evelyn's one year.

No matter where she ate, Madge always had home cooking. Turkey, noodles, dressing, mashed potatoes. She sometimes even brought her Golden Salad with marshmallows and pineap-ple and all kinds of good stuff. It made the best presentation if she set it up in a mold and undid it all fancy just before the meal. She had managed that the year at Evelyn's, thank the Lord.

This year, however, the Marvel women would be serving a turkey catered from Barkers. She and Alex had ordered it on the computer, along with several side dishes and three pies. Madge pretended the wasted money scandalized her, but she actually felt relieved not having to manage the kitchen with her walker.

Aspen spent all morning setting the table and making place cards. It would be quite a crowd. Jack had accepted an invitation because he didn't want to travel all the way to his family home just for the long weekend. Sounded to Madge like a good excuse to stay in town, for whatever reason.

At the last minute, Paige's family had decided to hold their feast a week later due to conflicting schedules. So, 'surprise' she could attend, too.

Madge kept trying to count the plates Aspen spread out, but she couldn't match them up to names. They were using the dining table with extra chairs, a small folding table, and Grace's high chair. She couldn't make it all add up in her mind. Maybe all that time in the hospital had her a little addled.

Paige arrived early. "I thought I could help with the last minute stuff," she said.

Alex took Paige's coat and tossed it in the laundry room. "Sure," she said, "you can cut the store-bought pies."

"I love pie in all forms," Paige said. "And, I brought a little something from the Rosedale family tradition." She held up a plate. "We start making sugar cookies at Thanksgiving because Christmas can't come soon enough. We just turn them into turkeys."

"Perfect." Aspen took the plate and perched it on top of a cake stand in the middle of the table. "Now it can be part of the centerpiece."

The doorbell rang, and Jack barged in before giving anyone time to answer. He shoved a huge basket of fruit ahead of him as he walked toward the kitchen. "I can't cook, but I did bring an offering," he said.

"Or, that could be our centerpiece," Aspen said. Paige grabbed the fruit before Jack could smash into the table with it, but he reached out and stopped her with a hand on one shoulder.

"Oh, wait," Jack said. "What is this?" He pulled a gauzy package from the center of the fruit basket and handed it to Paige. "Am I mistaken, or does this have your name on it?"

Madge leaned forward on her walker to watch Paige pull one of the twirly ribbons and unveil a box of fancy chocolates.

"Yummy," Aspen said, "I've never seen candy like that."

"It's European," Jack said. "Exotic and unique. Like Miss Rosedale." He said it with a little flip in his voice, but Madge caught the look in his eye when he smiled at Paige. The boy was catching on.

After everyone had tasted the exotic chocolate, the men stood around the stove and discussed how to best carve the turkey while the little girls shouted updates from the family room about the Macy's parade. Madge sat on the stool in one corner of the kitchen and watched the commotion.

Eventually, Alex started herding people toward the table. Aspen assigned seats, and Paige filled water glasses. Still, three places remained empty on Madge's side of the table. She started to reach out for the place card beside her but Aspen grabbed it.

"No peeking," she said.

The sound of the doorbell drowned out Madge's reply. A few minutes later, Pastor Cleveland walked into the room with Bess Caldwell on his arm. Madge heaved herself up and rolled the walker forward. She blinked as she crossed the floor. Probably getting smoke in her eyes from that oven. It needed cleaning.

Bess reached out and grabbed both of Madge's hands when they met. "They told me you hurt yourself," Bess said. "I've been worried sick."

"I'm just fine, Bess. Too ornery to stay down."

"Well, I'm awfully glad to see for myself. Pastor Cleveland was so kind to bring me to your house for Thanksgiving dinner. He said your family sent a special invitation." Bess looked around the table and smiled her best smile.

Madge looked, too. It was quite a sight. "Yes. I'm sure they did. They're sneaky that way. Now, come on and sit down, Bess. We want to eat while the rolls are warm."

"Oh, yes. Are they the recipe Catherine always used?"

"Why, it wouldn't be Thanksgiving without Catherine's rolls," Madge said.

"That's right. That's what I told Pastor Cleveland."

Madge watched Alex shove a wrapper from the Hawaiian rolls into the trash. She winked at Madge. Then she lowered her chin and nodded for Madge to look toward the entryway.

If she lived to be an old woman so rattled in her mind that she couldn't tell morning from night, Madge did not suppose she would ever forget the sight of Elmer Grigsby standing in the doorway. He wore a fine, Sunday suit. Not the skinny kind. His deep, blue tie hung perfectly straight. In one hand he held a dapper-looking hat, and in the other, a bouquet of purple mums.

Elmer gave a slight nod toward the crowd around the table and said, "Howdy."

Then, he turned to Madge. "I've brought you a little something for encouragement. I heard you fell down."

Madge had never been speechless in her life, but she found no words for this moment. She felt heat rising in her face as she tried to respond to the gesture. Alex saved her by diving forward and taking the flowers.

"Thank you so much, Mr. Grigsby," she said. "How kind. Madge, shall I put these in water for you?"

Madge couldn't even seem to nod. She just stood staring at Elmer Grigsby, and he smiled at her in return.

"Well, let's sit down," Luke said.

That broke the moment, and everyone started shuffling around the table to their spots. Once they were seated, Luke stood again.

"Before we eat or say grace," he said, "Aspen would like to make a presentation."

Aspen stood and went to the door of the staircase closet. She pulled out something wrapped in a sheet.

"This is my school project," she said. "I was supposed to do something to describe my family, and I chose to do a painting based on the meaning of our names. I'm not sure it worked."

She turned the canvas around and Madge leaned forward to

get a better view. A deep blue background set off the mountain scene they had been watching emerge. The Aspen tree stood in a grove this time. A young girl walked among the trees with a paintbrush in her hand.

A shining silver warrior with flowing hair stood on top of the mountain. Her sword pointed toward a dark dragon who was obviously flying away. Beside her stood a man dressed in armor. Beams of light exploded from the giant shield he held overhead.

"Dad's name means 'Of Light'," Aspen said. "And Mom's means 'Defender of Man.'" She glanced at Alex, who smiled almost as brightly as her armor in the painting.

"See how they are using their other hands to hold onto baby Grace?" The little girl standing between them obviously wore Grace's frilly white dress and black church shoes. Aspen continued her explanation.

"That's because, according to Madge and the dictionary, Grace is a free gift. A special favor coming from God. I think that is kind of poetic for our family."

Madge thought somebody should say something, but nobody did. Maybe nobody could. So, Aspen kept talking.

"Here are the little girls down below."

Quinn wore her Eskimo coat and held a spelling trophy. "That's me," she yelled. "You painted me."

"Yes, I did. And look, Peyton, I painted you, too." Aspen pointed to the princess with a peacock crown and a football.

Peyton laughed. "You're a good painter, Aspen."

Everyone grew quiet, and Aspen pulled back a little so the painting sat alone. Because one more person stood between the little girls in the painting. A woman with a wild crop of red hair. She wore a necklace with a giant pearl that Aspen had somehow managed to make glow.

"It's you," Aspen said to Madge. "Remember when Mom found out that your real name is Margaret? It means 'Pearl.' And pearls are made when something irritating, like a grain of sand, gets inside an oyster. The oyster sends out a fluid to coat the sand, and a pearl is formed."

"So, I'm an irritating grain of sand, am I?"

"No," Aspen spoke slowly. "You are the pearly fluid that comes out and covers all the hurting places."

Madge didn't know how long the silence stretched after that. She concentrated hard on the colors in the painting to keep herself from blubbering. Alex eventually broke the silence.

"And," she said, "I have the rest." She stood for a moment while everyone recovered. Then she did a little dance step toward the laundry room and came back with a purple frame. Although Madge supposed they would refer to that shade as violet.

"I've been watching this gorgeous painting, and I knew it needed the perfect frame. So, while Madge rested in the afternoons, I've been working on this." She turned the frame around. Inscribed in bright, yellow script were the words: *The Marvel Family, Established 2002: Here am I and the children whom the Lord has given me. We are a sign and wonder.*

"It's from the calendar," Quinn shouted.

"No," Luke said. "It's from the Bible." He reached out and took Alex's hand.

"Thanks, Mom," Aspen said. "It's perfect." She started to lean the painting into the frame, but Luke stopped her.

"Hey, wait a second," he said. He turned the frame over and rubbed his hand across remnants of lettering on the back. "Where did you get the lumber for this frame, Alexandra?"

Alex turned toward the kitchen and started to walk away. "Oh, I found this old *For Sale* sign out on the lawn, and I thought we didn't really need it anymore, so..."

"You know that's property damage, right? We're going to have to pay for it."

Alex turned and pointed a spoon in Luke's direction. "You worry too much. We'll be fine."

Everyone laughed, and Madge had a sudden, ridiculous urge to hug somebody. Fortunately, she resisted.

Discussion Questions

1. Do you have a group of Glory Circle sisters in your life? If so, describe those relationships.

2. How did you feel about Madge at the beginning of the story?

3. In the marriage struggle, did you empathize more with Luke or Alex? Why?

4. Which of the Marvel girls stole your heart? Why?

5. What do you think about the concept of a "Nest House"?

6. The meanings of names play a major role in this story. What does your name mean?

7. Can you describe a marvel God has done in your family?

8. Do you think Madge should get her license back? Why or why not?

9. What did you think when Elmer Grigsby showed up with flowers?

10. How did you feel about Madge at the end of the story?

AUTHOR BIO

Kathy Nickerson is an author, speaker, and eternal optimist who has been living happily-ever-after with her country doctor husband for more than forty years. They are the parents of four children who grew up to become their best friends and who have given them fourteen grandchildren, so far.

She is the author of three novels, including the award-winning *Thirty Days to Glory*, which is the first in the Glory Circle Sisters series. She has also written several short stories, magazine articles, and an e-book on parenting.
You can find her books at
www.amazon.com/author/kathynickerson
or wherever fine books are sold.

You can learn more about her writing and her reputation as an Eternal Optimist at her website www.kathynick.com or by finding her on social media:
www.facebook.com/kathynick
www.twitter.com/kathynick_

Made in the USA
Middletown, DE
02 December 2023

44400499R00166